THE SCAPEGOAT

THE
Scapegoat

RENÉ GIRARD

Translated by YVONNE FRECCERO

THE JOHNS HOPKINS UNIVERSITY PRESS BALTIMORE

THIS BOOK HAS BEEN BROUGHT TO PUBLICATION WITH THE
GENEROUS ASSISTANCE OF THE ANDREW W. MELLON FOUNDATION.

Originally published as *Le Bouc émissaire,* by Bernard Grasset, Paris
© Editions Grasset & Fasquelle, 1982

Johns Hopkins Paperbacks edition, 1989
9 8 7 6

The Johns Hopkins University Press
2715 North Charles Street
Baltimore, Maryland 21218-4363
www.press.jhu.edu

LIBRARY OF CONGRESS CATALOGING-IN-PUBLICATION DATA

Girard, René, 1923–
    The Scapegoat.

    Translation of: Le bouc émissaire.
    Includes bibliographical references and index.
    1. Violence — Religious aspects — Christianity.
2. Persecution. 3. Scapegoat. 4. Jesus Christ —
Passion. I. Title.
BT736.15.G5613 1986   261.8'3315   86-2699
ISBN 0-8018-3315-9 (alk. paper)
ISBN 0-8018-3917-3 (pbk.)

A catalog record for this book is available from the British Library.

Contents

THE SCAPEGOAT

CHAPTER ONE

Guillaume de Machaut
and the Jews

GUILLAUME DE MACHAUT was a French poet of the mid-fourteenth century. His *Judgment of the King of Navarre* deserves to be better known. The main part of the work is a long poem in the conventional, courtly style, but its opening is striking. Guillaume claims that he participated in a confusing series of catastrophic events before he finally closeted himself in his house in terror to await death or the end of the indescribable ordeal. Some of the events he describes are totally improbable, others only partially so. Yet the account leaves the impression that something must actually have happened.

There are signs in the sky. People are knocked down by a rain of stones. Entire cities are destroyed by lightning. Men die in great numbers in the city where Guillaume lives (he doesn't tell us its name). Some of these deaths are the result of the wickedness of the Jews and their Christian accomplices. How did these people cause such huge losses among the local population? They poisoned the rivers that provided the drinking water. Heaven-sent justice righted these wrongs by making the evildoers known to the population, who massacred them all. People continued to die in ever greater numbers, however, until one day in spring when Guillaume heard music in the street and men and women laughing. All was over, and courtly poetry could begin again.

Modern criticism, since its origin in the sixteenth and seventeenth centuries, has not relied blindly on texts. Many scholars today believe their critical insight develops in proportion to increasing skepticism. Texts that were formerly thought to contain real information are now suspect because they have been constantly reinterpreted by successive generations of historians. On the other hand, epistemologists and philosophers are experiencing an extreme crisis, which is undermining what was once called historical science. Scholars who used to sustain themselves on their texts now doubt the certainty of any interpretation.

At first glance, Guillaume de Machaut's text may seem susceptible to the prevailing skepticism concerning historical certainty. But after some moments' reflection even contemporary readers will find some real events among the unlikely occurrences of the story. They will not believe in the signs in the sky or in the accusations against the Jews, but neither will they treat all the unlikely themes in the same way, or put them on the same level. Guillaume did not invent a single thing. He is credulous, admittedly, and he reflects the hysteria of public opinion. The innumerable deaths he tallys are nonetheless real, caused presumably by the famous Black Death, which ravaged the north of France between 1349 and 1350. Similarly, the massacre of the Jews was real. In the eyes of the massacrers the deed was justified by the rumors of poisoning in circulation everywhere. The universal fear of disease gives sufficient weight to the rumors to unleash the massacres described. The following is the passage from the *Judgment of the King of Navarre* that deals with the Jews:

After that came a false, treacherous and contemptible swine: this was shameful Israel, the wicked and disloyal who hated good and loved everything evil, who gave so much gold and silver and promises to Christians, who then poisoned several rivers and fountains that had been clear and pure so that many lost their lives; for whoever used them died suddenly. Certainly ten times one hundred thousand died from it, in country and in city. Then finally this mortal calamity was noticed.

He who sits on high and sees far, who governs and provides for everything, did not want this treachery to remain hidden; he revealed it and made it so generally known that they lost their lives and possessions. Then every Jew was destroyed, some hanged, others burned; some were drowned, others beheaded with an ax or sword. And many Christians died together with them in shame.[1]

Medieval communities were so afraid of the plague that the word alone was enough to frighten them. They avoided mentioning it as long as possible and even avoided taking the necessary precautions at the risk of aggravating the effects of the epidemic. So helpless were they that telling the truth did not mean facing the situation but rather giving in to

1. Guillaume de Machaut, *Oeuvres*, Société des anciens textes français, vol. 1, *Le Jugement du Roy de Navarre* (Paris: Ernest Hoeppfner, 1908), pp. 144–45.

its destructive consequences and relinquishing all semblance of normal life. The entire population shared in this type of blindness. Their desperate desire to deny the evidence contributed to their search for "scapegoats."[2] La Fontaine, in *Animals Sickened by the Plague*, gives an excellent description of this almost religious reluctance to articulate the terrifying term and thereby unleash some sort of evil power on the community:

The plague (since it must be called by its name). . .[3]

La Fontaine introduces us to the process of collective bad faith which recognizes the plague as a divine punishment. The angry god is annoyed by a guilt that is not equally shared. To avert the plague the guilty must be identified and punished or, rather, as La Fontaine writes, "dedicated" to the god. The first to be interrogated in the fable are the beasts of prey, who describe their bestial behavior, which is immediately excused. Last comes the ass, the least bloodthirsty of them all, and therefore the weakest and least protected. It is the ass that is finally designated.

According to historians, in some cities Jews were massacred at the mere mention of the plague being in the area, even before it had actually arrived. Guillaume's account could fit this sort of phenomenon, because the massacre occurred well before the height of the epidemic. But the number of deaths the author attributes to the Jews' poisoning suggests another explanation. If the deaths are real—and there is no reason to think they are imagined—they might well be the first victims of that same plague. But Guillaume does not think so even in retrospect. In his eyes the traditional scapegoats remain the cause of *the first stages of the epidemic*. Only in the later stages does the author recognize the presence of a properly pathological phenomenon. Ultimately, the disaster is so great that it casts doubt on the likelihood of a single explanation of a conspiracy of poisoners, though Guillaume does not then reinterpret the whole chain of events from a rational perspective.

In fact, we might well ask to what extent the poet recognizes the existence of the plague, since he avoids writing the fatal word until the

2. J.-N. Biraben, *Les Hommes et la peste en France et dans les pays européens et mediterranéens*, 2 vols. (Paris-The Hague: Mouton, 1975–76); Jean Delumeau, *La Peur en Occident* (Paris: Fayard, 1978).
3. Jean La Fontaine, *Les Animaux malades de la peste* (Paris: Libraire Larousse, n.d.), bk. 7, no. 1.

very end. At the climactic moment he solemnly introduces the Greek word *epydimie*, which was uncommon at the time. The word obviously does not function in his text in the same way as it would in ours; it is not really a synonym for the dreaded word but rather a sort of euphemism, a new way of not calling the plague by its name. It is in fact a new but purely linguistic scapegoat. Guillaume tells us it was never possible to determine the nature and the cause of the disease from which so many people died in such a short time:

> Nor was there any physician or doctor who really knew the cause or origin, or what it was (nor was there any remedy), yet this malady was so great that it was called an epidemic.

On this score Guillaume prefers to refer to public opinion rather than to think for himself. The word *epydimie* in the fourteenth century had a certain scientific flavor which helped to ward off anxiety, somewhat like the vapors of the fumigation carried out at street corners to reduce the waves of pestilence. A disease with a name seems on the way to a cure, so uncontrollable phenomena are frequently renamed to create the impression of control. Such verbal exorcisms continue to appeal wherever science remains illusory or ineffective. By the refusal to name it, the plague itself becomes "dedicated" to the god. This linguistic sacrifice is innocent compared with the human sacrifices that accompany or precede it, but its essential structure is the same.

Even in retrospect, all the real and imaginary collective scapegoats, the Jews and the flagellants, the rain of stones and the *epydimie*, continue to play such an effective role in Guillaume's story that he never perceives in them the single entity that we call the "Black Death." The author continues to see a number of more or less independent disasters, linked only by their religious significance, similar in a way to the ten plagues of Egypt.

Almost everything I have said so far is obvious. We all understand Guillaume's text in the same way and my readers have no need of me. It is not useless, however, to insist on this reading, of which the boldness and forcefulness elude us, precisely because it is accepted by everyone and is uncontroversial. There has been agreement about it literally for centuries, all the more remarkable in that it involves a radical reinterpretation. We reject without question the meaning the author gives his text. We declare that he does not know what he is saying. From our several centuries' distance we know better than he and can correct what he has written. We even believe that we have discovered a truth not seen by the author and, with still greater audacity, do not hestitate to state that he provides us with this truth even though he does not perceive it himself.

What is the source of our amazing confidence in the statement that Jews were really massacred? An answer comes immediately to mind. We are not reading this text in a vacuum. Other texts exist from the same period; they deal with the same subjects; some of them are more valuable than Guillaume's. Their authors are less credulous. They provide a tight framework of historical knowledge in which Guillaume's text can be placed. Thanks to this context, we can distinguish true from false in the passage quoted.

It is true that the facts about the anti-Semitic persecutions during the plague are quite well known. There is an already recognized body of knowledge that arouses certain expectations in us. Guillaume's text is responding to those expectations. This perspective is not wrong from the point of view of our individual experience and our immediate contact with the text, but it does not justify us from the theoretical point of view.

Although the framework of historical knowledge does exist, it consists of documents that are no more reliable than Guillaume's text, for similar or different reasons. And we cannot place Guillaume exactly in this context because we lack knowledge of where exactly the events he describes took place. It may have been in Paris or Reims or even another city. In any case the context is not significant; even without that information the modern reader would end up with the reading I have given. He would conclude that there were probably victims who were unjustly massacred. He would therefore think the text is false, since it claims that the victims were guilty, but true insofar as there really were victims. He would, in the end, distinguish the truth from the false exactly as we do. What gives us this ability? Would it not be wise to be guided systematically by the principle of discarding the whole basket of apples because of the few rotten ones among them? Should we not suspect a certain lapse of caution or remnant of naïveté that, given the opportunity, will be attacked by overzealous contemporary critics? Should we not admit that all historical knowledge is uncertain and that nothing can be taken from a text such as ours, not even the reality of a persecution?

All these questions must be answered categorically in the negative. Out-and-out skepticism does not take into account the real nature of the text. There is a particular relationship between the likely and the unlikely characteristics of this text. In the beginning the reader cannot of course distinguish between true and false. He sees only themes that are incredible as well as others that are quite credible. He can believe in the increasing number of deaths; it could be an epidemic. But the massive scale of the poisonings described by Guillaume is scarcely credible. There were no substances in the fourteenth century capable of producing such harmful effects. The author's hatred for the supposedly guilty people is explicit and makes his thesis extremely suspect.

These two types of characteristics cannot be recognized without at least implicitly acknowledging that they interact with each other. If there really is an epidemic, then it might well stir up latent prejudices. The appetite for persecution readily focuses on religious minorities, especially during a time of crisis. On the other hand a real persecution might well be justified by the sort of accusation that Guillaume credulously echoes. Such a poet is not expected to be particularly sanguinary. If he believes in the stories he tells us, no doubt they are believed by the people around him. The text suggests that public opinion is overexcited and ready to accept the most absurd rumors. In short it suggests a propitious climate for massacres which the author confirms actually took place.

In a context of improbable events, those that are possible become probable. The reverse is also true. In a context of probable events, the unlikely ones cannot be ascribed to an imagination operating freely for the pleasure of inventing fiction. We are aware of the imaginary element, but it is the very specific imagination of people who crave violence. As a result, among the textual representations there is a mutual confirmation. This correspondence can only be explained by one hypothesis. The text we are reading has its roots in a real persecution described from the perspective of the persecutors. The perspective is inevitably deceptive since the persecutors are convinced that their violence is justified; they consider themselves judges, and therefore they must have guilty victims, yet their perspective is to some degree reliable, for the certainty of being right encourages them to hide nothing of their massacres.

Faced with a text such as Guillaume de Machaut's, it is legitimate to suspend the general rule by which the text as a whole is never worth more, as far as real information goes, than the least reliable of its features. If the text describes circumstances favorable to persecution, if it presents us with victims of the type that persecutors usually choose, and if, in addition, it represents these victims as guilty of the type of crimes which persecutors normally attribute to their victims, then it is very likely that the persecution is real. If this reality is confirmed by the text itself then there is little scope for doubt.

When one begins to understand the perspective of the persecutors, the absurdity of their accusations strengthens rather than compromises the informational value of the text, but only in reference to the violence that it echoes. If Guillaume had added stories of ritual infanticide to the episodes of poisoning, his account would be even more improbable without, however, in the least diminishing the accuracy of the massacres it reports. The more unlikely the accusations in this genre of text the more they strengthen the probability of the massacres: they confirm for us the psychosocial context within which the massacres must have taken place. Conversely, if the theme of massacres is placed alongside the theme of an epidemic it provides the historical context within which even the most precise scholar could take this account of poisoning seriously.

The accounts of persecutions are no doubt inaccurate, but in a way they are so characteristic of persecutors in general, and of medieval persecutors in particular, that the text can be believed in all the areas in which conjectures are prompted by the very nature of the inaccuracy. When potential persecutors describe the reality of their persecutions, they should be believed.

The combination of the two types of characteristics generates certainty. If the combination were only to be found in rare examples we could not be so certain. But its frequency is too great to allow doubt. Only actual persecution seen from the perspective of the persecutors can explain the regular combination of these characteristics. Our interpretation of all the texts is confirmed statistically.

The fact that certainty is statistically verifiable does not mean it is based only on an accumulation of equally uncertain documents. All documents like Guillaume de Machaut's are of considerable value because in them the probable and improbable interact in such a way that each explains and justifies the presence of the other. If there is a statistical character to our certainty it is because any document studied in isolation could be forged. This is unlikely, but not impossible, in the case of a single document. And yet it is impossible where a great number of documents are concerned.

The modern Western world chooses to interpret "texts of persecution" as real, this being the only possible way to demystify them. This solution is accurate and perfect because it makes allowance for all the characteristics found in this type of text. Solid intellectual reasoning is the basis, rather than humanitarianism or ideology. This interpretation has not usurped the almost unanimous agreement granted it. For the social historian reliable testimony, rather than the testimony of someone who shares Guillaume de Machaut's illusions, will never be as valuable as the unreliable testimony of persecutors, or their accomplices, which reveals more because of its unconscious nature. The conclusive document belongs to persecutors who are too naïve to cover the traces of their crimes, in contrast to modern persecutors who are too cautious to leave behind documents that might be used against them.

I call those persecutors naïve who are still convinced that they are right and who are not so mistrustful as to cover up or censor the fundamental characteristics of their persecution. Such characteristics are either clearly apparent in the text and are directly revealing or they remain hidden and reveal indirectly. They are all strong stereotypes and the combination of both types, one obvious and one hidden, provides us with information about the nature of these texts.

WE ARE ALL ABLE today to recognize the stereotypes of persecution. But what is now common knowledge scarcely existed in the fourteenth century. Naïve persecutors *are unaware of what they are doing.* Their conscience is too good to deceive their readers systematically, and they present things as they see them. They do not suspect that by writing their accounts they are arming posterity against them. This is true of the infamous "witch-hunts" of the sixteenth century. It is still true today in the backward regions of the world. We are, then, dealing with the commonplace, and my readers may be bored by my insistence on these first obvious facts. The purpose will soon be seen. One slight displacement is enough to transform what is taken for granted, in the case of Guillaume de Machaut, into something unusual and even inconceivable.

My readers will have already observed that in speaking as I do I contradict certain principles that numerous critics hold as sacrosanct. I am always told one must never do violence to the text. Faced with Guillaume de Machaut the choice is clear: one must either do violence to the text or let the text forever do violence to innocent victims. Certain principles universally held to be valid in our day, because they seem to guard against the excesses of certain interpretations, can bring about disastrous consequences never anticipated by those who, thinking they have foreseen everything, consider the principles inviolable. Everyone believes that the first duty of the critic is to respect the meaning of texts. Can this principle be sustained in the face of Guillaume de Machaut's work?

Another contemporary notion suffers in the light of Guillaume de Machaut's text, or rather from the unhesitating way we read it, and that is the casual way in which literary critics dismiss what they call the "referent." In current linguistic jargon the referent is the subject of the text; in our example it is the massacre of the Jews, who were seen as responsible for the poisoning of Christians. For some twenty years the referent has been considered more or less inaccessible. It is unimportant, we hear, whether we are capable or not of reaching it; this naïve notion of the referent would seem only to hamper the latest study of textuality. Now the only thing that matters is the ambiguous and unreliable relationships of language. This perspective is not to be rejected wholesale, but in applying it in a scholarly way we run the risk that only Ernest Hoeppfner, Guillaume's editor in the venerable Société des anciens textes, will be seen as the truly ideal critic of that writer. His introduction does in fact speak of courtly poetry, but there is never any mention of the massacre of the Jews during the plague.

The passage from Guillaume provides a good example of what I have called in *Des choses cachées depuis la fondation du monde* "persecution texts."[4] By that I mean accounts of real violence, often collective, told from the perspective of the persecutors, and therefore influenced by characteristic distortions. These distortions must be identified and corrected in order to reveal the arbitrary nature of the violence that the persecution text presents as justified.

We need not examine at length the accounts of witch trials to determine the presence of the same combination of real and imaginary, though not gratuitous, details that we found in the text of Guillaume de Machaut. Everything is presented as fact, but we do not believe all of it, nor do we believe that everything is false. Generally we have no difficulty in distinguishing fact from fiction. Again, the accusations made in trials seem ridiculous, even though the witch may consider them true and there may be reason to suspect her confession was not obtained by torture. The accused may well believe herself to be a witch, and may

4. René Girard, *Des choses cachées depuis la fondation du monde* (Paris: Grasset, 1978), 1:136–62.

well have tried to harm her neighbors by magical proceedings. We still do not consider that she deserves the death sentence. We do not believe that magic is effective. We have no difficulty in accepting that the victim shares her torturers' ridiculous belief in the efficacy of witchcraft but this belief does not affect us; our skepticism is not shaken.

During the trial not a single voice is raised to reestablish or, rather, to establish the truth. No one is capable of doing so. This means that not only the judges and the witnesses but also the accused are not in agreement with our interpretation of their own texts. This unanimity fails to influence us. The authors of these documents were there and we were not. We have access to no information that did not come from them. And yet, several centuries later, one single historian or even the first person to read the text feels he has the right to dispute the sentence pronounced on the witches.[5]

Guillaume de Machaut is reinterpreted in the same extreme way, the same audacity is exercised in overthrowing the text, the same intellectual operation is in effect with the same certainty, based on the same type of reasoning. The fact that some of the details are imagined does not persuade us to consider the whole text imaginary. On the contrary, the incredible accusations strengthen rather than diminish the credibility of the other facts.

Once more we encounter what would seem to be, but is not, a paradoxical relationship between the probable and improbable details that enter into the text's composition. It is in the light of this relationship, not yet articulated but no less apparent to us, that we will evaluate the quantity and quality of the information that can be drawn from our text. If the document is of a legal nature, the results are usually as positive or even more positive than in the case of Guillaume de Machaut. It is unfortunate that most of the accounts were burned with the witches. The accusations are absurd and the sentence unjust, but the texts have been edited with the care and clarity that generally characterize legal documents. Our confidence is therefore well placed. There is no suspicion that we secretly sympathize with those who conducted the witch-hunts. The historian who would consider all the details of a trial equally

5. J. Hansen, *Zauberwahn, Inquisition und Hexenprozess im Mittelalter und die Entstehung der grossen Hexenverfolgung* (Munich-Leipzig: Scientia, 1900); Delumeau, *La Peur en Occident*, vol. 2, chap. 2. On the end of the witchcraft trials, see Robert Mandrou, *Magistrats et sorciers* (Paris: Plon, 1968). See also Natalie Zemon Davis, *Society and Culture in Early Modern France* (Stanford, Calif.: Stanford University Press, 1975).

fantastic, on the excuse that some of them are tainted by the distortions of the persecutors, is no expert, and his colleagues would not take him seriously. The most effective criticism does not consist in rejecting even the believable data on the ground that it is better to sin by excess rather than lack of distrust. Once again the principle of unlimited mistrust must give way to the golden rule of persecution texts: the mind of a persecutor creates a certain type of illusion and the traces of his illusion confirm rather than invalidate the existence of a certain kind of event, the persecution itself in which the witch is put to death. To distinguish the true from the false is a simple matter, since each bears the clear mark of a stereotype.

In order to understand the reasons behind this extraordinary assurance evidenced in persecution texts, we must enumerate and describe the stereotypes. This is also not a difficult task. It is merely a question of articulating an understanding we already possess. We are not aware of its scope because we never examine it in a systematic fashion. The understanding in question remains captive in the concrete examples to which we apply it, and these always belong to the mainly Western historical domain. We have never yet tried to apply this understanding beyond that domain, for example to the so-called ethnological universe. To make this possible I am now going to sketch, in summary fashion, a typology of the stereotypes of persecution.

CHAPTER TWO
Stereotypes of Persecution

I SHALL CONFINE my discussion to collective persecutions and their resonances. By collective persecutions I mean acts of violence committed directly by a mob of murderers such as the persecution of the Jews during the Black Death. By collective resonances of persecutions I mean acts of violence, such as witch-hunts, that are legal in form but stimulated by the extremes of public opinion. The distinction is not, however, essential. Political terrors, such as the French Revolution, often belong to both types. The persecutions in which we are interested generally take place in times of crisis, which weaken normal institutions and favor *mob* formation. Such spontaneous gatherings of people can exert a decisive influence on institutions that have been so weakened, and even replace them entirely.

These phenomena are not always produced by identical circumstances. Sometimes the cause is external, such as an epidemic, a severe drought, or a flood followed by famine. Sometimes the cause is internal — political disturbances, for example, or religious conflicts. Fortunately, we do not have to determine the actual cause. No matter what circumstances trigger great collective persecutions, the experience of those who live through them is the same. The strongest impression is without question an extreme loss of social order evidenced by the disappearance of the rules and "differences" that define cultural divisions. Descriptions of these events are all alike. Some of them, especially descriptions of the plague, are found in our greatest writers. We read them in Thucydides and Sophocles, in Lucretius, Boccaccio, Shakespeare, Defoe, Thomas Mann, Antonin Artaud, and many others. Some of them are also written by individuals with no literary pretensions, and there is never any great difference. We should not be surprised since all the sources speak endlessly of the absence of difference, the lack of cultural differentiation, and the confusion that results. For example the Portuguese monk Fco de Santa Maria writes in 1697:

As soon as this violent and tempestuous spark is lit in a kingdom or a republic, magistrates are bewildered, people are terrified, the government thrown into disarray. Laws are no longer obeyed; business comes to a halt; families lose coherence, and the streets their lively atmosphere. Everything is reduced to extreme confusion. Everything goes to ruin. For everything is touched and overwhelmed by the weight and magnitude of such a horrible calamity. People regardless of position or wealth are drowning in mortal sadness. . . . Those who were burying others yesterday are themselves buried today. . . . No pity is shown to friends since every sign of pity is dangerous. . . .

All the laws of love and nature are drowned or forgotten in the midst of the horrors of such great confusion; children are suddenly separated from their parents, wives from their husbands, brothers and friends from each other. . . . Men lose their natural courage and, not knowing any longer what advice to follow, act like desperate blindmen, who encounter fear and contradictions at every step.[1]

Institutional collapse obliterates or telescopes hierarchical and functional differences, so that everything has the same monotonous and monstrous aspect. The impression of difference in a society that is not in a state of crisis is the result of real diversity and also of a system of exchange that "differentiates" and therefore conceals the reciprocal elements it contains by its very culture and by the nature of the exchange. Marriages for example, or consumer goods, are not clearly perceived as exchanges. When a society breaks down, time sequences shorten. Not only is there an acceleration of the tempo of positive exchanges that continue only when absolutely indispensable, as in barter for example, but also the hostile or "negative" exchanges tend to increase. The reciprocity of negative rather than positive exchanges becomes foreshortened as it becomes more visible, as witnessed in the reciprocity of insults, blows, revenge, and neurotic symptoms. That is why traditional cultures shun a too immediate reciprocity.

Negative reciprocity, although it brings people into opposition with each other, tends to make their conduct uniform and is responsible for

1. Fco de Santa Maria, *Historia de sagradas concregaçoes*... (Lisbon: M.L. Ferreyra, 1697); quoted by Delumeau, *La Peur en Occident*, p. 112.

the predominance of the *same*. Thus, paradoxically, it is both conflictual and solipsistic. This lack of differentiation corresponds to the reality of human relations, yet it remains mythic. In our own time we have had a similar experience which has become absolute because it is projected on the whole universe. The text quoted above highlights this process of creating uniformity through reciprocity: "Those who were burying others yesterday are themselves buried today. . . . No pity is shown to friends since every sign of pity is dangerous. . . children are suddenly separated from their parents, wives from husbands, brother and friends from each other." The similarity of behavior creates confusion and a universal lack of difference: "People regardless of position or wealth are drowning in mortal sadness. . . . Everything is reduced to an extreme confusion."

The experience of great social crisis is scarcely affected by the diversity of their true causes. The result is great uniformity in the descriptions that relate to the uniformity itself. Guillaume de Machaut is no exception. He sees in the egotistical withdrawal into the self and in the series or reprisals that result – the paradox of reciprocal consequences – one of the main causes of the plague. We can then speak of a stereotype of crisis which is to be recognized, logically and chronologically, as the first stereotype of persecution. Culture is somehow eclipsed as it becomes less differentiated. Once this is understood it is easier to understand the coherence of the process of persecution and the sort of logic that links all the stereotypes of which it is composed.

Men feel powerless when confronted with the eclipse of culture; they are disconcerted by the immensity of the disaster but never look into the natural causes; the concept that they might affect those causes by learning more about them remains embryonic. Since cultural eclipse is above all a social crisis, there is a strong tendency to explain it by social and, especially, moral causes. After all, human relations disintegrate in the process and the subjects of those relations cannot be utterly innocent of this phenomenon. But, rather than blame themselves, people inevitably blame either society as a whole, which costs them nothing, or other people who seem particularly harmful for easily identifiable reasons. The suspects are accused of a particular category of crimes.

Certain accusations are so characteristic of collective persecution that their very mention makes modern observers suspect violence in the air. They look everywhere for other likely indications – other stereotypes of persecution – to confirm their suspicion. At first sight the accusations seem fairly diverse but their unity is easy to find. First there are violent crimes which choose as object those people whom it is most criminal to attack, either in the absolute sense or in reference to the individual committing the act: a king, a father, the symbol of supreme authority, and in biblical and modern societies the weakest and most defenseless, especially young children. Then there are sexual crimes: rape, incest, bestiality. The ones most frequently invoked transgress the taboos that are considered the strictest in the society in question. Finally there are religious crimes, such as profanation of the host. Here, too, it is the strictest taboos that are transgressed.

All these crimes seem to be fundamental. They attack the very foundation of cultural order, the family and the hierarchical differences without which there would be no social order. In the sphere of individual action they correspond to the global consequences of an epidemic of the plague or of any comparable disaster. It is not enough for the social bond to be loosened; it must be totally destroyed.

Ultimately, the persecutors always convince themselves that a small number of people, or even a single individual, despite his relative weakness, is extremely harmful to the whole of society. The stereotypical accusation justifies and facilitates this belief by ostensibly acting the role of mediator. It bridges the gap between the insignificance of the individual and the enormity of the social body. If the wrongdoers, even the diabolical ones, are to succeed in destroying the community's distinctions, they must either attack the community directly, by striking at its heart or head, or else they must begin the destruction of difference within their own sphere by committing contagious crimes such as parricide and incest.

We need not take time to consider the ultimate causes of this belief, such as the unconscious desires described by psychoanalysts, or the Marxist concept of the secret will to oppress. There is no need to go that far. Our concern is more elementary; we are only interested in the mechanism of the accusation and in the interaction between representation and acts of persecution. They comprise a system, and, if knowledge of the cause is necessary to the understanding of the system, then the most immediate and obvious causes will suffice. The terror inspired in people by the eclipse of culture and the universal confusion of popular upris ings are signs of a community that is literally undifferentiated, deprived of all that distinguishes one person from another in time and space. As a result all are equally disordered in the same place and at the same time.

The crowd tends toward persecution since the natural causes of what troubles it and transforms it into a *turba* cannot interest it. The crowd by definition seeks action but cannot affect natural causes. It therefore looks for an accessible cause that will appease its appetite for violence. Those who make up the crowd are always potential persecutors, for they dream of purging the community of the impure elements that corrupt it, the traitors who undermine it. The crowd's act of becoming a crowd is the same as the obscure call to assemble or mobilize, in other words to become a *mob*. Actually this term comes from *mobile*, which is as distinct from the word *crowd* as the Latin *turba* is from *vulgus*. The word *mobilization* reminds us of a military operation, against an already identified enemy or one soon to be identified by the mobilization of the crowd.

All the stereotypes of accusation were made against the Jews and other scapegoats during the plague. But Guillaume de Machaut does not mention them. As we have seen, he accuses the Jews of poisoning the rivers. He dismisses the most improbable accusations, and his relative moderation can perhaps be explained by the fact that he is an "intellectual." His moderation may also have a more general significance linked to intellectual development at the end of the Middle Ages.

During this period belief in occult forces diminished. Later we shall ask why. The search for people to blame continues but it demands more rational crimes; it looks for a material, more substantial cause. This seems to me to be the reason for the frequent references to *poison*. The persecutors imagined such venomous concentrations of poison that even very small quantities would suffice to annihilate entire populations. Henceforth the clearly lightweight quality of magic as a cause is weighted down by materiality and therefore "scientific" logic. Chemistry takes over from purely demoniac influence.

The objective remains the same, however. The accusation of poisoning makes it possible to lay the responsibility for real disasters on people whose activities have not been really proven to be criminal. Thanks to poison, it is possible to be persuaded that a small group, or even a single individual, can harm the whole society without being discovered. Thus poison is both less mythical and just as mythical as previous accusations or even the ordinary "evil eye" which is used to attribute almost any evil to almost any person. We should therefore recognize in the poisoning of drinking water a variation of a stereotypical accusation. The fact that these accusations are all juxtaposed in the witch trials is proof that they all respond to the same need. The suspects are always convicted of nocturnal participation in the famous *sabbat*. No alibi is possible since the physical presence of the accused is not necessary to establish proof. Participation in criminal assemblies can be purely spiritual.

The crimes and their preparation with which the sabbat is associated have a wealth of social repercussions. Among them can be found the abominations traditionally attributed to the Jews in Christian countries, and before them to the Christians in the Roman Empire. They always include ritual infanticide, religious profanation, incestuous relationships, and bestiality. Food poisoning as well as offenses against influential or prestigious citizens always play a significant role. Consequently, despite her personal insignificance, a witch is engaged in activities that can potentially affect the whole of society. This explains why the devil and his demons are not disdainful of such an alliance. I will say no more about stereotypical accusations. It is easy to recognize the crisis caused by the lack of differentiation as the second stereotype and its link to the first.

I turn now to the third stereotype. The crowd's choice of victims may be totally random; but it is not necessarily so. It is even possible that the crimes of which they are accused are real, but that sometimes the persecutors choose their victims because they belong to a class that is particularly susceptible to persecution rather than because of the crimes they have committed. The Jews are among those accused by Guillaume de Machaut of poisoning the rivers. Of all the indications he gives us this is for us the most valuable, the one that most reveals the distortion of persecution. Within the context of other imaginary and real stereotypes, we know that this stereotype must be real. In fact, in modern Western society Jews have frequently been persecuted.

Ethnic and religious minorities tend to polarize the majorities against themselves. In this we see one of the criteria by which victims are selected, which, though relative to the individual society, is transcultural in principle. There are very few societies that do not subject their minorities, all the poorly integrated or merely distinct groups, to certain forms of discrimination and even persecution. In India the Moslems are persecuted, in Pakistan the Hindus. There are therefore universal signs for the selection of victims, and they constitute our third stereotype.

In addition to cultural and religious there are purely *physical* criteria. Sickness, madness, genetic deformities, accidental injuries, and even disabilities in general tend to polarize persecutors. We need only look around or within to understand the universality. Even today people cannot control a momentary recoil from physical abnormality. The very word *abnormal*, like the word *plague* in the Middle Ages, is something of a taboo; it is both noble and cursed, *sacer* in all senses of the word. It is considered more fitting in English to replace it with the word *handicapped*. The "handicapped" are subject to discriminatory measures that make them victims, out of all proportion to the extent to which their presence disturbs the ease of social exchange. One of the great qualities of our society is that it now feels obliged to take measures for their benefit.

Disability belongs to a large group of banal signs of a victim, and among certain groups – in a boarding school for example – every individual who has difficulty adapting, someone from another country or state, an orphan, an only son, someone who is penniless, or even simply the latest arrival, is more or less interchangeable with a cripple. If the disability or deformity is real, it tends to polarize "primitive" people against the afflicted person. Similarly, if a group of people is used to choosing its victims from a certain social, ethnic, or religious category, it tends to attribute to them disabilities or deformities that would reinforce the polarization against the victim, were they real. This tendency is clearly observable in racist cartoons.

The abnormality need not only be physical. In any area of existence or behavior abnormality may function as the criterion for selecting those to be persecuted. For example there is such a thing as social abnormality; here the average defines the norm. The further one is from normal social status of whatever kind, the greater the risk of persecution. This is easy to see in relation to those at the bottom of the social ladder.

This is less obvious when we add another marginal group to the poor and outsiders – the marginal insider, the rich and powerful. The monarch and his court are often reminiscent of the *eye* of the hurricane. This double marginality is indicative of a social organization in turmoil. In normal times the rich and powerful enjoy all sorts of protection and privileges which the disinherited lack. We are concerned here not with normal circumstances but with periods of crisis. A mere glance at world history will reveal that the odds of a violent death at the hands of a frenzied crowd are statistically greater for the privileged than for any other category. Extreme characteristics ultimately attract collective destruction at some time or other, extremes not just of wealth or poverty, but also of success and failure, beauty and ugliness, vice and virtue, the ability to please and to displease. The weakness of women, children, and old people, as well as the strength of the most powerful, becomes weakness in the face of the crowd. Crowds commonly turn on those who originally held exceptional power over them.

No doubt some people will be shocked to find the rich and powerful listed among the victims of collective persecution under the same title as the poor and weak. The two phenomena are not symmetrical in their eyes. The rich and powerful exert an influence over society which justifies the acts of violence to which they are subjected in times of crisis. This is the holy revolt of the oppressed.

The borderline between rational discrimination and arbitrary persecution is sometimes difficult to trace. For political, moral, and medical reasons certain forms of discrimination strike us as reasonable today, yet they are similar to the ancient forms of persecution; for example, the quarantine of anyone who might be contagious during an epidemic. In the Middle Ages doctors were hostile to the idea that the plague could spread through physical contact with the diseased. Generally, they belonged to the enlightened group and any theory of contagion smacked too much of a persecutor's prejudice not to be suspect. And yet these doctors were wrong. For the idea of contagion to become established in the nineteenth century in a purely medical context, devoid of any association with persecution, it was necessary for there to be no suspicion that it was the return of prejudice in a new disguise.

This is an interesting question but has nothing to do with our present work. My only goal is to enumerate the qualities that tend to polarize violent crowds against those who possess them. The examples I have given unquestionably belong in this category. The fact that some of these acts of violence might even be justifiable today is not really important to the line of analysis I am pursuing.

I am not seeking to set exact boundaries to the field of persecution; nor am I trying to determine precisely where injustice begins or ends. Contrary to what some think, I am not interested in defining what is good and bad in the social and cultural order. My only concern is to show that the pattern of collective violence crosses cultures and that its broad contours are easily outlined. It is one thing to recognize the existence of this pattern, another to establish its relevance. In some cases this is difficult to determine, but the proof I am looking for is not affected by such difficulty. If a stereotype of persecution cannot be clearly recognized in a particular detail of a specific event, the solution does not rest only with this particular detail in an isolated context. We must determine whether or not the other stereotypes are present along with the detail in question.

Let us look at two examples. Most historians consider that the French monarchy bears some responsibility for the revolution in 1789. Does Marie Antoinette's execution therefore lie outside our pattern? The queen belongs to several familiar categories of victims of persecution; she is not only a queen but a foreigner. Her Austrian origin is mentioned repeatedly in the popular accusations against her. The court that condemns her is heavily influenced by the Paris mob. Our first stereotype can also be found; all the characteristics of the great crisis that provoke collective persecution are discernible in the French Revolution. To be sure historians are not in the habit of dealing with the details of the French Revolution as stereotypes of the one general pattern of persecution. I do not suggest that we should substitute this way of thinking in all our ideas about the French Revolution. Nonetheless it sheds interesting light on an accusation which is often passed over but which figures explicitly in the queen's trial, that of having committed incest with her son.[2]

Let's look at another example of a condemned person, someone who has actually committed the deed that brings down on him the crowd's violence: a black male who actually rapes a white female. The collective violence is no longer arbitrary in the most obvious sense of the term. It is actually sanctioning the deed it purports to sanction. Under such circumstances the distortions of persecution might be supposed to play no role and the existence of the stereotypes of persecution might no longer bear the significance I give it. Actually, these distortions of persecution are present and are not incompatible with the literal truth of the accusation. The persecutors' portrayal of the situation is irrational. It inverts the relationship between the global situation and the individual trans-

2. I am grateful to Jean-Claude Guillebaud for drawing my attention to this accusation of incest.

gression. If there is a causal or motivational link between the two levels, it can only move from the collective to the individual. The persecutor's mentality moves in the reverse direction. Instead of seeing in the microcosm a reflection or imitation of the global level, it seeks in the individual the origin and cause of all that is harmful. The responsibility of the victims suffers the same fantastic exaggeration whether it is real or not. As far as we are concerned there is very little difference between Marie Antoinette's situation and that of the persecuted black male.

WE HAVE SEEN the close relationship that exists between the first two stereotypes. In order to blame victims for the loss of distinctions resulting from the crisis, they are accused of crimes that eliminate distinctions. But in actuality they are identified as victims for persecution because they bear the signs of victims. What is the relationship of the third type to the first two stereotypes? At first sight the signs of a victim are purely differential. But cultural signs are equally so. There must therefore be two ways of being different, two types of differences.

No culture exists within which everyone does not feel "different" from others and does not consider such "differences" legitimate and necessary. Far from being radical and progressive, the current glorification of difference is merely the abstract expression of an outlook common to all cultures. There exists in every individual a tendency to think of himself not only as different from others but as extremely different, because every culture entertains this feeling of difference among the individuals who compose it.

The signs that indicate a victim's selection result not from the difference within the system but from the difference outside the system, the potential for the system to differ from its own difference, in other words not to be different at all, to cease to exist as a system. This is easily seen in the case of physical disabilities. The human body is a system of anatomic differences. If a disability, even as the result of an accident, is disturbing, it is because it gives the impression of a disturbing dynamism. It seems to threaten the very system. Efforts to limit it are unsuccessful; it disturbs the differences that surround it. These in turn become *monstrous*, rush together, are compressed and blended together to the point of destruction. Difference that exists outside the system is terrifying because it reveals the truth of the system, its relativity, its fragility, and its mortality.

The various kinds of victims seem predisposed to crimes that eliminate differences. Religious, ethnic, or national minorities are never actually reproached for their difference, but for not being as different as expected, and in the end for not differing at all. Foreigners are incapable of respecting "real" differences; they are lacking in culture or in taste, as the case may be. They have difficulty in perceiving exactly what is different. The *barbaros* is not the person who speaks a different language but the person who mixes the only truly significant distinctions, those of the Greek language. In all the vocabulary of tribal or national prejudices hatred is expressed, not for difference, but for its absence. It is not the other *nomos* that is seen in the other, but anomaly, nor is it another norm but abnormality; the disabled becomes deformed; the foreigner becomes the *apatride*. It is not good to be a cosmopolitan in Russia. Aliens imitate all the differences because they have none. The mechanisms of our ancestors are reproduced unconsciously, from generation to generation, and, it is important to recognize, often at a less lethal level than in the past. For instance today anti-Americanism pretends to "differ" from previous prejudices because it espouses all differences and rejects the uniquely American virus of uniformity.

We hear everywhere that "difference" is persecuted. This is the favorite statement of contemporary pluralism, and it can be somewhat misleading in the present context.

Even in the most closed cultures men believe they are free and open to the universal; their differential character makes the narrowest cultural fields seem inexhaustible from within. Anything that compromises this illusion terrifies us and stirs up the immemorial tendency to persecution. This tendency always takes the same direction, it is embodied by the same stereotypes and always responds to the same threat. Despite what is said around us persecutors are never obsessed by difference but rather by its unutterable contrary, the lack of difference.

Stereotypes of persecution cannot be dissociated, and remarkably most languages do not dissociate them. This is true of Latin and Greek, for example, and thus of French or English, which forces us constantly in our study of stereotypes to turn to words that are related: *crisis, crime, criteria, critique,* all share a common root in the Greek verb *krino,* which means not only to judge, distinguish, differentiate, but also to accuse and condemn a victim. Too much reliance should not be placed on etymology, nor do I reason from that basis. But the phenomenon is so constant it deserves to be mentioned. It implies an as yet concealed relationship between collective persecutions and the culture as a whole. If such a relationship exists, it has never been explained by any linguist, philosopher, or politician.

CHAPTER THREE
What Is a Myth?

EACH TIME AN oral or written testament mentions an act of violence that is directly or indirectly collective we question whether it includes the description of a social and cultural crisis, that is, a generalized loss of differences (the first stereotype), crimes that "eliminate differences" (the second stereotype), and whether the identified authors of these crimes possess the marks that suggest a victim, the paradoxical marks of the absence of difference (the third stereotype). The fourth stereotype is violence itself, which will be discussed later.

The juxtaposition of more than one stereotype within a single document indicates persecution. Not all the stereotypes must be present: three are enough and often even two. Their existence convinces us that (1) the acts of violence are real; (2) the crisis is real; (3) the victims are chosen not for the crimes they are accused of but for the victim's signs that they bear, for everything that suggests their guilty relationship with the crisis; and (4) the import of the operation is to lay the responsibility for the crisis on the victims and to exert an influence on it by destroying these victims or at least by banishing them from the community they "pollute."

If this pattern is universal it should be found in virtually all societies. Historians do in fact find it in all the societies included in their studies which today embrace the entire planet, but previously were confined to Western society and prior to that specifically to the Roman Empire. And yet ethnologists have never come to recognize this pattern of persecution in the societies they study. Why is that? Two answers are possible. "Ethnological" societies are so little given to persecution that the type of analysis applied to Guillaume de Machaut is not applicable to them. Contemporary neoprimitivism which tends toward this solution places the superior humanity of all other cultures in opposition to the inhumanity of our society. But no one dares argue that persecution fails to exist in non-Western societies. The second possible answer is that persecution exists but we do not recognize it, either because we are not in possession of the necessary documents, *or because we do not know how to decipher the documents we do possess.*

I consider the second of these two hypotheses to be the correct one. Mythical, ritualistic societies are not exempt from persecution. We possess documents that allow us to prove this: they contain the stereotypes of persecution that I have named, they emerge from the same total pattern as the treatment of the Jews in Guillaume de Machaut. If our logic is consistent we should apply the same type of interpretation to them. These documents are myths.

To make my task easier I shall begin with a myth that is exemplary. It contains all the stereotypes of persecution and nothing else, and it contains them in a startling form. It is Sophocles' account of the myth of Oedipus in *Oedipus Rex*. I shall then turn to myths that reproduce the pattern of persecution but in a form that is harder to decipher. Finally, I shall turn to myths that reject this pattern but do so in such an obvious way as to confirm its relevance. By proceeding from easy to more difficult I intend to show that all myths must have their roots in real acts of violence against real victims.

I begin with the myth of Oedipus. The plague is ravaging Thebes: here we have the first stereotype of persecution. Oedipus is responsible because he has killed his father and married his mother: here is the second stereotype. The oracle declares that, in order to end the epidemic, the abominable criminal must be banished. The finality of persecution is explicit. Parricide and incest serve openly as the intermediaries between the individual and the collective; these crimes are so oblivious of differences that their influence is contagious to the whole society. In Sophocles' text we establish that to lack difference is to be plague-stricken.

The third stereotype has to do with the signs of a victim. The first is disability: Oedipus limps. This hero from another country arrived in Thebes unknown to anyone, a stranger in fact if not in right. Finally, he is the son of the king and a king himself, the legitimate heir of Laius. Like many other mythical characters, Oedipus manages to combine the marginality of the outsider with the marginality of the insider. Like

Ulysses at the end of the *Odyssey* he is sometimes a stranger and a beggar and sometimes an all-powerful monarch.

The only detail without an equivalent in historical persecutions is the exposed infant. But the whole world agrees that an exposed infant is a victim at an early stage, chosen because of the signs of abnormality which augur badly for his future and which evidently are the same as the signs that indicate the selection of a victim mentioned above. The fatal destiny determined for the exposed child is to be expelled by his community. His escape is only ever temporary, his destiny is at the best deferred, and the conclusion of the myth confirms the infallibility of the signs of the oracle that dedicate him, from earliest infancy, to collective violence.

The more signs of a victim an individual bears, the more likely he is to attract disaster. Oedipus's infirmity, his past history of exposure as an infant, his situation as a foreigner, newcomer, and king, all make him a veritable conglomerate of victim's signs. We would not fail to observe this if the myth were a historical document, and we would wonder at the meaning of all these signs, together with other stereotypes of persecution. There would be no doubt about the answer. We would certainly see in the myth what we see in Guillaume de Machaut's text, an account of persecution told from the perspective of naïve persecutors. The persecutors portray their victim exactly as they see him—as the guilty person—but they hide none of the objective traces of their persecution. We conclude that there must be a real victim behind the text, chosen not by virtue of the stereotypical crimes of which he is accused, crimes which never spread the plague, but because of all the characteristics of a victim specified in that text which are most likely to project on him the paranoiac suspicion of a crowd tormented by the plague.

In the myth, as in Guillaume and in the witchcraft trials, the accusations are truly *mythological*: parricide, incest, the moral or physical poisoning of the community. These accusations are characteristic of the way in which frenzied crowds conceive of their victims. But these same accusations are juxtaposed with criteria for the selection of a victim which may well be real. How can we not believe that a real victim lies behind a text which presents him in this way and which makes us see him, on the one hand, as the persecutors generally see him and, on the other hand, as he should really be to be chosen by real persecutors. For even greater certainty, his banishment is said to take place in a time of extreme crisis which favors real persecution. All the conditions are present that will automatically prompt the modern reader, as we have described above for *historical* texts, to reach the same interpretation we would make of texts written from the perspective of persecutors. Why do we hesitate in the case of myths?

Just as in medieval persecutions, stereotypical persecutors are always found in myths and are statistically too prevalent to ignore. The myths are too numerous for us to be able to attribute the repetition of the model to anything but real persecutions. Any other conclusion would be as absurd as to think that Guillaume de Machaut's account of the Jews was pure fiction. As soon as we are confronted with a text that is perceived to be historical we know that only the behavior of a persecutor, seen through a persecutor's mind, can generate the collection of stereotypes we find in many myths. Persecutors believe they choose their victims because of the crimes they attribute to them, which make them in their eyes responsible for the disasters to which they react by persecution. Actually, the victims are determined by the criteria of persecution that are faithfully reported to us, not because they want to inform us but because they are unaware of what they reveal.

In the case of a text written by the persecutors the only elements of it that should be believed are those that correspond (1) to the real circumstances of the texts coming into being, (2) to the characteristic traits of its usual victims, and (3) to the results that normally follow collective violence. If these authors describe not merely parricide and incest as the cause of plagues but also everything that goes with this type of belief in the real world and all the resulting sorts of behavior, then they are probably right on all these points because they are wrong about the first one. These are our four stereotypes of persecutors, the same combination of the likely and the unlikely that we saw in the historical texts, and we cannot expect it to have another significance than the one stated above. It is the partly accurate and partly false perspective of persecutors who are convinced of their own persecution.

This conclusion is not the result of naïveté. Real naïveté is buried under the extremes of skepticism, which is incapable of identifying the stereotypes of persecution and of resorting to the daring yet legitimate interpretation they require. The myth of Oedipus is not just a literary text, or a psychoanalytic text, but a persecution text and should be interpreted as such. It will be objected that an interpretive method that was invented in and for history cannot be applied to myth. I agree, but as I have shown above, genuine historical evidence plays no more than a secondary role in deciphering representations of persecution. If they had been dependent on history, they would never have been deciphered, a process that has only just begun in the modern era.

If we consider that the victims mentioned by the witch-hunters are real, we do not usually do so because we have information on them from independent, unbiased sources. Admittedly, we place the text in a framework of knowledge, but that framework would not exist if we treated historical persecution texts as we treat the myth of Oedipus.

As already mentioned, we do not know exactly where the events described by Guillaume de Machaut took place; even if we knew almost nothing, including the existence of the Black Death, we would still conclude that such a text must reflect a phenomenon of real persecution. Just the combination of persecutor stereotypes would give sufficient indication. Why is the situation different in the case of myth?

My hypothesis relies on nothing historical in the critics' sense. It is purely "structural" as in our interpretation of historical representations of persecution. We assert that certain texts are based on a real persecution because of the nature and the disposition of the persecutor stereotypes they portray. Without this origin it is impossible to explain why and how the same themes keep recurring in the same pattern. If we accept this thesis the obscurity of the text is immediately dispelled. The themes are all easily explained and no serious objection can be raised. For this reason we have unhesitatingly accepted the thesis as the origin of all the historical texts that follow the pattern of persecution we have described. As a result we no longer see it as controversial but as the pure and simple truth of these texts. And we have good reason. It remains to find out why such a solution does not occur to us in the case of a myth like that of Oedipus.

That is the real problem. The lengthy analysis I have just given of the type of interpretation that automatically results in the identification of stereotypes of persecution was necessary in order to understand that problem. As long as we are talking of historical texts the interpretation presents no problem, and there is no need to detail each step of the process. But this attitude is precisely the obstacle to our taking the necessary step backward to reflect on our *understanding* of the representations of persecution. We have not completely mastered that understanding because it has never been made totally explicit.

Everything I have said about mythology would appear to be obvious, almost too obvious in the case of a "historical" document. If my readers are not convinced I shall convince them now by a very simple example. I am going to draw a rough sketch of the story of Oedipus; I shall remove his Greek clothing and substitute Western garb. In so doing, the myth will descend several steps on the social ladder. I will give no details of the place or the precise date of the event. The reader's good will will provide the rest. My tale falls naturally into some part of the Christian world between the twelfth and thirteenth centuries; that is all that is needed to release, like a spring, the operation that no one has thought of applying to a myth, as long as we have been calling it precisely that, a myth.

Harvests are bad, the cows give birth to dead calves; no one is on good terms with anyone else. It is as if a spell had been cast on the village. Clearly, it is the cripple who is the cause. He arrived one fine morning, no one knows from where, and made himself at home. He even took the liberty of marrying the most obvious heiress in the village and had two children by her. All sorts of things seemed to take place in their house. The stranger was suspected of having killed his wife's former husband, a sort of local potentate, who disappeared under mysterious circumstances and was rather too quickly replaced by the newcomer. One day the fellows in the village had had enough; they took their pitchforks and forced the disturbing character to clear out.

NO ONE WILL have the slightest hesitation in this instance. Everyone will instinctively give the explanation I have mentioned. Everyone understands that the victim most certainly did not do what he was accused of but that everything about him marked him as an outlet for the annoyance and irritation of his fellow citizens. Everyone will understand easily the relationship between the likely and unlikely elements in this little story. No one will suggest that it is an innocent fable; no one will see it as a casual work of poetic imagination or of a wish to portray "the fundamental mechanisms of man's thought."

And yet nothing has changed. It has the same structure as the myth since it is a rough sketch of it. Thus the interpretation does not rest on whether it is or is not set in a framework of historical detail. A change of setting is enough to redirect the interpreter to a reading that he indignantly rejects when the text is presented in a "true" mythological form. If we transported our story to the Polynesians or American Indians we would see the same ceremonious respect that the Hellenists had for the Greek version of the myth, accompanied by the same obstinate refusal to have recourse to the most effective interpretation. The latter is reserved exclusively for our historical universe, for reasons we shall try to uncover later.

We are dealing with cultural schizophrenia. My hypothesis would have served a purpose if it had only revealed just that. We interpret texts not by what they really are but by their external trappings (I am almost tempted to call it their commercial wrapping). A slight modification of the presentation of a text is enough to inhibit or release the only truly radical demystification available to us, and no one is aware of the situation.

SO FAR I have only spoken of a myth that I myself recognize to be exemplary in regard to representations of persecution. Those myths that are not must also be discussed. They do not bear an obvious resemblance to persecution texts, but if we look for the four stereotypes we shall find plenty of them without difficulty, though in a rather more transfigured form.

Often the beginning of the myth can be reduced to a single characteristic. Day and night are confused; heaven and earth communicate; gods move among men and men among gods. Among god, man, and beast there is little distinction. Sun and moon are twins; they fight constantly and cannot be distinguished one from the other. The sun moves too close to the earth; drought and heat make life unbearable. At first sight, there is nothing in these beginnings of myth that has any connection with reality. Clearly, however, myth involves a lack of differentiation. The great social crises that engender collective persecutions are experienced as a lack of differentiation. This is the characteristic that I uncovered in the preceding chapter. We might well ask whether this is not our first stereotype of persecution, in an extremely stylized and transfigured form, reduced to its simplest expression.

Lack of differentiation in myth sometimes has idyllic connotations, of which I will speak later. Usually, its character is catastrophic. The confusion of day and night signifies the absence of sun and the withering of everything. The sun's too close proximity to the earth indicates that existence is equally unbearable but for the opposite reason. Myths that are thought to "invent death" in reality invent nothing but rather distinguish it from life when "in the beginning" both are confused. I believe this to mean that it is impossible to live without dying or, once again, that existence is unbearable.

"Primordial" lack of differentiation and the "original" chaos conflict strongly in character. Those elements that are indistinguishable often have conflictual connotations. This theme is particularly developed in the post-Vedic texts of Brahman India. Everything always begins with an interminable, indecisive battle between gods and demons who are so alike one can hardly tell them apart. In short, that too rapid and visible evil reciprocity makes all behavior the same in the great crises of society that are apt to trigger collective persecutions. The undifferentiated is only a partially mythical translation of this state of affairs. We must associate with it the theme of twins or fraternal enemies who illustrate the conflict between those who become undifferentiated in a particularly graphic fashion. No doubt this is why the theme provides the most classic beginning for myths everywhere.

Lévi-Strauss was the first to identify the unity of numerous mythical beginnings in terms of a lack of differentiation. For him the undifferentiated is purely rhetorical; it serves as a background for the display of differences. There is no question of relating this, then, to real social conditions. And until now there would seem to be no evidence of any hope of finding in myth any concrete relationship with reality. Our four stereotypes of persecution have now modified this state of affairs. If we find three of them in the myths which begin in the way I have described, we might legitimately conclude that the initial lack of differentiation constitutes a schematic but nevertheless recognizable version of the first.

We need not dwell on this. All the crimes that persecutors attribute to their victims can generally be found in myths. In certain, especially Greek, mythologies these crimes are often not treated as crimes; they are seen as mere pranks; they are excused and made light of but they are nevertheless present and, at least in letter if not in spirit, they correspond perfectly to our stereotype. In the myths that appear most "primitive"—if I dare use the term—the chief characters are formidable criminals and are treated as such. Because of this they incur a punishment that bears a strange resemblance to the fate of the victims of collective persecutions (it is often a question of lynching). On this one main point the myths which I call "primitive" are even closer than the myth of Oedipus to the crowd phenomena with which I am comparing them.

There is only one stereotype we must find in these myths: the mark that identifies the selection of a victim for persecution. I need not point out that world mythology swarms with the lame, the blind, and the crippled or abounds with people stricken by the plague. As well as the heroes in disgrace there are those who are exceptionally beautiful and free of all blemish. This means not that mythology literally is meaningless but that it usually deals in extremes; and we have already noted that this is a characteristic of the polarization of persecution.

The whole range of victim signs can be found in myths, a fact unnoticed because we focus on the victim's ethnic or religious minority. That particular sign cannot appear in the same form in mythology. We find neither persecuted Jews nor blacks. But their equivalent can be found in a theme that plays a central role in all parts of the world, that of the *foreigner* banished or assassinated by the community.[1]

The victim is a person who comes from elsewhere, a well-known stranger. He is invited to a feast which ends with his lynching. Why? He has done something he should not have done; his behavior is perceived as fatal; one of his gestures was misinterpreted. Here again we have only to imagine a real victim, a real stranger, and everything becomes clear. If the stranger behaves in a strange or insulting way in the eyes of his hosts, it is because he conforms to other customs. Beyond a certain threshold of ethnocentrism, the stranger becomes, for better or worse, truly mythological. The smallest misunderstanding can be disastrous. Beneath this myth of an assassinated stranger who is made a god we can trace a form of "provincialism" so extreme that we can no longer identify it, just as we no longer can see the sounds and colors of an electromagnetic wave beyond a certain length. Again, to bring our overphilosophical interpretations down to earth, we need only place these mythical themes against a Western, rural background. One immediately grasps the meaning, just as in the transposition of the Oedipus myth a moment ago. A little suitable intellectual gymnastics, and especially a little less icy veneration for all that does not belong to the modern Western world, and we will quickly learn how to enlarge our field of recognition and understanding in mythology.

A close examination of myths is not necessary to establish that a great number of them contain our four stereotypes of persecution; there are others, of course, that contain only three, two, one or even none. I do not overlook them but am not yet able to analyze them successfully.

---

1. See the three myths examined in *Des choses cachées depuis la fondation du monde,* pp. 114–40.

We are beginning to see that the representations of persecution we have already deciphered are for us an Ariadne's thread to guide us through the labyrinth of mythology. They will enable us to trace the real origin in collective violence of even the myths that contain no stereotypes of persecution. We shall see later that, instead of gainsaying our thesis or demanding questionable feats to maintain it, those myths that are entirely void of stereotypes of persecution will provide us with the most astounding verification. For the time being we must continue our analysis of the myths that contain our stereotypes but under a form that is less easy to identify, because it is somewhat more transfigured, than in the medieval persecutions or the myth of Oedipus. This more extreme transfiguration does not create an insurpassable abyss between myths and persecutions that have already been deciphered. One word is sufficient to define the type to which they belong: monstrous.

Ever since the romantic movement we have tended to see in the mythological monster a true creation ex nihilo, a pure invention. Imagination is perceived as an absolute ability to conceive of forms that exist nowhere in nature. Examination of mythological monsters reveals no such thing. They always consist of a combination of elements borrowed from various existing forms and brought together in the monster, which then claim an independent identity. Thus the Minotaur is a mixture of man and bull. Dionysus equally, but the god in him commands more attention than the monster or than the mixture of forms.

We must think of the monstrous as beginning with the lack of differentiation, with a process that, though it has no effect on reality, does affect the perception of it. As the rate of conflictual reciprocity accelerates, it not only gives the accurate impression of identical behavior among the antagonists but it also disintegrates perception, as it becomes dizzying. Monsters are surely the result of a fragmentation of perception and of a decomposition followed by a recombination that does not take natural specificity into account. A monster is an unstable hallucination that, in retrospect, crystallizes into stable forms, owing to the fact that it is remembered in a world that has regained stability.

We saw earlier that the representations of historical persecutions resemble mythology. A transition to the monstrous is made in the extreme representations we have mentioned, such as in the crisis caused by the lack of differentiation, or in signs like deformity that mark a victim for persecution. There comes a point at which physical monstrosity and moral monstrosity merge. The crime of bestiality, for example, engenders monstrous mixtures of men and animals; in the hermaphroditism of a Tiresias, physical monstrosity cannot be distinguished from moral monstrosity. The stereotypes themselves merge, in other words, to form the mythological monsters.

In the mythological monster the "physical" and the "moral" are inseparable. The two are so perfectly combined that any attempt to separate them seems doomed to failure. Yet, if I am right, there is a distinction to be made. Physical deformity must correspond to a real human characteristic, a real infirmity. Oedipus's wounds or Vulcan's limp are not necessarily less real in their origins than the characteristics of medieval witches. Moral monstrosity, by contrast, actualizes the tendency of all persecutors to project the monstrous results of some calamity or public or private misfortune onto some poor unfortunate who, by being infirm or a foreigner, suggests a certain affinity to the monstrous.

My analysis may seem strange, for the monstrous character is generally perceived as being the final proof of the absolutely fictitious and imaginary character of mythology. Yet in the monster we recognize the false certainty and the true possibility that I have been discussing. It will be said that the presence of stereotypes in such confusion discounts my argument. If they are examined all at once, however, they do form a sort of unity; they create a particular climate that is specific to mythology, and we should do nothing to dissociate the elements even for aesthetic reasons. Nor have our best interpreters ever separated them, though some scholars are moving in the direction of a definitive separation of the (imaginary) crimes of the victims and the (possibly real) signs that indicate a victim. Here is a representative text, of Mircea Eliade's on Greek mythology, that begins with the latter and ends with the former:

[the heroes] are distinguished by their *strength* and *beauty* but also by *monstrous characteristics* ([gigantic] stature – Heracles, Achilles, Orestes, Pelops – but also stature [much shorter] than the average); or they are [theriomorphic] (Lycaon, the "wolf") or able to *change themselves into animals*. They are *androgynous* (Cecrops), or *change their sex* (Teiresias), or *dress like women* (Heracles). In addition, the heroes are characterized by numerous *anomalies* (*acephaly* or *polycephaly*; Heracles has *three rows of teeth*); they are apt to be *lame, one-eyed* or *blind*. Heroes often fall victim to *insanity* (Orestes, Bellerophon, even the exceptional Heracles, when he *slaughtered his sons* by Megara). As for their *sexual behavior*, it is *excessive* or *aberrant*: Heracles *impregnates the fifty daughters of Thespius in one night*; Theseus is famous for his *numerous rapes* (Helen, Ariadne, etc.); Achilles *ravishes Stratonice.* The heroes commit *incest with their daughters or their mothers* and indulge in *massacres* from envy or anger or often for no reason at all: *they even slaughter their fathers and mothers or their relatives.*[2]

This text is important because it contains so many relevant traits. Under the sign of the monstrous the author unites the marks that identify a victim and the stereotypical crimes without mixing them. Something here seems to resist conflating the two rubrics. There is an actual, though not justified, separation.

Physical and moral monstrosity go together in mythology. Their connection seems normal, and is even suggested by language. But in a similar situation in our historical universe we would not exclude the possibility of the victims being real, making the perpetual juxtaposition of the two kinds of monstrosity odious; we would suspect that its origin lay in the mentality of persecution. But what else could be its source? What other force might always be responsible for converging the two themes? For reassurance it is attributed to the *imagination.* We always rely on the imagination in order to avoid reality. Yet I'm not referring to the imagination of the aesthetician but, rather, to that of Guillaume de Machaut's at its most confused, to the sort of imagination, which, precisely because it is confused, brings us back to the real victims. It is always the imagination of the persecutors. Physical and moral monstrosity are heaped together in myths that justify the persecution of the infirm. The fact that other stereotypes of persecution surround them leaves no room for doubt. If this were a rare conjunction it might be dubious, but innumerable examples can be found; it is the daily fare of mythology.

Except in the case of certain exemplary myths, that of Oedipus in particular, mythology cannot be *directly* assimilated to the pattern of representations of persecution that can be decoded, but it can be so *indirectly.* Instead of bearing certain faintly monstrous characteristics, the victim is hard to recognize as a victim because he is totally monstrous. This difference should not lead us to decide that the two types of texts cannot have a common source.

After detailed examination it becomes clear that we are dealing with a single principle of distorted presentation, though in mythology the mechanism operates in a higher register than in history. It is undeniably

2. Mircea Eliade, *A History of Religious Ideas* (Chicago: University of Chicago Press, 1978), 1:288 (italics mine).

and universally true that the less rational the persecutors' conviction the more formidable that conviction becomes. But in historical persecutions the conviction is not so overwhelming as to conceal its character and the process of accusation from which it stems. Admittedly, the victim is condemned in advance; he cannot defend himself, his trial has already taken place, but at least there is a trial no matter how prejudiced. The witches are hunted legally; even the persecuted Jews are explicitly charged, charged with crimes that are less unlikely than those of the mythical heroes. The desire for relative probability which conjures up "the poisoning of rivers," paradoxically helps us to make the distinction between truth and falsity. Mythology demands the same operation, though in a more daring form because the circumstances are more confused.

In historical persecutions the "guilty" remain sufficiently distinct from their "crimes" for there to be no mistake about the nature of the process. The same cannot be said of myth. The guilty person is so much a part of his offense that one is indistinguishable from the other. His offense seems to be a fantastic essence or ontological attribute. In many myths the wretched person's presence is enough to contaminate everything around him, infecting men and beasts with the plague, ruining crops, poisoning food, causing game to disappear, and sowing discord around him. Everything shrivels under his feet and the grass does not grow again. He produces disasters as easily as a fig tree produces figs. He need only be himself.

The definition of victim as sinner or criminal is so absolute in myth, and the causal relationship between crime and collective crisis is so strong, that even perceptive scholars have as yet failed to disassociate these details and to identify the accusatory process. The persecution text, whether medieval or modern, provides the needed Ariadne's thread. Even those historical texts that retain the strongest sense of persecution reflect only very slight conviction. The more relentlessly they struggle to demonstrate the justice of their wrongdoing, the less convincing they sound. If the myth were to state "Undoubtedly Oedipus killed his father; it is certain that he had intercourse with his mother," we would recognize the type of lie it embodies; it would be written in the style of historical persecutors, from a basis of belief. But it speaks tranquilly of an unquestionable fact: "Oedipus killed his father; he had intercourse with his mother," in the same tone one would say: "Night follows day" or "The sun rises in the East."

The distortions in persecution become weaker as we move from myths to persecutions in the Western world. This weakening has in fact allowed us to decipher the latter. Our task is to use this decoding in order to gain access to mythology. I will use as my guide the text of Guillaume de Machaut and the others we have already encountered because they are easier to read, to help interpret the myth of Oedipus, first of all, and then increasingly more difficult texts. As we proceed we will recognize all the stereotypes of persecution and so reach the conclusion that there are real acts of violence and real victims behind themes that seem so fantastic that it is difficult to think that one day we may no longer consider them purely and simply imaginary.

Our medieval ancestors took the most incredible fables seriously— the poisoning of fountains by the Jews or by lepers, ritual infanticide, witches' broomsticks, and moonlight diabolical orgies. The mixture of cruelty and credulity seems insurpassable to us. And yet myths surpass them; historical persecutions are the result of degraded superstitions. We think we are free of mythical illusions because we have sworn not to be hoodwinked by them.

We are in the habit of considering necessarily fictional even the most plausible characteristics of mythological heroes because of their association with other improbable characteristics. Similarly, if we were to permit it, the same false notion of prudence and the same attitude toward fiction would prevent us from recognizing the reality of the anti-Semitic massacres in Guillaume de Machaut. We do not doubt the reality of the massacres on the excuse that they are juxtaposed with all sorts of more or less significant fables. There is equally no good reason to doubt the reality in the case of myths.

The face of the victim shows through the mask in the texts of historical persecutions. There are chinks and cracks. In mythology the mask is still intact; it covers the whole face so well that we have no idea it is a mask. We think there is no one behind it, neither victim nor persecutor. We are somewhat like Polyphemus's brothers, the Cyclopes, to whom he calls in vain for help after Ulysses and his companions blinded him. We save our only eye, if we have one, for what we call history. As for our ears, if we have them, they only hear this *no one, no one*...that is so deeply embedded in collective violence that we take it for nothing, nonexistent, pure fabrication by a Polyphemus in a vein of poetic improvisation.

We no longer consider mythological monsters as a supernatural or even natural species; there are no longer theological or even zoological genres. They belong instead to the quasi-genres of the imaginary, "archetypes" of fable heaped in an unconsciousness that is even more mythical than the myths themselves. There was a time when no one could read even the distortions of persecution found in our own history. Finally we did learn. We can put a date to this achievement. It goes back to the beginning of the modern era and seems to constitute only the first stage in a process that has never really been interrupted but has been marking time for centuries because it lacked a truly fruitful direction that would stretch back to mythology.

Now we must discuss an essential dimension of myth that is almost entirely absent from historical persecutions: that of the sacred. Medieval and modern persecutors do not worship their victims, they only hate them. They are therefore easy to identify as victims. It is more difficult to spot the victim in a supernatural being who is a cult object. Admittedly, the glorious adventures of the hero can hardly be distinguished from the stereotypical crimes of collective victims. Like those victims, moreover, the hero is hunted and even assassinated by his own people. But the experts are in agreement that such annoying incidents are not important. They are merely minor escapades in a career that is so noble and transcendental it is poor taste to notice them.

Myths exude the sacred and do not seem comparable with texts that do not. No matter how striking the similarities mentioned in the preceding pages they pale before this dissimilarity. I am trying to explain myths by discovering in them more extreme distortions of persecution than those of historical persecutors as they recall their own persecutions. The method has been successful until now since I have uncovered in myths the warped forms of everything that appears equally in persecution texts. We may wonder whether we are missing the essential. Even if on a lower level mythology is vulnerable to my comparative method, idealists will say that at a higher level it escapes through the transcendental dimension that is beyond reach.

This is not so for the following two reasons. Beginning with the similarities and differences between our two types of texts, the nature of the sacred and the necessity of its presence in myths can literally be deduced by a simple process of reasoning. I will go back to the persecution texts and show that, despite appearances, they contain traces of the sacred that correspond exactly to what is to be expected, if we were to recognize, as I did earlier, the degenerated and half-decomposed myths in these texts.

In order to understand that existence of the sacred, we must begin by recognizing a true belief in what I have called the stereotype of accusation, the guilt and the apparent responsibility of the victims. Guillaume de Machaut sincerely believed that the rivers were poisoned by the Jews. Jean Bodin sincerely believed that France was exposed to danger by sorcery in his day. We do not have to sympathize with the belief by admitting its sincerity. Jean Bodin was an intelligent man and yet he believed in sorcery. Two centuries later such a belief makes people of even mediocre intelligence laugh. What, then, is the source of the illusions of a Jean Bodin or a Guillaume de Machaut? Clearly, they are social in nature. They are illusions shared by a great number of people. In most societies belief in witchcraft is not the act of certain individuals only, or even of many, but the act of everyone.

Magical beliefs flourish amid a certain social consensus. Even though it was far from unanimous in the sixteenth and even in the fourteenth century, the consensus was broad, at least in certain milieus. It acted as a sort of constraint on people. The exceptions were not numerous, and they were not influential enough to prevent the persecutions. The representation of these persecutions retains certain characteristics of a collective representation in the sense used by Durkheim. We have examined the makeup of this belief. Vast social groups found themselves at the mercy of terrifying plagues such as the Black Death or sometimes less visible problems. Thanks to the mechanism of persecution, collective anguish and frustration found vicarious appeasement in the victims who easily found themselves united in opposition to them by virtue of being poorly integrated minorities.

We owe our comprehension of this to the discovery of stereotypes of persecution in a text. Once we understand we almost always exclaim: *The victim is a scapegoat.* Everyone has a clear understanding of this expression; no one has any hesitation about its meaning. Scapegoat indicates both the innocence of the victims, the collective polarization in opposition to them, and the collective end result of that polarization. The persecutors are caught up in the "logic" of the representation of persecution from a persecutor's standpoint, and they cannot break away. Guillaume de Machaut no doubt never participated himself in collective acts of violence, but he adopts the representation of persecution that feeds the violence and is fed in return. He shares in the collective effect of the scapegoat. The polarization exerts such a constraint on those polarized that the victims cannot prove their innocence.

We use the word "scapegoat" therefore to summarize all that I have said so far on collective persecutions. By mentioning "scapegoat" when discussing Guillaume de Machaut we indicate that we are not taken in by his representation and that we have done what is necessary to break down the system and substitute our own reading. "Scapegoat" epitomizes the type of interpretation I would like to extend to mythology. Unfortunately, the expression and the interpretation suffer the same fate. Because everyone uses it no one bothers to determine its exact significance, and the misconceptions multiply. In the example of Guillaume de Machaut and persecution texts in general, this use has no direct connection with the rite of the scapegoat as described in Leviticus, or with other rites that are sometimes described as belonging to the "scapegoat" because they more or less resemble that of Leviticus.

As soon as we begin to study the "scapegoat" or think about the expression apart from the context of the persecutor, we tend to modify its meaning. We are reminded of the rite; we think of a religious ceremony that unfolds on a fixed date and is performed by priests; we imagine a deliberate manipulation. We think of skillful strategists who are fully aware of the mechanisms of victimization and who knowingly sacrifice innocent victims in full awareness of the cause with Machiavellian ease.

Such things can happen, especially in our time, but they cannot happen, even today, without the availability of an eminently manipulable mass to be used by the manipulators for their evil purposes, people who will allow themselves to be trapped in the persecutors' representation of persecution, people capable of belief where the scapegoat is concerned. Guillaume de Machaut is obviously no manipulator. He is not intelligent enough. If manipulation exists in his universe, he must be numbered among the manipulated. The details that are so revealing in his text are not revealing for him, evidently, but only for those who understand their real significance. Earlier I spoke of naïve persecutors; I could have spoken of their lack of awareness.

Too conscious and calculating an awareness of all that the "scapegoat" connotes in modern usage eliminates the essential point that the persecutors believe in the guilt of their victim; they are imprisoned in the illusion of persecution that is no simple idea but a full system of representation. Imprisonment in this system allows us to speak of an unconscious persecutor, and the proof of his existence lies in the fact that those in our day who are the most proficient in discovering other people's scapegoats, and God knows we are past masters at this, are never able to recognize their own. Almost no one is aware of his own shortcoming. We must question ourselves if we are to understand the enormity of the mystery. Each person must ask what his relationship is to the scapegoat. I am not aware of my own, and I am persuaded that the same holds true for my readers. We only have legitimate enmities. And yet the entire universe swarms with scapegoats. The illusion of persecution is as rampant as ever, less tragically but more cunningly than under Guillaume de Machaut. *Hypocite lecteur, mon semblable, mon frère . . .*

If we are at the point where we compete in the penetrating and subtle discovery of scapegoats, both individual and collective, where was the fourteenth century? No one decoded the representation of persecution as we do today. "Scapegoat" had not yet taken on the meaning we give it today. The concept that crowds, or even entire societies, can imprison themselves in their own illusions of victimage was inconceivable. Had we tried to explain it to the men of the Middle Ages, they would not have understood. Guillaume de Machaut was much more influenced by the scapegoat effect than we are. His universe was more deeply immersed in its unawareness of persecution than we are, but even so, it was less so than the world of mythology. In Guillaume, as we have seen, just a small portion, and not the worst, of the Black Death is blamed on scapegoats: in the myth of Oedipus it is the entire plague. In order to explain epidemics, mythological universes have never needed anything more than stereotypical crimes and of course those who are guilty of them. Proof can be found in ethnological documents. Ethnologists are shocked by my blasphemies yet for a long time they have had at their disposal the necessary evidence to confirm them. In so-called ethnological societies the presence of an epidemic immediately rouses the suspicion that there has been an infraction of the basic rules of the community. We are not permitted to call such societies primitive, yet we are expected to describe as primitive everything that perpetuates the mythological type of beliefs and behaviors that belong to persecution in our universe.

The representation of persecution is more forceful in myths than in historical accounts and we are disconcerted by that strength. Compared with such granitelike belief ours seems paltry. The representations of persecution in our history are always vacillating and residual, which is why they are so quickly demystified, at least within several centuries, instead of lasting for millennia, like the myth of Oedipus, which toys with our efforts to understand it. Such formidable belief is foreign to us today. At best we can try to imagine it by tracing it in the texts. We are led, then, to the determination that the sacred forms a part of that blind and massive belief.

Let us examine this phenomenon, beginning with the conditions that make it possible. We do not know why this belief is so strong, but we suspect that it corresponds to a more effective scapegoat mechanism than our own, to a system of persecution that functions at a higher level than our own. To judge by the numerical preponderance of mythological universes, this higher system is more the norm for humanity than our own society which constitutes the exception. Such a strong belief could not be established and perpetuated, after the death of the victim, in the persecutors' commemoration in their myths, if there were any doubt left in the relationships at the heart of the community, in other words if there were not total reconciliation. In order for all the persecutors to be inspired by the same faith in the evil power of their victim, the latter must successfully polarize all the suspicions, tensions, and reprisals that poisoned those relationships. The community must effectively be emptied of its poisons. It must feel liberated and reconciled within itself. This is implied in the conclusion of most myths. We see the actual return to the order that was compromised by the crisis, or even more often the birth of a completely new order in the religious union of a community brought to life by its experience.

The perpetual conjunction in myths of a very guilty victim with a conclusion that is both violent and liberating can only be explained by the extreme force of the scapegoat mechanism. This hypothesis in fact solves the fundamental enigma of all mythology: the order that is either absent or compromised by the scapegoat once more establishes itself or is established by the intervention of someone who disturbed it in the first place. It is conceivable that a victim may be responsible for public disasters, which is what happened in myths as in collective persecutions, but in myths, and only in myths, this same victim restores the order, symbolizes, and even incarnates it.

Our specialists have not yet gotten over this. The transgressor restores and even establishes the order he has somehow transgressed in anticipation. The greatest of all delinquents is transformed into a pillar of society. In some myths this paradox is diminished, censured, or camouflaged, no doubt by the faithful whom it scandalizes almost as much as our contemporary ethnologists, but it is no less transparent beneath the camouflage. This is eminently characteristic of mythology. Plato was troubled by this precise enigma when he complained of the immorality of the Homeric gods. Interpreters have stumbled over this enigma for centuries. It is identical with the enigma of the *primitive* sacred, the beneficial return from the harmful omnipotence attributed to the scapegoat. To understand this return and solve the enigma, we have to reexamine our conjunction of themes, our four stereotypes of persecution, somewhat deformed, *plus* the conclusion that reveals for us the persecutors reconciled. *They really must be reconciled.* There is no reason to doubt it since they commemorate their experiences after the death of the victim and always attribute them unhesitatingly to him.

On further thought this is not surprising. How could the persecutors explain their own reconciliation and the end of the crisis? They cannot take credit for it. Terrified as they are by their own victim, they see themselves as completely passive, purely reactive, totally controlled by this scapegoat at the very moment when they rush to his attack. They think that all initiative comes from him. There is only room for a single cause in their field of vision, and its triumph is absolute, it absorbs all other causality: it is the scapegoat. Thus nothing happens to the persecutors that is not immediately related to him, and if they happen to become reconciled, the scapegoat benefits. There is only one person responsible for everything, one who is absolutely responsible, and he will be responsible for the cure because he is already responsible for the sickness. This is only a paradox for someone with a dualistic vision who is too remote from the experience of a victim to feel the unity and is too determined to differentiate precisely between "good" and "evil."

Admittedly, scapegoats cure neither real epidemics nor droughts nor floods. But the main dimension of every crisis is the way in which it affects human relations. A process of bad reciprocity is its own initiator; it gains nourishment from itself and has no need of external causes in order to continue. As long as external causes exist, such as an epidemic of plague for example, scapegoats will have no efficacy. On the other hand, when these causes no longer exist, the first scapegoat to appear will bring an end to the crisis by eliminating all the interpersonal repercussions in the concentration of all evildoing in the person of one victim. The scapegoat is only effective when human relations have broken down in crisis, but he gives the impression of effecting external causes as well, such as plagues, droughts, and other objective calamities.

Beyond a certain threshold of belief, the effect of the scapegoat is to reverse the relationships between persecutors and their victims, thereby producing the sacred, the founding ancestors and the divinities. The victim, in reality passive, becomes the only effective and omnipotent cause in the face of a group that believes itself to be entirely passive. If groups of people can, as a group, become sick for reasons that are objective or that concern only themselves, if the relationships at the heart of these groups can deteriorate and then be reestablished by means of victims who are unanimously despised, obviously these groups will commemorate these social ills in conformance with the illusory belief that the scapegoat is omnipotent and facilitates the cure. The universal execration of the person who causes the sickness is replaced by universal veneration for the person who cures that same sickness.

We can trace in myths a system of representation of persecutions similar to our own but complicated by the effectiveness of the process of persecution. We are not willing to recognize that effectiveness because it scandalizes us on the levels of both morality and intelligence. We are able to recognize the first evil transfiguration of the victim, which seems normal, but we cannot recognize the second beneficent transfiguration; it is inconceivable that it can unite with the first without destroying it, at least initially.

People in groups are subject to sudden variations in their relationships, for better or worse. If they attribute a complete cycle of variations to the collective victim who facilitates the return to normal, they will inevitably deduce from this double transference belief in a transcendental power that is both double and will bring them alternatively both loss and health, punishment and recompense. This force is manifest through the acts of violence of which it is the victim but is also, more importantly, the mysterious instigator.

If this victim can extend his benefits beyond death to those who have killed him, he must either be resuscitated or was not truly dead. The causality of the scapegoat is imposed with such force that even death cannot prevent it. In order not to renounce the victim's causality, he is brought back to life and immortalized, temporarily, and what we call the transcendent and supernatural are invented for that purpose.[3]

3. René Girard, *Violence and the Sacred* (Baltimore: Johns Hopkins University Press, 1972) pp. 85–88; *Des choses cachées depuis la fondation du monde*, pp. 32–50.

CHAPTER FOUR
Violence and Magic

IN ORDER TO explain the sacred, I have compared persecutors' representations of persecution which involve the sacred with those which do not.
I have examined what was specific to mythological compared with
historical persecutions, but I have neglected the relative quality of that
specificity. I have discussed historical distortions as if they had no connection with the sacred. But they do. Although increasingly less apparent, the sacred still persists in medieval and modern texts. I have
omitted these instances of survival in order not to minimize the distance
between mythology and my chosen texts. Reliance on approximate
similarities is all the more annoying in a context where a perfect explanation for dissimilarities exists—the scapegoat mechanism, the real
origin of the various kinds of distortions found in persecution, both
unintelligible and intelligible, mythological or otherwise, according to
the order within which persecution is operating.

Now that I have identified this difference in order, I can return to
the traces of the sacred that persist in intelligible distortions and consider whether they function as they do in myths.

Hatred plays a prominent role in medieval persecutions, and it is
easy to see nothing but hatred, especially where the Jews are concerned.
During this period, however, Jewish medicine enjoyed exceptional prestige, which can be explained by the real superiority of their practi-
tioners, who were more open than others to scientific progress. But in
the particular case of the plague this explanation is scarcely convincing.
The best medicine is no more effective than the worst. Both the
aristocrats and the common people preferred Jewish doctors because
they associated their power to cure with the power to cause sickness.

This medical practice, therefore, cannot be viewed as an example of individuals who are distinguished from others by their lack of prejudice. Prestige and prejudice seem to be two faces of the same attitude, indicating the survival of a primitive form of the sacred. Even in our own time the almost sacred fear inspired by doctors is not altogether independent of their authority.

If a person shows ill will to the Jew, he might infect him with the plague. If, on the other hand, he shows good will, the Jew might spare him or even cure him if he is already stricken. He is seen therefore as the last resource because of, and not in spite of, the evil he can do or has already done. The same is true in the case of Apollo; if the Thebans beg him (rather than some other god) to cure them of the plague, they do so because they hold him ultimately responsible. Apollo should not therefore be seen as a particularly benevolent, peaceful, or serene god in the sense Nietzsche and the aestheticians give to the word Apollonian. Like so many others they were misled by the ultimate fading of the Olympian gods. Despite appearances and weakened theories this tragic Apollo remains "the most abominable" of all the gods, the formula Plato reproached Homer for using, as if the poet had indulged in a personal fantasy.

Apart from certain intense beliefs, the scapegoat no longer appears to be merely a passive receptacle for evil forces but is rather the mirage of an omnipotent manipulator shown by mythology to be sanctioned unanimously by society. Once the scapegoat is recognized as the unique cause of the plague, then the plague becomes his to dispose of at will, either as punishment or reward, according to his displeasure or pleasure.

Queen Elizabeth of England's Jewish doctor, Lopez, was executed at the height of his influence for his attempts at poisoning and for his practice of magic. The slightest failure or denunciation can cause a newcomer to fall far lower than the heights he has climbed. Thus, Oedipus, the savior of Thebes and a licensed healer, who bears the signs of a victim, is crushed during times of trouble, just at the moment of his greatest glory, a victim of one of the stereotypical accusations we have identified.[1]

1. Joshua Trachtenberg, *The Devil and the Jews* (New Haven: Yale University Press, 1943), p. 98; H. Michelson, *The Jew in Early English Literature* (Amsterdam: A.J. Paris, 1928), p. 88ff. On the portrayal of the Jew in the Christian world, see the works of Gavin I. Langmuir: "Qu'est-ce que 'les juifs' signifiaient pour la société médiévale?" in *Ni juif ni Grec: Entretiens sur*

The supernatural aspect of the offense is coupled with a crime in the modern sense, in response to the demand for rationality that is characteristic of a time in which belief in magic is dwindling. The important detail is the fact that it is poisoning, a crime that deprives the accused of any legal protection just as bluntly as any accusation directly involving magic. Poisoning is so easy to conceal, especially for a doctor, that it is impossible to prove the crime and *therefore there is no need to prove it.*

This brings us back to all of our examples at once. It contains features which recall the myth of Oedipus, others which remind us of Guillaume de Machaut and all the persecuted Jews, and still others which are reminiscent of the false myth I concocted to "historicize" that of Oedipus and demonstrate that the decision to define a text as historical or mythological is arbitrary.

Because of the historical context we automatically demystify it with a psychosociological interpretation. We sense a cabal organized by jealous rivals, and we immediately lose awareness of those aspects that remind us of the sacred in mythology.

Lopez, like Oedipus, and like Apollo himself, is both master of life and master of death, for he controls this terrible plague, the sickness. One moment Lopez miraculously dispenses cures, the next, no less miraculously, sickness which is within his capability to cure if he so pleases. It is inevitable that the historical requirements of the text remind us of the sort of interpretation that is considered blasphemous and almost inconceivable in mythology, particularly Greek mythology. Presented in the form of myth it becomes a powerful symbol of the human condition, of the heights and depths of destiny. How the humanists rejoice! Put the story in an Elizabethan setting and it is nothing more than a sordid palace scandal, typical of the frenzied ambitions, hypocritical violence, and superstition that are rife only in the modern Western world. The second vision is certainly more accurate than the first, but still not entirely so, given that a remnant of unconscious persecution still plays a role in the Lopez affair. No allowance is made for this. What is more, a shadow is cast on our historical universe

---

le racisme, ed. Léon Poliakov (Paris–The Hague: Mouton/De Gruyter, 1978), pp. 179–90; "From Ambrose of Milan to Emicho of Leiningen: The Transformation of Hostility against Jews in Northern Europe," in *Gli Ebrei nell'alto Medioevo* (Spoleto: Atti, Centro Studi Alto Medioevo, 1980), pp. 314–67.

by presenting real crimes against a false background of Rousseau-like innocence of which it alone is deprived.

Behind the warrior gods there are always victims, and victims are usually linked to medicine. Just as in the case of the Jews, the same men who denounce the witches go to them for help. All persecutors attribute to their victims both the capacity to do harm and its reverse.

All aspects of mythology can be found in a less extreme form in medieval persecutions. This is true in the case of the monstrous, which can be easily recognized if the effort is made to compare phenomena that, out of ignorance, have been considered incomparable.

The confusion of animals and men provides mythology with its most important and spectacular modality of the monstrous. The same confusion can be found in medieval victims. Sorcerers and witches are thought to have a particular affinity with the goat, an extremely evil animal. During the trials, suspects' feet are examined to see if they are cloven; their foreheads are tapped for any trace of a horn. The gradual disappearance of the borderline between animal and man in those who are marked as victims is an important concept. If the alleged witch possesses a pet, a cat, a dog, or a bird, she is immediately thought to resemble that animal, and the animal itself seems almost an incarnation, a temporary embodiment or a useful disguise to ensure the success of certain enterprises. These animals play exactly the same role as Jupiter's swan in the seduction of Leda, or the bull with Pasiphae. We are distracted from the resemblance by the extremely negative connotations of monstrosity in the medieval world which are almost always positive in later mythology and in our modern conception of mythology. During recent centuries, writers, artists, and even contemporary anthropologists have completed the process of mitigation and criticism begun in the so-called classical era. I will return to this later.

The almost mythological figure of the old witch is a good example of the tendency to merge moral and physical monstrosities that was mentioned in our discussion of mythology. She is lame and bandylegged, and her face is covered with warts and various excretions that emphasize its ugliness. Everything about her attracts persecution. The same was clearly true for the Jews in medieval and modern antiSemitism. All that is needed is a number of victims' signs centered in a group of individuals who then become the target for the majority.

The Jew is also thought to be connected with the goat and certain other animals. The concept of the suppression of differences between man and animal reappears in this context in an unexpected form. In 1575, for example, the illustrated *Wunderzeitung* of Johann Fischart, of Binzwangen, near Augsburg, shows a Jewish woman contemplating two little pigs to whom she has just given birth.[2]

Although this type of thing is found throughout world mythology the similarity eludes us because the scapegoat mechanism is not functioning within the same order in the two cases and the social result cannot be compared. The higher order of mythology ends with the victim becoming sacred, thereby concealing from us, and in some cases totally eliminating, the distortions of persecution.

Let us look at a myth that is very important throughout the northwest of Canada, in an area around the Arctic Circle. It is the original myth of the Dogrib Indians. I will quote Roger Bastide's summary of it in the volume *Ethnologie générale* of the *Encylopédie de la Pléiade* (p. 1065).

A woman has intercourse with a dog and gives birth to six puppies. Her tribe banishes her and she is forced to hunt for her own food. One day as she returns from the bush she discovers that the puppies are children and that they shed their animal skins the moment she leaves the house. So she pretends to leave and when her children are as it were undressed she takes their skins away, forcing them to keep their human identity from now on.

All the stereotypes of persecution we have identified exist in this story though they are somewhat difficult to distinguish. Even their fusion is revealing. The general loss of differences that I term crisis is indicated here in the mother's hesitation between human and dog, and that same hesitation is seen in the children, who represent the community. The fact that she is a woman is the stereotypical victim's sign, and the stereotypical crime is bestiality. The woman is certainly responsible for the crisis since she gives birth to a monstrous community. But the myth tacitly admits the truth. There is no difference between the woman criminal and the community: both are undifferentiated, and the community existed before the crime, since it is the community that punishes the crime. This is therefore an example of a scapegoat accused of a stereotypical crime and treated accordingly: *her tribe banishes her and she is forced to hunt for her own food. . . .*

We don't recognize the connection with the Jewish woman from Binzwangen accused of giving birth to pigs because the scapegoat mech-

---

2. Trachtenberg, *The Devil and the Jews*, pp. 52–53.

anism is at work throughout and becomes fundamental; it turns into something positive. That is why the community exists both before and after the crime it is punishing: it is born of this crime, not of its monstrosity which is temporary in nature, but of its humanity which is well defined. Thanks to the scapegoat who is at first accused of causing the community to vacillate between human and animal, the difference between the two is permanently settled. The woman-dog becomes a great goddess who punishes not only bestiality but also incest and all other stereotypical crimes, all infractions of society's fundamental rules. The apparent cause of disorder becomes the apparent cause of order because she is a victim who rebuilds the terrified unity of a grateful community, at first in opposition to her, and finally around her.

There are two stages in myths, but interpreters have failed to distinguish them. The first is the act of accusing a scapegoat who is not yet sacred to whom all evil characteristics adhere. Then comes the second stage when he is made sacred by the community's reconciliation. I have succeeded in identifying this first stage by means of its equivalent in historical texts that reflect the perspective of the persecutor. These texts are all the more appropriate for guiding an interpreter toward this first stage because they are almost exclusively limited to it.

Texts of persecution indicate that myths comprise a first transfiguration similar to that of our persecutors that is really only the substructure of the second transfiguration. Mythological persecutors, more credulous than their historical equivalents, are so taken with what is accomplished by their scapegoats that they are truly reconciled, and their fear of the victim and hostility toward him are supplemented by adoration. It is difficult to understand this second transfiguration which has almost no equivalent in our universe. But once it has been clearly distinguished from the first it can be analyzed logically, beginning with the differences between the two types of texts being compared, especially in the conclusion. Finally, I have confirmed the accuracy of this analysis of establishing that the faint traces of the sacred still clinging to historical victims bear too close a resemblance to the vanished forms of the sacred for them to have evolved from an independent mechanism.

Collective violence must therefore be recognized as a mechanism that is still creating myths in our universe, but, for reasons we shall learn more about, is functioning less and less well. The second of the two mythical transfigurations is obviously the most fragile since it has almost entirely disappeared. Modern Western history is characterized by the decay of mythic forms that only survive as phenomena of persecution and are almost entirely limited to the first transfiguration. If the mythological distortion is directly proportional to the belief of the persecutors, this decline might well constitute the other side of our growing yet imperfect ability to decode. This ability to decode began with the decomposition of the sacred and then developed into our ability to read the partially decomposed forms. As our ability grows we are encouraged to go back to the forms that are still intact and decode the meaning of real myths.

Apart from the complete reversal involved in the conversion to the sacred, there are no greater distortions of persecution in the Dogrib myth than in our passage from Guillaume de Machaut. It is primarily the element of the sacred that interferes with our understanding. If we do not recognize the double transfiguration of the scapegoat, then undoubtedly the phenomenon of the sacred, illusory as it seems to us, will be no less impenetrable than it was for the faithful of the Dogrib cult. Myths and rites contain everything necessary to analyze this phenomenon but we do not recognize it.

Will we trust the myth too much if we assume that their victims and scapegoats are real? That criticism will certainly be made, but the same situation faces the interpreter of the Dogrib texts as in the preceding examples. It contains too many stereotypes of persecution for the text to be purely imaginary. Extreme distrust is as destructive to the understanding of myths as an excess of belief. My interpretation seems rash only if judged by standards that cannot be applied to the stereotypes of persecution.

I could of course be mistaken in the particular myth I have chosen, that of the woman-dog. This myth could have been made up of various pieces for reasons similar to those that led me earlier to invent a "false" myth of Oedipus. The mistake in that case would be purely local and would not compromise the accuracy of the whole interpretation. Even if the Dogrib myth were not the result of actual collective violence it would be the work of a competent imitator, capable of reproducing the textual effects of this type of violence; it would therefore still provide a valuable example like my false myth of Oedipus. If I were to assume there was a real victim behind the text I have just invented I would be making a huge mistake, but my error would not, in fact, be any less faithful to the truth of the majority of texts containing the same stereotypes and similar structure. It is statistically inconceivable that all these texts could have been forgeries.

Clearly, the same concept can be applied when we consider the example of the Jewish woman of Binzwangen accused of giving birth to monsters. A slight change of decor and a weakening of the positive quality of the sacred would point my critics in the direction of an interpretation they consider unacceptable. The type of interpretation demanded of myths is suddenly gone from their minds; and if it is imposed on them they themselves denounce its mystifying character. All interpretations that do not attempt to demystify persecution are in fact regressive despite their noisy avant-garde posture.

ETHNOLOGISTS BELIEVE their work is far removed from my thesis, but in certain areas it comes very close. Ethnology has long recognized in what it calls "magical thought" a supernatural explanation, and *of the causal type*. Hubert and Mauss saw in magic "a gigantic variation on the theme of the principle of causality." This type of causality precedes and somewhat heralds that of science. In accord with the ideological mind-set of the time the ethnologists insist on the similarities rather than the differences between the two types of interpretation. The differences are important to those who boast of the superiorities of science; the similarities, on the other hand, are important to those who insist on the unity of human thought.

Lévi-Strauss belongs to both groups. In *The Savage Mind*, he takes Hubert and Mauss's formula and defines rites and magical beliefs as "so many expressions of an act of faith in a science yet to be born."[3] Although the intellectual aspect interests him, in support of what he has to say he quotes a text of Evans-Pritchard which immediately clarifies the identity of magical thought and of the *witch-hunt*:

Notions of witchcraft comprise natural and moral philosophies. As a natural philosophy it reveals a theory of causation. Misfortune is due to witchcraft co-operating with natural forces. If a buffalo gores a man, or the supports of a granary are undermined by termites so that it falls on his head, or he is infected with cerebro-spinal meningitis, Azande say that the buffalo, the granary, and the dis-

3. Claude Lévi-Strauss, *The Savage Mind* (Chicago: University of Chicago Press, 1966), p. 19.

ease, are causes which combine with witchcraft to kill a man. Witchcraft does not create the buffalo and the granary and the disease for these exist in their own right, but it is responsible for the particular situation in which they are brought into lethal relations with a particular man. The granary would have fallen in any case, but since there was witchcraft present it fell at the particular moment when a certain man was resting beneath it. Of these causes the only one which permits intervention is witchcraft, for witchcraft emanates from a person. The buffalo and the granary do not allow intervention and are, therefore, whilst recognized as causes, not considered the socially relevant ones.[4]

The term *natural philosophy* invokes the image of Rousseau's "noble savage," who wonders innocently about the "mysteries of nature." In reality magical thought does not originate in disinterested curiosity. It is usually the last resort in a time of disaster, and provides principally a system of accusation. It is always the *other* who plays the role of the sorcerer and acts in an unnatural fashion to harm his neighbor.

Evans-Pritchard illustrates what I have illustrated myself but in the language of ethnologists. Magical thought seeks "a significant cause on the level of social relations," in other words a human being, a victim, a scapegoat. It is not necessary to identify the exact nature of the *corrective intervention* that results from the magical explanation. Everything he mentions is applicable not only to the normal phenomena of magic in the ethnological universe but also to the whole range of persecution of phenomena, from medieval violence to mythology proper.

Thebes is not unaware that epidemics strike human communities from time to time. But the people of Thebes ask why our city at this particular time? Those who are suffering are not interested in natural causes. Only magic makes "corrective intervention" possible, and everyone eagerly seeks a magician who can put things right. There is no remedy against the plague as is, or against Apollo if you will. On the other hand, there is nothing to prevent the cathartic correction of the unfortunate Oedipus.

Lévi-Strauss makes the same suggestion in his essays on magical thought, but he pushes the art of litotes even further than Evans-Pritchard. He admits that despite certain results "of good scientific standing" magic generally cuts a poor figure compared with science but not for the reasons imagined by the devotees of "primitive thought."

4. E. E. Evans-Pritchard, "Witchcraft," *Africa* 8 (1955): 418–19.

...magical thought...can be distinguished from science not so much by any ignorance or contempt of determinism but by a more imperious and uncompromising demand for it which can at the most be regarded as unreasonable and precipitate from the scientific point of view.[5]

Magical thought is generally perceived as a defensive action against magic; it results in the same type of behavior as displayed by the witchhunters or by the Christian mobs during the Black Death. Moreover, we rightly describe all these people as reasoning in *magical* fashion, or even *mythological* fashion, as I recall. The two terms are synonymous and equally justifiable. This is unwittingly demonstrated by Evans-Pritchard. There is no essential difference between the representation and behavior of magic in history and in mythology.

The moral attitude of the two disciplines, history and ethnology, makes all the difference. Historians emphasize the dimension of persecution and loudly denounce the intolerance and superstition that make such things possible. The ethnologists are only interested in the epistemological aspects and the theory of causes. One need only reverse the fields of application without changing the language to assert once more the schizophrenic nature of our culture. This assertion inevitably makes us uneasy; it affect the values that are dear to us and are considered inviolable. This is no reason to transfer that uneasiness to those who identified it and treat them as scapegoats. Yet the reason is the same, basic, immemorial reason—only in its modern, intellectualized version. All this tends to set the *unconscious* mechanism in motion once again. In order to fill the cracks and holes in the system, we resort *more or less unconsciously* to the generative and regenerative mechanism of this same system. In our day, the emphasis is on the less, rather than the more. Even though there are more and more persecutions, there are less *unconscious* persecutors and truly unperceived distortions in the representation of the victims. Because of this there is less resistance to the truth, and all of mythology will soon be understood.

MYTHS REPRESENT persecutions similar to those we have already interpreted, but they are more difficult to decode because they contain greater distortions. The transfigurations are stronger in mythology. The victims become monstrous and display fantastic power. After sowing disorder, they reestablish order and become founding fathers or gods. This addi-

5. *The Savage Mind*, p. 10.

tional element of transfiguration, however, does not prevent the comparison of myths with historical persecutions. The explanation lies in the mechanism identified in those representations already decoded, from which we must now seek an even more effective function. The return to peace and order is ascribed to the same cause as the earlier troubles – to the victim himself. That is what makes the victim sacred and transforms the persecution into a point of religious and cultural departure. The whole process, in effect, serves as: (1) a model for mythology in which it is commemorated as a religious epiphany; (2) a model for ritual which is forced to reproduce it on the principle that the action or experience of the victim, in that it was beneficial, must always be repeated; and (3) a countermodel for the forbidden, by virtue of the principle that one must never repeat the actions of this same victim, insofar as they were harmful.

There is nothing in mythico-ritual religions that does not unfold logically from the fact that the scapegoat mechanism functions on a higher order than in history. There was good reason for past ethnology to assume a close relationship between myths and rituals, but the enigma of this relationship was never resolved because it was never understood that the phenomena of persecution provided both the model and the countermodel for every religious institution. The first detail, of which the second is only the reflection, was sometimes identified in myths and sometimes in rituals. By dint of failure the ethnologists gave up questioning the nature and relationship of religious institutions.

The effect of the scapegoat resolves a problem that contemporary ethnologists do not even recognize. To understand the magnitude of my proposed solution we must consider the relationship to the actual event described of the account given by the persecutors of their own persecution. A detached observer who is present at, but does not participate in, an episode of collective violence, only sees a helpless victim mistreated by a hysterical crowd. But if he asks the members of that crowd what is happening he will scarcely recognize what he has seen with his own eyes. He will be told about the extraordinary power of the victim, the occult influence he exercised and possibly still exercises on the community, for he has no doubt escaped death, etc.

The distance between what actually happened and the way it is perceived by the persecutors must be further enlarged in order to understand the relationship between myths and rituals. In the most primitive rites we see a disorderly crowd that gradually focuses on one victim and ends by flinging itself on him. The myth describes the story of a formidable god who saved the faithful by some sacrifice, or by dying after spreading disorder in the community.

The faithful of these cults declare that they are reenacting in their rites what happened in the myths. We cannot understand this statement since we see in the rites an unleashed mob that harms a victim, and the myths speak of an all-powerful god who dominates a community. We do not understand that it is the same person in both cases because we cannot conceive of distortions of persecution powerful enough to consecrate the victim.

Past ethnology is right to suspect that the most brutal rites are the most primitive. They may not be the most ancient on an absolute scale of chronology, but they are the closest to their violent origin, and therefore the most revealing. Although myths use as their model the same sequence of persecution as rites, they resemble them least at the moment of greatest resemblance. The words in this case are more deceptive than actions, and invariably deceive the ethnologists. They see only that the very same episode of collective violence is much closer to what actually takes place in the ritual than in the myth. Indeed in rituals the faithful repeat the collective violence of their predecessors; they imitate that violence, and their representation of what happened does not influence their behavior as much as their words. The words are entirely determined by the representation of persecution, that is, by the symbolic power of the appointed victim, whereas the ritual actions are directly patterned on the actions of the crowd of persecutors.

CHAPTER FIVE

Teotihuacan

MY CRITICS CONSTANTLY accuse me of switching back and forth between the representation and the reality of what is being represented. Readers who have been following the text attentively will understand that I do not deserve the reproach or, if I do, we all deserve it equally because we affirm the existence of real victims behind the almost mythological texts of medieval persecutors.

I shall now turn to myths that are more problematic for my thesis, at least on the surface, since they deny the relevance of collective murder for mythology. One of the ways of denying that relevance is by affirming that, although they are dead, the victims went to their death willingly. How should the myths of self-sacrifice in primitive societies be interpreted? Let us look at a great American myth of self-sacrifice, the Aztec myth of the creation of the sun and moon. Like almost everything else we know about the Aztecs we owe this to Bernardino de Sahagún, the author of *Historia general de las cosas de la Nueva España*. Georges Bataille has given in *La Part maudite* a paraphrased translation of the myth, which I will cite in abbreviated form:

They say that before there was day in the world, the gods came together in that place which is named Teotihuacan. They said to one another: "O gods, who will have the burden of lighting the world?" Then to these words answered a god named Tecuciztecatl, and he said: "I shall take the burden of lighting the world." Then once more the gods spoke, and they said: "Who will be another?" Then they looked at one another, and deliberated on who the other should be. And none of them dared offer himself for that office. All were afraid and declined. One of the gods, to whom no one was paying any attention, and who was covered with pustules, did not speak but listened to what the other gods were saying. And the others spoke to him and said to him: "You be the one who is to give light, little pustule-covered one." And right willingly he obeyed what they commanded, and he answered: "Thankfully I accept what you have commanded me to do. Let it be as you say." And then both began to perform penances for four days. . . .

And midnight having come, all the gods placed themselves about the hearth, called *teotexcalli*. In this place the fire blazed four days. The aforementioned gods arranged themselves in two rows, some at one side of the fire, some at the other side. And then the two gods above mentioned placed themselves before the fire, between the two rows of gods, all of whom were standing. And then the gods spoke, and said to Tecuciztecatl: "How now, Tecuciztecatl! Go into the fire!" And then he braced himself to cast himself into the fire.

And since the fire was large and blazed high, as he felt the great heat of the fire, he became frightened and dared not cast himself into the fire. He turned back. Once more he turned to throw himself into the fire, making an effort and drawing nearer, to cast himself into the flames. But, feeling the great heat, he held back and dared not cast himself into it. Four times he tried, but never let himself go. Since he had tried four times, the gods then spoke to Nanauatzin, and said to him: "How now, Nanauatzin! You try!" And when the gods had addressed him, he exerted himself and with closed eyes undertook the ordeal and cast himself into the flames. And then he began to crackle and pop in the fire like one who is roasted.

And when Tecuciztecatl saw that Nanauatzin had cast himself into the flames, and was burning, he gathered himself and threw himself into the fire. And it is said that an eagle entered the blaze and also burned itself; and for that reason it has dark brown or blackened feathers. Finally a tiger entered; it did not burn itself, but singed itself; and for that reason remained stained black and white. . . .

And they say that after this the gods knelt down to wait to see where Nanauatzin, become sun, would rise. . . . And when the sun came to rise, he looked very red. He appeared to waddle from one side to the other. No one could look at him, because he snatched sight from the eyes. He shone and cast rays of light from him in grand style. His light and his rays he poured forth in all directions. And thereafter the moon rose on the horizon. Having hesitated, Tecuciztecatl was less brilliant. . . . Later the gods all had to die. The wind *Kwetzalcoatl* killed them all; it tore out their hearts and gave life to the newborn stars.[1]

The first god is not chosen by anyone—he truly volunteers—but this is not true for the second god. Later on, the reverse is true. The second god throws himself into the fire immediately without being

1. Quoted in *The Savage Mind*, pp. 101–3.

urged, which is not true of the first. In each case there is an element of constraint in the behavior of these two gods. As we look from one to the other we see reversals that are translated into both differences and symmetries. We must not forget the former but, contrary to what the structuralists think, it is never the difference but rather the symmetries—the aspects shared by the victims—that are the most revealing.

The myth emphasizes the free and voluntary aspect of their decision. The gods are great, and they give themselves to death essentially of their own free will, to secure the continued existence of the world and of mankind. Nevertheless there is an obscure element of constraint in both cases that gives us pause. The little pockmarked god shows great docility. He exalts in the idea of dying for such a wonderful cause as the birth of the sun but he is not a volunteer. Unquestionably, all the gods share in the weakness. They are frightened, intimidated, and dare not "offer themselves for that job." The weakness might be said to be very slight, but later we shall see a tendency in myths to minimize the weaknesses of the gods. In any case it is a weakness that the pockmarked one displays briefly before he courageously undertakes the mission entrusted to him.

Nanauatzin possesses a distinctive feature that cannot fail to attract our attention, the pocks or sores that make him a leper, someone stricken with the plague, the embodiment of contagious disease. From my perspective of collective persecution we must recognize in this a preferential sign for the selection of a victim. The question follows whether it is not this sign that determines the choice of victim, in which case it would be a question of a victim and a collective murder rather than a self-sacrifice. The myth, of course, does not say this, but we must not expect the myth to reveal this type of truth. The myth does, however, confirm Nanauatzin's probable role as a scapegoat by presenting him as a god "to whom no one was paying any attention"; he stands to one side and remains silent.

We should note in this passage that the Aztec sun-god is also the god of pestilence, like the Greek god Apollo. Apollo's resemblance to the Aztec god might be greater if Olympian censure had not cleansed him of all the stigmata of a victim. There are many examples of this combination. What do pestilence and the sun have in common? To understand this we must break away from the insipid concepts of symbolism and of the unconscious, whether collective or individual. If we select only what we want to see then inevitably we find what we want to find. Instead we should confront the scene in question. It is common for plague victims to be burned because fire has always been considered the most effective means of purification. This connection is not made explicitly in our myth, but we can sense its presence which becomes explicit in other American myths. Fire appears more frequently as the contagion becomes more menacing. Add to this the scapegoat mechanism and the torturers who already hold their victim responsible for the epidemic will now hold him responsible for the cure.

Sun-gods must be people so sick that men turn to a great fire such as Teotihuacan's to destroy them. If then the epidemic recedes, the victim becomes divine in that he is burned and becomes one with the fire that instead of destroying him mysteriously transforms him into a force for good. The victim is thus transformed into that inextinguishable flame that shines on humanity. Where can this flame be found thereafter? The answer is immediately apparent. It can only be in the sun, or possibly in the moon and the stars. Only the celestial bodies give man light permanently; but there is no guarantee they will always do so. To assure their benevolent collaboration they must be nourished and provided with victims, to assure their regeneration, victims will always be needed.

Obviously, by the same process of shooting rays on the crowd the god confers benefits and inflicts harm. They bring light, heat, and fertility but they also bring disease. They become the darts hurled at the Thebans by an irritated Apollo. All these themes can be found in the worship of Saint Sebastian at the end of the Middle Ages and form a part of the representation of persecution. They are generated by a much weaker version of the scapegoat mechanism.[2]

Saint Sebastian is thought to protect one against the plague because he is *covered with arrows,* and arrows seem to have the same significance as they had for the Greeks and no doubt for the Aztecs: they imply the sun's rays or pestilence. Epidemics are frequently portrayed as a rain of arrows hurled at men by the Eternal Father and even by Christ. There is affinity between Saint Sebastian and the arrows, or rather the pestilence; the faithful hope that his presence in their churches will attract the wandering arrows to him and spare them. Saint Sebastian is offered

2. Delumeau, *La Peur en Occident,* p. 107.

as the preferred target for the malady; he is brandished like the serpent of brass in front of the Hebrews.

The saint thus plays the role of scapegoat: he protects because he is tainted; he is consecrated in the primitive double sense of cursed and blessed. Like all primitive gods, the saint protects as long as he monopolizes and incarnates the plague. The evil aspect of this incarnation has almost disappeared. We must therefore be careful not to say: "It is exactly the same as in the case of the Aztecs." It is not the same because violence plays no role, but it is certainly the same mechanism and is more readily identified because of the much reduced level of belief at which it is operating.

If we compare Saint Sebastian with the persecuted Jews and doctors we see that the evil and beneficial aspects are in inverse proportion. Real persecutions and the "pagan" primitive aspects of the cult of saints are unequally affected by the decomposition of mythology. The only fault with which we can reproach Nanauatzin is that he waits passively to be selected. On the other hand the god unquestionably possesses one of the preferential signs of victims. The opposite is true of Tecuciztecatl who does not bear the mark of a victim but who proves to be both extremely boastful and extremely cowardly. Even if he has not committed a crime against nature, his constant boastfulness during the four days of penance make him guilty of *hubris* in a sense similar to that of the Greeks.

There would be no sun or moon without victims; the world would be plunged in obscurity and chaos. This is the basis of the whole of Aztec religion. The point of departure in our myth is the total lack of difference between day and night. In this we have a classic stereotype of crisis, the social setting most favorable for the scapegoat mechanism. We now have three of the four stereotypes: a crisis, faults if not crimes, one of the preferential signs of a victim, and two violent deaths which literally produce the differentiating decision. The result is not only the appearance of two luminous and very distinct stars but also the specific coloration of two kinds of animals, the eagle and the tiger.

The only stereotype missing is collective murder. The myth assures us that there is no murder since death is voluntary. But I have pointed out the fortuitous inclusion of an element of constraint in the free will of the two victims. Finally, if we need to be convinced of the presence of collective murder, however superficially denied or camouflaged, we need only look at the crucial scene. The gods are lined up menacingly on two sides. They have organized the whole affair and regulate every detail. They always act in unison and speak with a single voice, first to choose the second "volunteer" and then to order the two victims to throw themselves "voluntarily" into the fire. What would happen if the fainthearted volunteer did not choose to follow his companion's example? Would the gods around him allow him to resume his place among them as if nothing had happened? Or would their forms of encouragement become more brutal? The idea that the victims could freely escape from their demiurgic task seems unlikely. If one of them sought to escape, the two parallel lines of gods could quickly form a circle and push the victim into the fire by closing in on him. I would like the reader to remember this circular or almost circular configuration which will reappear, with or without the fire, and with or without any apparent victim, in a great many of the myths I shall be discussing.

The sacrifice of the two victims is in essence presented to us as an act of free will, a self-sacrifice, but in both cases a subtle element of constraint eats away at that freedom on two different occasions. This element of constraint is decisive. It provides yet another detail in this text to suggest the phenomenon of persecution, mythologized by the perspective of the persecutors. Three of the four stereotypes are present, and the fourth is strongly suggested as much by the victims' death as by the general configuration of the scene. If we were to see this same scene as a silent living tableau we would have no doubt that the victims were put to death and that their consent was of almost no concern for those making the sacrifice. Our doubts would be confirmed by the knowledge that human sacrifice was a typical religious activity of the Aztec civilization. Some experts have mentioned as many as twenty thousand victims a year at the time of Cortes's conquest. Even if considerable allowance is made for exaggeration, human sacrifice still plays a monstrous role among the Aztecs. As a people they were constantly occupied with fighting not for the expansion of territory but to obtain the victims necessary for the innumerable sacrifices recounted by Bernardino de Sahagún.

Ethnologists have known these facts for centuries, ever since the first deciphering of the representations of persecution in the Western world. But they have not drawn the same conclusions. They spend most of their time minimizing, if not actually justifying, among the Aztecs what they rightly condemn in their own universe. Once again we see the different means of measurement characteristic of anthropology when dealing with both historical and ethnological societies. Our inability to decode more mystifying representations of persecution in myths than the ones we can demystify is not merely the result of the complexity of the undertaking or the extreme transfiguration of the data. Scholars show an extraordinary reluctance to examine so-called ethnological societies as ruthlessly as they do their own.

Admittedly, ethnologists have a difficult task. "Their" cultures shatter on the slightest contact with modern Western society to the point of scarcely existing any more. Such a situation constantly triggers a form of oppression that increases in bitterness the more it is scorned. Modern intellectuals are obsessed by scorn and feel compelled to present vanished worlds in the most favorable light. Our ignorance sometimes becomes a resource. How can we criticize the religious life of these people? We do not know enough to contradict when their victims are presented as volunteers, as believers who silently allowed themselves to be massacred in order to prolong the existence of the world. There exists an ideology of sacrifice among the Aztecs which is revealed for what it is in our myth. Without victims, the world would be plunged in darkness and chaos. The first victims are not enough. At the end of the passage quoted, the sun and moon shine in the sky but do not move; to force them to move, first every single god must be sacrificed, and then the anonymous crowds which are substituted for them. Everything depends on the sacrifice.

There is certainly "some truth" in the myth of the consenting victim, and the myth reveals it. The boastful god overestimated his strength; he recoiled at the crucial moment: this recoil suggests that all the victims might not be as willing as the ethnologists would have us believe. Tecuciztecatl ultimately overcomes his cowardice, and it is his companion's example that makes the difference between the early failures and the final success. This is the moment of revelation of the force that dominates groups of men: imitation, mimesis. I have not mentioned it until now because I wanted to demonstrate in the simplest possible way the relevance of collective murder for the interpretation of mythology; I wanted to introduce only those details that were strictly indispensable, which cannot be said of mimesis. I will now indicate the truly remarkable role it plays in our myth.

The future moon-god is obviously driven to volunteer by the wish to outstrip all the other gods, the spirit of mimetic rivalry. He wants to be without a rival, the first among them, one who acts as a model for others without having a model himself. This is *hubris*, so exaggerated a form of mimetic desire that he claims to be beyond all mimesis, to want no other model than himself. If the moon-god cannot obey the injunction to throw himself into the fire it is clear that, having achieved the first place that he claimed, he finds himself without a model; he can no longer follow someone's guidance and must guide others. The very reason that made him claim that first place is the reason that he is incapable of holding it: he is so totally mimetic. The second god, on the other hand, the future sun, did not try to put himself forward; he is less hysterically mimetic, which is why when his turn comes he resolutely takes the initiative that his fellow god was unable to take. He is able to become an effective model for one who cannot act without a model.

Mimetic elements can be found circulating through myths in a hidden fashion. The moral of the fable does not exhaust them. The two characters are contrasted within an even wider circle of imitation, the assembled gods who are unified in mimesis and control the whole scene. Everything the gods do is perfect because it is unanimous. Freedom and constraint are bound inextricably by their subordination to the mimetic power of the united gods. I have described the act of free will of the one who in response to the gods' appeal goes voluntarily or throws himself unhesitatingly into the fire, but this freedom is no more than the divine will that continually says: "Go throw yourself into the fire." It is the equivalent of an immediate or delayed imitation of divine will. The spontaneous act of will is the same as the irresistible hypnotic power of the example. For our pockmarked god the message "Go throw yourself into the fire" is immediately transformed into action; it already exerts an exemplary force. For the other god the message is not enough; the additional spectacle of action is needed. Tecuciztecatl throws himself into the fire because he sees his companion do so. He would appear at first glance to be more mimetic but perhaps ultimately he is less mimetic.

The mimetic collaboration of victims with their executioners continues in the Middle Ages and even into our own time, though now the forms are weaker. We are told that in the sixteenth century witches chose their own stake; they were made to understand the horror of their misdeeds. Heretics too often called for the punishment merited by their abominable beliefs; it would be lacking in charity to deprive them of it. In our own time all forms of Stalinism find viperous victims who will confess far more than is asked of them, and rejoice in the just punishment that awaits them. Fear is an insufficient explanation for this type of behavior. Even Oedipus joins in the unified chorus that declaims his abominable defilement. He asks the city of Thebes to spew him forth in the same way as he causes himself to vomit.

When such attitudes appear in our society, we indignantly deny them, yet we do not even wince at attributing them to the Aztecs or other primitive people. Ethnologists eagerly describe the enviable lot of these victims. In the time preceding their sacrifice they enjoy extraordinary privileges so that they go to their death serenely, perhaps even joyously. Jacques Soustelle, among others, warns his readers not to interpret this religious butchery in the light of our current concepts. That terrible sin of ethnocentrism is lying in wait for us and, no matter what exotic societies do, we must guard against the slightest negative judgment.[3]

However laudable is the desire to "rehabilitate" unappreciated nations, some discernment should be used. The current excesses are as ridiculous as the former arrogant exaggerations, but in reverse. It is the same condescension in the end. The reason we do not apply the same criteria to those societies as we do to our own results from the demagogic reversal typical of our contemporary era. Otherwise our sources are worthless and we would do well to remain silent. We either know nothing about the Aztecs and never will; or our sources have value, and honesty demands that we recognize that the Aztec religion has not yet taken its rightful place in our planet's museum of human horror. Antiethnocentric zeal errs in justifying bloody orgies by accepting the obviously misleading self-image these people present.

Despite its sacrificial ideology, this atrocious and magnificent myth of Teotihuacan is a powerful witness against the vision of mystification. If anything can humanize this text it is not the false idyll of victims and executioners in our post-war era patterned on Rousseau and Nietzsche. The hesitations I have identified, despite the false evidence surrounding them, run counter to this hypocritical vision without openly contradicting it. The myth's disturbing beauty cannot be separated from the kind of tremulousness that takes possession of it. We must expand on this tremulousness to rock the structure and bring it crashing down.

3. Jacques Soustelle, *La Vie quotidienne des Aztèques* (Paris: Hachette, 1955), pp. 126–29.

CHAPTER SIX

Ases, Curetes, and Titans

I HAVE BEEN discussing a myth in which collective murder is absent. I shall now select a number of examples from myths, or the endless variants of myths, in which the central scene clearly depicts collective murder but in which such an effort is made to avoid defining the deed that the scene becomes a near caricature. The configuration of the scene is always the same—the murderers are in a circle around their victim—but the obvious or intentional significance of the scenes can vary widely. It may share only a single characteristic: the awareness that they do not signify collective murder.

My second example belongs to Scandinavian mythology. Baldr is the best of all the gods: he has no faults, is rich in virtues, and is incapable of violence. He is disturbed by dreams warning him that a threat of death is hanging over him. He shares his anguish with his companions, the Ases, who decide to "claim protection for Baldr against all danger." To achieve this, Frigg, his mother: "makes all animate and inanimate creatures – fire, water, metals, stones, earth, wood, diseases, quadrupeds, birds, snakes. . . . swear to do him no harm. Thus protected, Baldr enjoys an extraordinary game with the Ases in the public square. They hurl things at him and strike him with their swords but nothing wounds him."

The synopsis I have quoted is Georges Dumézil's in *Mythe et epopée*.[1] It is easy to understand why the eminent scholar considers the game the Ases are playing astonishing. A little further on he will

---

1. Georges Dumézil, *Mythe et epopée* (Paris: Bibliothèque des sciences humains, 1968), p. 224.

describe this same game as both "spectacular" and "fake." He arouses our curiosity without satisfying it. What is there about this myth that provokes our astonishment? Is the scene unusual or, on the contrary, very familiar, totally ordinary, yet endowed with an unusual significance? The game appears fake, but we cannot call it that without revealing something else, another scene that is not usually hidden and is surely known to all ethnologists, even if they make no direct mention of it. By suggesting that the game of the Ases is fake, without explaining his meaning, G. Dumézil could be said to be speaking about the scene indirectly. It is clearly a question of collective violence. If Baldr were not invulnerable he would obviously not survive the treatment inflicted on him by the Ases; the very event Baldr fears, and is feared by all the Ases, will obviously take place. Baldr will perish, like so many gods, the victim of collective murder. There is nothing to distinguish the myth of Baldr from the countless myths in which collective murder provides the central drama.

We are surprised by the myth precisely because it adds nothing truly original or unexpected, and the game seems fake because it resembles so exactly the most frequently found and hackneyed scene in all mythology, collective murder. The convention of an invulnerable Baldr merely transforms the representation of a murder into an inoffensive game. Is this a simple coincidence, an accidental similarity? The sequence proves it is not. To understand the myth's close relationship to other myths that *contain collective murder* we must proceed to the end of this seemingly inoffensive game of the Ases and determine whether the final consequences would be the same had the game been played for real. Baldr falls, struck dead by one of the gods who are supposed to remain innocent of the deed even though, in the end, they truly cause his death.

What has happened? We shall learn as we read on in *Mythe et epopée*. There is one god or, rather, one demon, Loki, the trickster or cheat of Scandinavian mythology, who does not join in the make-believe game and tries to break it up. Faithful to his sources, G. Dumézil writes, "This spectacle displeased Loki." The feigned lynching of Baldr arouses strong reactions among all the spectators, displeasure in Loki, and astonishment in Dumézil. And it is the fault of Loki, as always, that the feigned lynching of Baldr, the childish game of the Ases, ultimately brings about the same consequence as an actual lynching.

The Scandinavian trickster disguises himself as a woman and goes to Frigg to ask whether there is any exception to the universal oath not to harm Baldr. And he learns from Frigg that a young shoot of *mistilteinn* (mistletoe) had seemed so young to her that she had not asked it to take the oath. Loki takes the shoot, returns to the *thing* [the sacred spot where the lynching will take place] and gives it to Baldr's blind brother, Hoehr, who had refrained from hitting his brother until then because he could not see him. Loki guides his hand toward the victim who is assassinated by a simple twig of mistletoe.

Loki's treachery thus cancels the effect of the measures taken by the gods to "protect" Baldr from all violence. Why does this myth take such a strange and circuitous route to arrive at almost the same result as thousands of other myths, the violent death of a god struck by other gods, his companions who are all joined against him. Since the result is so familiar why not take the familiar route to it? The only feasible or even conceivable response seems to be that the version of the myth we are analyzing *is not the first*. It must stem from older versions in which Baldr is the victim of the most banal and classic of all collective murders. It must be the work of people who cannot tolerate the traditional representation of the murder because it makes all the gods, the victim aside, into criminals. The original gathering of gods is no different from a band of assassins, and in a sense the faithful want none of it but they have no other sacred text; they cling to it; they are passionately attached to their religious representations. They want to keep these representations but they also want to get rid of them or, rather, to overthrow them in an effort to eliminate that essential stereotype of persecution, collective murder. The effort to reconcile the two imperatives results in myths, such as Baldr's that are so curiously structured.

The answer lies in the idea that the ancestors saw clearly what there was to see in the primordial epiphany *but interpreted it wrongly*. Naïve and uncivilized as they were, they did not understand the subtlety of what was happening. They believed it was collective murder, falling into the trap set by the demon Loki, the only real assassin and deceiver. Loki becomes the unique receptacle for the violence that was formerly shared by all the lynchers, but which clearly becomes perverse when it is concentrated within a single individual. The reputation of the loner, Loki, is sacrificed for the rehabilitation of all the other gods. The choice of Loki is paradoxical if, as it would seem, he really was the only one of all the gods in the originial scene who does not join in the lynching.

This would seem to suppose a manipulation of the myth to the moral detriment of a single god for the benefit of all the others. There are several other small indications of the desire to clear the original murderers of guilt such as the strange way in which Baldr is actually put to death. All the details of the incident are clearly meant to remove any trace of responsibility from the person who is most likely to be seen as the criminal, since it is by his hand—he is even called *handbani*, or one who kills by hand, elsewhere in the myth—that Baldr dies. Presumably, in collective murder not all the participants are equally guilty; if the person who deals the fatal blow can be identified, as in this case, then he unquestionably bears the greater responsibility. The myth must take exceptional measures to prove the innocence of Hoehr, since obviously he is the most guilty, having dealt the blow. Greater effort is needed to prove his innocence than for all the other gods put together.

Once this is understood the other details of the murder become clear. In the first place, Hoehr is blind: "He had until then refrained from striking his brother because he could not see him." For him to touch his brother someone has to guide his hand toward the target; Loki of course obliges. Hoehr has no reason to believe that his blow might kill Baldr. Like the other gods he believes that his brother is invulnerable to all conceivable weapons and projectiles. He is even further reassured by the object that Loki puts in his hand, which is extremely light and too insignificant to be considered a fatal weapon. Even the most anxious and concerned of brothers for the well-being and security of his brother could not foresee the terrible consequences of Hoehr's action. In other words the myth heaps on the excuses in an effort to prove Hoehr's innocence. In place of the simple denial that is sufficient for the other gods, Hoehr's responsibility is denied on at least three successive occasions. Each time it is Loki who bears the brunt of it. Three times guilty of the murder of which he is technically innocent, Loki cynically manipulates the unfortunate Hoehr who on each of the three occasions is innocent of the murder for which he alone is technically to blame.

If you try too hard to prove something you prove nothing. This is the case in the myth of Baldr: guilty people make too many excuses. They fail to realize that a simple excuse is more effective than many excellent ones. If you want to deceive your audience you had better not let them see what you are trying to do. Too great an effort to hide something always reveals the deception. The intention becomes more obvious because it removes everything that might distract and immediately reveals the hidden object. Nothing is likely to arouse suspicion more than the many elements of irresponsibility that are heaped strangely on the head of the real culprit.

It is clearly possible to interpret the myth of Baldr by explaining absolutely every detail, relying on the simplest and most economical principle, but it is only possible by seeking that principle in an aversion to the representation of a collective murder. The myth is clearly obsessed and completely determined by this representation that nevertheless does not figure explicitly among its themes. Mythologists do not perceive this aversion because they do not realize the importance of collective murders in mythology. Once we realize this importance, all the enigmatic aspects of our particular myth, and of many others, begin to make sense...they make even more sense, of course, in the context of the many Germanic myths that contain a collective murder in its classical form. We might be wise to listen to myths, especially when they contradict ideas that we take for granted.

It remains to prove that the myth of Baldr is not an aberration or exception in mythology. Similarities are to be found not everywhere but in enough important traditions that are both too close to what we have just studied in probable intent yet too different in the solution adopted—the thematic content of the version that has come down to us—not to reinforce the concept that a stage of development and adaptation in their evolution may exist in which the significance of "collective murder" is effaced. This desire to obliterate is remarkable because it is usually associated with a religious conservatism that is anxious to keep earlier representations intact, although their object could only be collective murder.

I shall now turn to a second example taken, this time, from Greek mythology: the birth of Zeus. The god, Kronos, is devouring all his children and is looking for his last-born, Zeus, whom Rhea, the mother, has hidden from him. The Curetes, fierce warriors, hide the baby by forming a circle around him. The cries of the terrified baby Zeus could lead his father to his hiding-place. To drown out his crying and deceive the devouring monster, the Curetes clash their weapons and behave in as noisy and threatening a way as possible.[2] The more frightened the baby becomes, the shriller his cries, and the more the Curetes, in order to protect him, must behave in a way that frightens him. The more

2. Strabo *Strabonis Geographica* 10:468. Jane Harrison, *Themis* (Cambridge: Cambridge University Press, 1912).

actual reassurance and protection they provide, the more frightening they appear. It looks as if they are forming a circle around the baby to kill him, whereas they are actually saving his life.

Again, collective violence is absent from this myth, but not in the same way a thousand other things are absent that have not even been considered. Its absence is similar but not identical to the absence I have just analyzed in the myth of Baldr. The situation involving the infant Zeus is clear, but the configuration and behavior of the Curetes are reminiscent of collective murder. What else would we imagine listening to the wild cries and the brandishing of weapons in the direction of a defenseless creature? If this were a spectacle without words, a living tableau, we would not hestitate to give it the meaning that the myth denies. Like the fake game of the Ases, or the suicide of the Aztecs, the playacting of the Curetes and the frightened reaction of the infant come as close as one could conceive to the drama that statistically dominates world mythology. Yet this myth and that of Baldr assure us that the resemblance is an illusion.

Both myths give the group of murderers the role of "protector" in order to eliminate the violent significance of the scene. But the similarity ends there. In the Scandinavian myth the collective murder that is presented as unreal has the same consequences as if it were real. It has no consequence in the Greek myth. The dignity of Zeus is incompatible with his death at the hands of the Curetes. I imagine there is an earlier version of this myth, too, that contains collective murder. In the metamorphosis the murder has disappeared without modifying, or modifying extensively, the representations that suggest it. The problem is the same, but the Greek solution is both more elegant and more radical than the Scandinavian solution. It succeeds in giving the lynching scene, the circle around the victim, the significance of a protective role. The Scandinavian myth, as we have seen, has no other recourse but to represent it as a game that even observers who reject the concept of collective murder recognize as "fake" or, in other words, as possessing *another meaning*.

The two solutions are too original for one myth to have influenced the other. Here we have two religious thoughts pursuing not exactly the same but very similar objectives at a similar stage in their evolution. Before such evidence there can be no question about the evolution of mythology, or rather successive stages of evolution limited to a small number of religious traditions.

Like the myth of Baldr the myth of the Curetes must originate with interpreters who are genuinely convinced that they have received their mythological tradition in an altered form. In their eyes collective murder is too scandalous to be authentic. They do not consider it a falsification of the text when they reinterpret that scene in their own fashion. They consider the transmission of the myth at fault. Instead of faithfully reporting the tradition handed down to them, their forefathers must have corrupted it because they could not understand it. In this myth, too, the violence that was formerly shared by many is attributed to one god only, Kronos, who as a result of this transference becomes truly monstrous. This sort of caricature is unusual in myths that portray collective murder. There is a certain sharing of *good* and *evil*: moral dualism appears as *collective* violence is eliminated. The fact that evil is attributed to a god of the preceding generation in Olympian mythology no doubt reflects the negative opinion held by a new religious sensibility of the representation it transforms.

My interpretation of the myth of Zeus and the Curetes is entirely based on an *absence*, the absence of collective murder. I have treated the absence of murder as a given even though it is of course speculative, even more than in the case of Baldr, since Zeus is spared and there are no consequences of collective murder. Although strengthened by the similarity of the two myths, my interpretation of the Greek myth is certainly weaker than that of the Scandinavian myth. For support it needs the discovery of a second myth, in its own general category, which would be closely similar to it but different in that the collective murder of the infant god would not have been eliminated. The scene that has been so cleverly transfigured in the myth of the Curetes would be left to exist in the fullness of its original sense. The chances of there really being a transfiguration, and of my interpretation being accurate, would be considerably increased. Is this too much to ask? Of course not. There is a myth in Greek mythology that is homologous to that of the Curetes except in one point: it contains collective violence that is directed against an infant god; it still retains the sense that *is clearly lacking* in the case of the Curetes. Let's put it to the test:

In order to attract the young Dionysus into their circle, the Titans shake a kind of rattle. Fascinated by the brilliant objects, the child advances toward them, and the monstrous circle closes around him. Altogether, the Titans assassinate Dionysus; after which they roast and eat him. Zeus, father of Dionysus, destroys the Titans and revives his son.[3] Between the Curetes and the Titans most of the significance is reversed. The father is a protector among the Titans, destructive and cannibalistic among the Curetes. The group in the myth of the Titans is destructive and cannibalistic; in the myth of Curetes the group is protective. In both myths objects are shaken in front of the child. In the myth of the Titans they seem harmless but are deadly; among the Curetes they seem deadly but are in fact harmless.

Mythology is a game of transformations. Lévi-Strauss has made a most important contribution in revealing this. But the ethnologists believe—wrongly, I think—that the passage can be interpreted in any way. Everything is on the same level. Nothing essential is ever either lost or gained. The arrows of time do not exist. The inadequacy of this concept can be clearly seen. Our two myths are clearly transformations of each other; as I have just shown. After shuffling his cards, the magician spreads them out again in a different order. At first we have the impression that they are all there, but is it true? If we look closer we shall see that there is actually always one missing, and it is always the same one, the representation of collective murder. Everything that happens is of less importance than this disappearance, and to see everything else is to see what is not essential. Moreover, it is impossible to penetrate unless the secret design to which it responds is understood.

Structural analysis rests on the single principle of differentiated binary opposition. It does not allow for the identification of the extreme importance for mythology of the "all against one" of collective violence. Structuralism perceives it as one among many oppositions and traces it to a common law. It attaches no particular significance to the existing representation of violence, and therefore certainly not to its absence. It is too rudimentary a method of analysis to understand what has been lost in the course of a transformation such as I have just described. When the magician shuffles the cards long enough and displays them in a different order he is preventing us from thinking about what has disappeared, and makes us forget the disappearance if we happened to have noticed it. The magician of mythologies and religions has a very good audience in our structuralists.

Identifying the disappearance of collective murder in the passage

---

3. Eliade, *A History of Religious Ideas*, 1:382–87.

from the myth of the Titans to the myth of the Curetes brings the understanding that this type of transformation can only be brought about in
the one way I have indicated. Collective murder may certainly disappear
from mythology. It does in fact nothing else; but once gone it cannot
reappear, it will not spring, fully armed, from some pure combination,
like Minerva from the head of Zeus. Once a myth has been transformed
from its Titan form to that of Baldr or of the Curetes, it never returns
to its former state; that would be inconceivable. There is, in other words,
a *history* of mythology. This fact can be acknowledged without the danger of the old illusions of historicism. The necessary historical, or diachronic, stages result from a purely textual and "structural" analysis.
Mythology eliminates collective murder but does not reinvent it, because all evidence indicates it was not invented in the first place.

None of this is meant to imply that the myth of the Curetes
originates in the myth of the Titans or that it is the transformation of
that myth rather than another. A closer look at the myth of the Titans
reveals a correspondence to a religious vision that is perhaps not so
different from that of the myth of Zeus. And if it had retained the
representation of collective murder, this myth also would have been the
object of a certain manipulation. There is to be found in it, always to
Zeus's advantage, the same division between *good* and *evil* as in the myth
of the Curetes. Collective violence persists but is declared evil akin to
cannibalism. As in the myth of the Curetes violence is attributed to an
older mythological generation and to a religious system now seen to be
"barbarous" and "primitive."

Children and naïve people experience a feeling of fear and revulsion
when confronted with the myth of the Titans. Ethnologists today would
say that they allow themselves to be dominated by the affectivity. I
myself have lapsed into an *affective* ethnology entirely absorbed by a sentimental lack of coherence or so they say. Like the realist novelists of the
mid-nineteenth century our human scientists identify cold humanity
and impassivity as the most fitting state of mind in which to acquire
scientific knowledge. The mathematical exactitude of the so-called hard
sciences arouses an admiration that all too often takes the metaphor of
hardness too literally. Research disdains sentiments that cannot be
ignored without risk since they play an essential role in the very object
being studied, in this case the mythological text. Even if the analysis of
"structures" can be kept completely separated from affectivity there is
still no point to maintaining that separation. The sentiments scorned by

ethnology must be considered if we are to understand the secret behind the transformation of the myths in our two examples. Feigning toughness in order not to be disarmed is in fact to give up one's best weapons.

The real triumphs over mythology have nothing in common with this feigned impassiveness. They belong to an earlier period when the aim pursued was purely moral. They are the anonymous work of those early critics of the witch-hunts and persecutions by intolerant mobs. Even in a purely formal reading that retained all the strong points of today's school, a successful interpretation would not be possible without taking into account either collective murder, wherever it is present, or the uneasiness caused by its disappearance: all the images are arranged around its absence. Unless we recognize this uneasiness, *even those aspects relating strictly to the combination and transformation of the relationships among certain myths* must remain hidden.

CHAPTER SEVEN
The Crimes of the Gods

THE EVOLUTION OF mythology is governed by the determination to eliminate any representation of violence. To gain a clearer understanding we must follow the process beyond the stage, just defined, in which only *collective* violence is at work. Each time it disappears it is replaced by *individual* violence. There may be a second stage, especially in Greek and Roman mythology, in which even individual violence is suppressed, so that all forms of violence in mythology become unacceptable. Those who go beyond this stage, whether they know it or not — and it would seem that usually they do not — are all pursuing the same goal: the elimination of the very last traces of collective murder, the elimination of traces of traces, so to speak. Plato's attitude provides a significant example of this new stage. His intention to remove any trace of mythological violence is quite explicit in the *Republic*. This is especially noticeable in the character of Kronos in a text that is particularly relevant to my analysis:

and then there is the tale of Kronos's doings and of his son's treatment of him. Even if such tales were true, I should not have supposed they should be lightly told to thoughtless young people. If they cannot be altogether suppressed, they should only be revealed in a mystery, to which access should be as far as possible restricted by requiring the sacrifice, not of a pig, but of some victim such as very few could afford. It is true: those stories are objectionable.[1]

Clearly, it is not collective murder that shocks Plato, since it has disappeared, but the individual violence that has taken its place.

1. Plato *Republic*, trans. Francis MacDonald Cornford (New York: Oxford University Press), 378 a–b.

The determination to eliminate all violence, by its very explicitness, becomes a form of censorship, a deliberate mutilation of the mythological text. It no longer has the force of structural reorganization and the extraordinary coherence it possessed in the preceding stage, and therefore does not succeed in modifying the mythological text. Plato foresaw that failure and proposed a kind of compromise mixed with the most interesting religious precautions. The recommendation that the sacrificial victim should be of significance and value is not merely motivated by the desire to reduce to the minimum the number of witnesses to the misdeeds of Kronos and Zeus. This recommendation is to be expected, within the context of a religion in which sacrifice still existed, from a sincerely religious person confronted with a violence that he feels may be contaminating. A similar but legitimate and sacred form of violence is needed as a counterbalance, and is found in the sacrifice of as important a victim as possible. Thus in Plato's text the circle of violence and the sacred is almost explicitly closed before our very eyes.

The censorship that Plato demanded was never imposed in the way he imagined; but it was imposed and still is imposed today in a different and more effective form, incorporated in the discipline of ethnology. The Platonic stage, as opposed to the preceding one, does not culminate in an actual re-creation of the myth, though it is just as fundamental. Another culture is founded, no longer truly mythological but "rational" and "philosophical," forming the very text of philosophy. Mythology is condemned by many ancient writers, generally in the trite forms taken from Plato which illustrate well the true nature of the scandal. Varro, for example, talks of a "theology of the poets" which he found particularly annoying because it asks the faithful to admire "thieving and adulterous gods, gods who are slaves of a man; in other words all man's pitfalls are attributed to the gods, even the most despicable."[2]

According to Varro what Plato calls the theology of the poets is that very primitive dual quality of the sacred which unites blessed with cursed. All the passages from Homer criticized by Plato show the evil aspects of divinity as well as the good. Plato's wish for differentiation does not permit moral ambiguity in the divine. Exactly the same can be seen today in Lévi-Strauss and in structuralism, except that Plato's moral grandeur has disappeared and been replaced by a certain linguisti-

---

2. Quoted by Georges Dumézil, *La Religion romaine archaïque* (Paris: Payot, 1966), p. 108.

cal and logical concern, a philosophy of the mixture that is impossible because it does not conform to the "laws of language and thought." The idea that men might not always think in exactly the same way never occurs. Dionysius of Halicarnassus also complains of myths that present gods as "wicked, evildoers, indecent, unworthy of honest people, never mind divine beings. . ." In fact all these ancient authors share the premonition that their gods may become the despised and trampled victims of men. This is what they must prevent. They reject the possibility in horror, for, unlike the prophets of the Jews and then the Gospels, they cannot imagine that such a victim could be innocent.

Plato openly condemns mythology and deflects it from its traditional themes. His text is full of the sort of motifs mentioned earlier in explanation of the disappearance of collective murder from the myth of the Curetes. The first transformations date from a prephilosophical stage and evolved from the original myths. We have no other evidence aside from these transformed myths, which become immediately comprehensible when they are understood to be the result of transformation. Plato's philosophical decree is thus not the result of individual whim but reveals retroactively the evolution of all mythology. Plato clearly had both recent and distant predecessors who were involved in cleaning up myths, but they all worked mythologically, within the framework of mythology and traditional religion, transforming mythological narrative.

The stereotype of violence to which the gods and heroes were subjected is first weakened by the loss of its brutally and spectacularly collective character and then almost entirely disappears as it becomes a sort of individual violence. Other stereotypes of persecution undergo comparable evolutions and for the same reasons. Men who cannot tolerate the collective murder of a god would be equally shocked by the crimes that justify the murder. The texts I have quoted show that the two go together. Varro complains of the poets *who attribute to the gods all man's weaknesses, particularly those of the most despised of men.* The poets, of course, are not responsible for the attribution since it is found everywhere in mythology. Even then, as today, the "poets," the interpreters of the preceding period, provide the best available scapegoats, and the betrayals of which they are accused in turn bring about further censorship.

From now on gods must be neither criminals nor victims and, because they are not recognized as scapegoats, their acts of violence and criminality—the signs that point to them as victims—including the crisis itself, must be gradually eliminated. Sometimes the meaning of the crisis is inverted, and the lack of distinction between gods and men is endowed with the utopian sense to which I have alluded.

As a community moves away from its violent origins, the sense of ritual weakens and moral dualism is reinforced. Gods and their deeds, even the most evil, served originally as models in the rites. On important ritual occasions religions make a place for disorder, though always in subordination to order. There comes a time, however, when men want only models of morality and demand gods purified of all faults. The complaints of Plato should not be taken lightly, nor those of Euripides, who also wanted to reform the gods. They reflect the disintegration of the primitive notion of the sacred, the tendency toward dualism that only wants to retain the beneficent aspect of the gods. This leads to the development of an ideology that consists either in transferring the sacred to demons, in order to distinguish them more and more from the gods, as in the Brahman religion, or in belittling or nullifying evil, implying that it was added to an *earlier* religion which alone conforms to the ideal of the reformer. In fact, the reformer is creating an origin by relegating his ideal to a purely imaginary past. By this act of relegation he transfigures the original crisis into an idyll and a utopia. The conflict that results from the absence of distinction becomes a happy resolution.

The tendency to idealize transforms or effaces all the stereotypes: the crisis, the signs that indicate a victim, collective violence, and of course the victim's crime. This can be seen clearly in the myth of Baldr. The god who is not collectively killed cannot be a guilty god. He is a god whose crime has been completely effaced, a perfectly sublime god, devoid of all fault. It is no accident that the two stereotypes are suppressed simultaneously; this results from a single *inspiration* on the part of the faithful. The punishment and its cause are connected and must disappear together, since the reason for their disappearance is the same.

Am I right in insisting that something has been actively eliminated and that this is more than a pure and simple absence? I proved it in the case of collective murder, but the argument only related indirectly to the crime that I assumed was originally attributed to all the gods. I implied that an original "criminal" Baldr must have existed in a more primitive version of the myth. As we have seen, the myth of Baldr contains all that is necessary to confirm the tremendous relevance of the collective murder that is absent, and thereby the manipulation of that murder in the version handed down to us. This does not quite hold true for the crime that is also *absent*. In order to prove that the stereotypes of persecution are truly universal we must demonstrate their great relevance for myths, particularly those that *do not contain them*.

Take first the stereotype of the crime. The study of myths suggests that there was a very strong tendency, especially in Greek mythology, to minimize and even suppress the crimes of the gods long before Plato and the philosophers articulated the concept. Even a superficial reading will reveal immediately that myths cannot be divided into two categories according to divine misdoing: guilty gods on the one hand and innocent gods on the other. There are a multitude of variations between the two, forming a continuum from the most atrocious crimes to perfect innocence by way of unimportant mistakes, blunders, and carelessness, which, however, have just as disastrous consequences as the most serious crimes.

This range cannot be looked on as static. Its evolutionary character becomes clear when we notice how many themes clearly share one feature in common: the wish to minimize and excuse a fault. The literal definition of the fault always remains the same, but we are left with so different an impression even today that the fundamental identity of all these crimes is not apparent. The Olympian gods of classical Greece are no longer victims, as we have seen, but they still commit most of the stereotypical crimes that would justify putting the guilty person to death in other mythologies. Their actions, however, are treated so favorably, with so much indulgence and refinement, that their effect on us today is very different from our reaction to them in so-called ethnological myths.

When Zeus turns into a swan to become Leda's lover we do not think of the crime of bestiality, when the Minotaur marries Pasiphae we think nothing of it, or at most consider the author in bad taste; yet there is no difference between these two myths and the Dogrib myth of the woman-dog or even the horrible medieval fiction of the Jewish woman of Binzwangen giving birth to a litter of pigs. We react to the same fables in different ways, depending on whether we see in them, or are made to see in them, the results of persecution. Aesthetic and poetic treatment lends itself to a million and one ways of elaborating on the stereotypes of persecution or of concealing anything that might reveal the original scapegoat mechanism that created the text.

Plato, like all Puritans, misses the goal, which is to reveal the mechanism of the victim and the demystification of the representations of persecution. But at least he has more greatness and depth than the morally lax poets or the aesthetes among contemporary critics who dissolve the essential of the problematic. Plato not only objects to attributing all the typical crimes to the gods, he is also opposed to the poetic treatment of those crimes so that they appear to be no more than minor faults, simple escapades, and trivial pranks.

The Aristotelian notion of "hamartia" conceptualizes the poetic minimization of the crime. It suggests simple negligence, a fault by omission rather than the fullness of evil of the ancient myths. The "tragic flaw" of the translation evokes a very minor fault, a single chink in a homogeneous mass of irreproachable virtue. The baleful dimension of the sacred is still present, though reduced to a minimum, just as it is logically indispensable to the justification of the invariably disastrous consequences. This is a long way from the myths in which good and evil are balanced. Most of the so-called primitive myths have come down to us in that first stage of balance, and past ethnology has rightly classified them primitive; it senses their affinity to the scapegoat mechanism on which they are based and which achieves results through a successful projection of all evil.

If the crime is not to be completely obliterated in an attempt to excuse the god—something that Plato openly called for—then an enduring force is needed which would treat the traditional text with extreme respect. Only the prolonged effect of the scapegoat can achieve this, with the logic that belongs to the ritual and sacrificial phase of primitive religion. The god incarnates the scourge, as I said earlier; he is this side of good and evil, not beyond them. The difference he incarnates is not yet defined in terms of moral distinctions; the victim's transcendence has not yet been fragmented into a good and divine power on one side and a bad demoniacal power on the other.

It is inevitable that this division will take place as a result of all the different pressures brought to bear on the original mythical collection. From the moment of division the balance in myths is broken, sometimes in favor of the evil, sometimes in favor of the good, sometimes in both directions at once. In this case the ambiguous primitive god is split into a perfectly good hero and a perfectly bad monster who ravages the community: Oedipus and the sphinx, Saint George and the dragon, the water snake of the Arawak myth and the liberator who kills him. The monster inherits all that is detestable in the episode, the *crisis*, the *crime*, the *criteria* for choosing a victim, the first three stereotypes of persecution. The hero incarnates the fourth stereotype only: murder, the sacrificial decision, which is all the more clearly liberating because fully justified by the evil of violence of the monster.

This type of division evidently occurs at a late stage since it is found in fairy tales and legends, mythical forms which have degenerated to such a degree that they are no longer the object of truly religious belief. Let us turn back.

It is not a question of an immediate suppression of the god's crime. If censored carelessly, it would eliminate one problem only to create another. Religious adapters of myths are more perceptive than ethnologists and understand clearly that the violence inflicted on their god is justified by a fault he committed previously. If this justification is eliminated purely and simply, then the most sacred character in the myth is exonerated, but the community that punished him, deprived of its justification, then becomes criminal. This community of murderers is almost as sacred as the original victim, for it engenders the community of the faithful. The attempt to moralize myths ends in a dilemma. We can easily deduce this dilemma from primordial mythic themes, but we can also read the results clearly in more developed texts. The frequently subtle nuances of divine culpability which have been incomprehensible until now suddenly appear to be rather ingenious solutions invented by the faithful throughout the ages, and myths simultaneously designed to free all the actors in the sacred drama of blame.

The simplest solution is to retain the victim's crimes but claim they were not intended. The victim did indeed do what he is accused of, but *he did not do it intentionally*. Oedipus killed his father and went to bed with his mother, but he thought he was doing something else. No one in fact is to blame, and all the moral exigencies are satisfied with respect to *almost* all of the traditional text. At a *critical* stage of their evolution, or rather of their interpretation, myths frequently reveal innocent culprits, like Oedipus, juxtaposed with communities that are innocently guilty.

The situation is somewhat similar in the case of the Scandinavian god Hoehr, analyzed earlier. Although he is physically responsible for the murder of the noble Baldr, he is, if anything, even more innocent than Oedipus. There are many good reasons why he sees his murderous action as only a harmless imitation or an amusing parody with no untoward consequences for his brother, the target at which he is aiming. Hoehr has absolutely no way of anticipating what will happen.

Thus the primitive gods, who are fully guilty, are succeeded by gods of limited or even nonexistent culpability. The absolution, however, is never truly universal. The elimination of the fault in one place generally means its reappearance somewhere else, usually on the periphery and in an exacerbated form. Thus we see a god or a kind of demon appear who is even more guilty, a Loki or a Kronos who plays the role of a secondary scapegoat. Although this is a textual creation it nevertheless constitutes a trace of the real victim.

There are other ways of reducing the guilt of the gods without attributing it to a violent community and above all without revealing the mechanism of the scapegoat which can never be revealed. Victims are introduced who are guilty of the actions without being intrinsically bad. Because they have not been informed of certain circumstances, they bring about unintentionally the state of affairs required to justify the use of collective violence against them. This is really only a variation of the crime without criminal intention.

The supreme form of this double justification can be found in the interaction of the victim with the community of killers in terms of pure and simple misunderstanding and communication wrongly interpreted.

It also happens that the crimes of the gods are seen as real, but they are given, in the myths, a subsidiary reason such as a natural but irresistible force which compels the god to evil action without his wanting any part of it. He may be made to take an intoxicating drink, or be stung by a poisonous insect. This is a summary of what Eliade wrote in his *History of Religious Ideas* about a Hittite god stung by a bee:

Because the beginning of the story has been lost we do not know why Telipinu decides to "disappear". . . But the results of his disappearance are immediately felt. Hearth fires are extinguished, gods and men feel "overwhelmed"; the sheep forsakes her lamb and the cow her calf; "the barley and corn no longer ripen," animals and men couple no longer; pastures grow barren and springs dry up. . . . Finally the mother-goddess sends the bee; it finds the god sleeping in a wood and wakes him with a sting. In his fury Telipinu provokes such calamities on the country that the gods are afraid and resort to magic to calm him. Telipinu is purged of anger and of "evil" by magic formulae and ceremonies. Finally pacified he returns to the gods—and life resumes its normal rhythm.[3]

3. Eliade, *History of Religious Ideas* 1:156–57.

Two of the stereotypes of persecution are very much in evidence: the crisis and the guilt of the god who precipitates the crisis. Divine responsibility is both increased and diminished by the bee sting. Instead of collective violence directly reversing evil into good, this is its ritual equivalent. The magic action nevertheless signifies that violence; it always tries to reproduce the original effect of the scapegoat, and it is always collective in nature. *All the other gods* are afraid and intervene *against* Telipinu to put an end to his destructive actions. But the violence of this intervention is hidden; the gods are no more enemies of Telipinu than Telipinu is really the enemy of the people. There is disorder in the community and the cause of it is divine, but there is no truly bad intention on the part of anyone, neither in Telipinu's relationship with the people nor in the other gods' relationship with Telipinu.

We should include among the variations on the theme of the minimized fault the actions of the North American trickster and all the "deceiving" gods found everywhere. These gods are as much scapegoats as the others. All their good deeds stem from a social pact formed at the expense of the victim. They are always preceded by actions clearly perceived as wrong and justly punished. Again, this is the paradox of the god who is helpful because he is harmful, a force of order because he creates disorder. As long as the mythological representation of persecution remains intact there are bound to be questions about the intentions of the gods. Why should a god put those he wants to help and protect into such difficulties; moreover, why does he put himself in that position? Apart from the gods who do evil unwittingly and the gods who are forced irresistibly to do evil, there is inevitably a third solution, the god who enjoys doing evil and is amused by it. Although he always helps in the end, he is delighted when things go badly and continues to enjoy it. He is known for his games. He pushes his playfulness so far that he loses control of the consequences. He is the sorcerer's apprentice who sets fire to the world by lighting a very small flame and who drowns the earth with his urine. Thus he justifies every *effort to correct* and, by virtue of these efforts, he is transformed into a benefactor.

The trickster is sometimes seen as wicked, but sometimes he is so stupid and clumsy in carrying out his mission that accidents happen, whether he wants them to or not. These both compromise the desired result and yet ensure its outcome by creating the unanimous opposition to the blunderer necessary for the good of the community.

We must recognize in the trickster one of the two great theologies to evolve as a result of the sacralization of the scapegoat: the theology of *divine caprice*. The other theology is *divine anger*, which provides still another solution to the problem that faces religious belief when the victim whom it thinks is truly guilty becomes the means of reconciliation. If those who benefited from the mechanism were able to challenge the scapegoat's responsibility, there would be no reconciliation and no divinity.

In this perspective the god is fundamentally good but is temporarily transformed into a wicked god. He crushes the faithful in order to bring them back to the straight path; he corrects their weaknesses which prevent him from immediately showing his beneficence. He who loves greatly punishes greatly. This solution, though less happy than the preceding one, is more profound in that it introduces the rare idea among men that their scapegoat is not the only incarnation of violence. The community shares the responsibility for evil with the god; it begins to be guilty of its own disorders. The theology of anger comes very close to the truth, but it is still closely tied to the representation of persecution. The solution lies in an analysis of the scapegoat mechanism which will untie the knot that keeps the mythological representation closed within itself.

To conclude this discussion of the guilt of the god and to show that we need not divide the solutions into rigid categories, I would like to discuss a myth that is found in very different parts of the world and that ingeniously manages to combine all the advantages from which the above solutions had to choose.

Cadmus, the ancestor of all Theban mythology, after killing the dragon, sows the dragon's teeth in the earth, from which armed warriors immediately spring up. This new menace, born of the previous one, clearly illustrates the relationship between the crisis of persecution within human communities on the one hand, and all the dragons and fabled beasts on the other. Cadmus resorts to a very simple ruse to rid himself of the warriors. Surreptitiously he picks up a pebble and throws it into the middle of the troop. It hits none of the warriors, but the noise of the fall makes each one think the other has provoked him; in a moment they are at each other's throats and kill each other to the last man. Cadmus is seen here as a kind of *trickster*. In one sense he causes the social crisis, the great disorder that ravages a group of men to the point of complete destruction. In itself his action is not outrageous, the pebble did not hurt anyone; the trick only becomes truly wicked because of the stupid brutality of the warriors and their blind tendency to react antagonistically. An evil reciprocity feeds and exasperates the conflict all the more quickly in that the participants are unaware of it.

This myth reveals in a spectacular way how reciprocity, as discussed earlier, eliminates differences as it accelerates and takes over societies in crisis. But the wondrous thing is that it implicitly reveals both the justification for the scapegoat and the explanation of his effectiveness. Once set in motion, the mechanism of evil reciprocity can only become worse for the very reason that all the harm which does not exist at that precise moment is about to become real. At least half of the combatants always believe that justice has been done since they have been avenged, while the other half try to reestablish that same justice by striking those who are provisionally satisfied with a blow that will finally achieve their vengeance. The circumstances are so confused that they will only be brought to an end by both sides recognizing the evil reciprocity. It is asking too much to expect them to understand that the relationships within the group not only feed their misfortune but generate it. A community may pass from good to evil reciprocity for petty reasons, but the reasons may be so powerful and convincing that it amounts to the same thing. Everyone is more or less equally responsible but no one will admit it. Even if men were truly aware of their evil reciprocity they would still want to identify the author, a real and punishable source; they might allow that his role was less significant, but they would still want an original cause *which could be rectified*, as Evans-Pritchard writes, *a pertinent cause on the plane of social relationships*.

It is easy to understand why and how the mechanism of the scapegoat can sometimes interrupt this process. The blind instinct for reprisals, the stupid recriprocity which pits each one against the nearest or most visible adversary, is not based on anything specific; thus everything can converge at almost any time, on almost anyone, but preferably at the moment of greatest hysteria. Something must trigger the incident, either accidentally or by some sign that points to a victim. A possible target need only be slightly more attractive than others for the whole group suddenly to come together in total agreement without the slightest feeling of doubt or contradiction. . . . Since in such cases there is never any reason for violence except everyone's belief in that other reason, it is enough for everyone to focus on that other reality, the scapegoat, who then becomes everyone's "other." *The intervention* no longer *seems to be*, but *is* effective, by simply extinguishing all possible desire for reprisals among the survivors. Only the scapegoat could want to be avenged, and he is obviously in no position to get satisfaction.

In other words, in order to end the reciprocal destruction in the myth of Cadmus the warriors need only recognize Cadmus's role as agent provocateur and become reconciled at his expense. It does not matter whether the agent is real or not as long as everyone is convinced of his reality and identity. How can anyone be sure that the victim is really guilty since all that happened was a small stone falling, the noise of a simple stone hitting other stones? A similar incident could happen at any time without the person responsible intending any harm, in fact without anyone being responsible at all. What is important is the more or less intense and universal faith ultimately inspired by the scapegoat in his will and in his capability to sow disorder and therefore to reestablish order. If the warriors had not discovered what had actually happened, or, if you prefer, if the scapegoat had not been so convincing, they would not have stopped fighting and the crisis would have ended in total annihilation.

The survivors represent the community that arises out of the myth of Cadmus; the dead represent only disorder as apart from Cadmus himself. In the myth Cadmus represents both the power that created disorder—he sowed the dragon's teeth—and the power that created order—he saved humanity by destroying first the dragon and then the multitude of warriors, *draco redivivus*, the new monster of a thousand heads issued from the remains of the former monster. Cadmus therefore is one of those gods who always provoke disorder but "only" in order to put an end to it. Cadmus therefore is not a scapegoat explicitly in and for this myth; he is implicitly a scapegoat, made sacred by the myth itself, the god of the Thebans. This myth is merely ingenious; it does not and cannot reveal finally the secret of its own creation but must rely on the mechanism of the scapegoat.

Myths of the category "small causes, big results," or if you like "minor scapegoats, major crisis," can be found all over the world and often in such unique forms that it will not do to explain them away by invoking "experiences." The Indian version of the myth of Cadmus might be traced to Indo-European influence, but it is impossible in the South American version which is mentioned in Lévi-Strauss's *Mythologiques*. Invisible in a tree, an anthropomorphous parrot sows discord beneath him by dropping things from his beak. It is difficult to argue that all these myths have only their one purely logical and distinctive significance, and that they have absolutely nothing to do with human violence.

COLLECTIVE MURDER has not been eliminated from all the texts of ancient mythology. There are important exceptions among religious commentators, great writers (especially those who wrote tragedies), and historians as well. In reading the commentary we must remember my analysis above. It would seem to me to shed new light both on the rumors about Romulus and all similar rumors concerning certain founders of cities and religions. Freud is the only major modern author who took these rumors seriously. In his *Moses and Monotheism* he uses, unfortunately too polemically, the "rumors" found on the periphery of Jewish tradition, according to which Moses may have also been the victim of collective murder. But he fails to draw the obvious conclusion from the remarkable similarity of the rumors about Moses and those about so many other religious lawgivers and founders (an unusual omission for the author of *Totem and Taboo*, one that may be explained by his overly partial critique of the Jewish religion). According to certain sources Zarathustra was murdered by members, disguised as wolves, of one of these ritual associations whose sacrificial violence he opposed, a violence that had always had the collective and unanimous character of the original murder which it reenacted. In the margins of official biographies there often lingers a more or less "esoteric" tradition of collective murder.

Modern historians do not take these stories seriously. They can hardly be criticized, not having the means to incorporate them into their analyses. They choose to interpret them either within the framework of a single author, in which case they must agree with what their sources ironically or cautiously call unidentifiable gossip and "old wives' tales," or else within the framework of mythology or universal history. In this case they are obliged to recognize that the theme, although far from being universal, recurs too frequently to be ignored. Nor can collective violence be called mythological since it categorically contradicts the myths. Does this mean that our critics are forced finally to face the problem and acknowledge its existence? Not at all (there are endless ways to avoid the truth). In their denial of the true meaning they resort to their ultimate weapon, their deathblow: the disturbing theme is treated simply as rhetoric. Any insistence on the absence of collective violence or continuing concern is purely decorative. We are naïve if we allow ourselves to be convinced. None of the lifeboats is so unsinkable. After a long disappearance the theme has resurfaced in our day, and the storms of our apocalypse wash over it in vain. Even though it carries more passengers than the raft of the *Medusa* it will not sink; how can it be sunk?

No one in fact attaches any importance to collective murder. Let us return to Livy, who is of more interest than the university that made him hostage. This historian tells us how, in a great storm, Romulus "was enveloped in such a thick cloud that he disappeared from the gaze of the assembly. Since that time he has never again appeared on earth." After a moment of dumb dejection "the young Romans acclaim Romulus as a new god." But "I believe there were, from that time, skeptics who maintained quietly that the king had been torn to pieces by the Fathers with their bare hands: in fact, this is also said, in the great mystery; the other version became popular because of the hero's prestige and dangers of the time."[4]

Plutarch notes many versions of Romulus's death, three of them forms of collective murder. According to one, Romulus was suffocated in his bed by his enemies; according to another he was torn to pieces by the senators in the Temple of Vulcan. In still another version the murder took place in the Goat Marsh, during a great storm mentioned by Livy, a storm that drove the crowds of people away while the *senators closed their ranks*. As in Livy's version it is the senators, that is the murderers, who establish the cult of the new god *because they closed their ranks against him*:

Most of the populace accepted this story, and were happy to hear the news, adoring Romulus in their hearts in good faith, as they went about their business; but there were some who set about harshly and bitterly to find out the truth, and they disturbed the patricians greatly, letting it be known that they were abusing the simple people with their empty and foolish arguments and that it had been they who had killed the king with their own hands.[5]

The legend, as such, is an antilegend. It is the result of an explicit effort to demystify, reminiscent of Freud. The official version had to become legend in order to consolidate the authority of the rulers. Romulus's death resembles that of Pentheus in *the Bacchae*: "And yet some thought that the senators had all rushed on him . . . and that after tearing

4. Livy, *The History of Rome* (Cambridge, Mass.: Harvard University Press, 1935), 1:16.

5. Plutarch, "Life of Romulus," *Plutarch's Lives*, trans. John Dryden, rev. Arthur Hugh Clough (New York: Modern Library, 1864), p. 44.

him to pieces, each had carried away a piece in the folds of his robe." This ending recalls the Dionysiac *diasparagmos* in which the victim is torn to death by the mob. There are therefore unquestionably mythological and religious echoes, but the *diasparagmos* happens spontaneously among crowds gripped with a murderous frenzy. The account of the great riots among the French people during the wars of religion teem with examples similar to Plutarch's text. The rioters even fight over the last remains of their victim, which they consider precious relics and which could later be sold for the most exorbitant prices. There are endless examples which suggest a close relationship between collective violence and a process in which a victim becomes sacred without necessarily already being powerful and renowned. The metamorphosis of remains into relics has also been documented in the case of racial lynchings in modern times.

The point of the "rumors" about Romulus is that the murderers themselves transform their victim into a sacred object. The account has a particularly modern ring to it, for they see in this affair a kind of political plot, a story put together from many elements by people who never lost their heads and knew exactly what they were doing. The text reflects the perspective of the populace. In their struggle against the aristocracy, the people reduce Romulus's becoming a god to a kind of plot against the people, an instrument of propaganda for the senators. The idea that, by making someone a god, the sordid reality of an event can be transfigured is very important. Nevertheless, no matter how seductive the argument of a deliberate cover-up may be to the modern mind, whose tendencies it foreshadows, it cannot totally satisfy observers who are aware of the essential role the phenomenon of mobs and their extreme collective mimesis does play in the genesis of the sacred. By making the mythological process a conscious fabrication at every stage, the *rumors* mentioned by Livy and Plutarch will, if taken literally, lead us to make the same mistakes as modern rationalists did about religion. Their true relevance lies in the implied relationship between the birth of myth and the unleashed mob. No nineteenth-century scholar ever went that far; he would only retain what was untrue in the rumors: religion was reduced to a plot of the powerful against the weak.

Every trace of collective violence must be examined, compared, and criticized. In our analysis of the *rumors* we have revealed a dimension that goes beyond the rough alternatives of traditional positivism, "true" and "false," historical and mythological. The *rumors* cannot fit the framework of these alternatives, so no one is capable of interpreting them. For historians, they are even more suspect than all their own accounts of the origins of Rome. Livy himself is aware of this. Nor can the mythologists be interested in something that is presented as anti-mythological rather than mythological. Rumors fall between the cracks of organized knowledge, as always happens to the traces of collective violence. As culture evolves, these traces are always expelled and eliminated. Philology and modern criticism thus finish the work of the later mythologies. Such is the process of so-called knowledge.

Collective violence continues to be concealed among us today by the same insidious and irresistible process as in the past. For proof of this we should turn once more to the body of myths concerning Romulus and Remus. It will reveal that the process is in full operation among us today and will help us understand that we ourselves are unconscious intermediaries in concealing the traces as we interpret Livy's text.

Most of my readers are convinced, I suppose, that the heretical versions of the death of Romulus are *the only* representation of collective murder in the whole of his myth. Everyone knows that there is another violent death in the myth, which is always presented as a murder but as an *individual* murder, namely, the death of Remus. Romulus alone is the murderer. Ask any of your cultured friends and they will all tell you that this is so. Romulus kills his brother in a moment of anger because that brother mockingly leaped over the symbolic boundaries of the city of Rome which Romulus had just finished tracing.

This version of the murder is found in Livy, but it is neither the first nor the only version. The first version contains collective murder. Compared with the second, it is a classic example of a myth that has not yet eliminated the representation of collective murder. The first version is based on a quarrel over auguries. The flight of birds does not succeed in deciding between Romulus and Remus, the enemy twins. This story is well known; it has not been concealed, because it fits so easily with the second version of the myth which always provides the ending. Unaware, we all choose it *because it is the version that eliminates collective murder.* After describing how the two brothers conceive of the idea of building a new city on the very spot where "they were abandoned and reared," Livy adds:

To these subjects is soon added the hereditary passion, the thirst to reign, and this passion makes what was originally a peaceful enterprise into a criminal conflict. Since it is impossible to choose between the twins, even from the vantage of age, it was up to the gods who protected the place to indicate by auguries the one who would give his name to the new city, who would found it and rule it.

First, Remus received an augury: six vultures. He had just announced it when double the number appeared to Romulus. Each was proclaimed king by his supporters. One claimed royalty by being first, the other because of the number of birds. An argument ensues, which comes to blows; anger degenerates into a murderous struggle. It is, then, *in the scuffle* that Remus falls dead.[6]

Everything is always equal between twins; there is conflict because there is competition and rivalry. The conflict is caused not by difference but by its absence. This is why structuralism, which interprets in terms of binary opposites and differences, is no more capable of understanding enemy twins than psychoanalysis "structured like a language." Like Greek tragedians who write of that other set of twins, Eteocles and Polynices, Livy understands that the conflict of the twins cannot be resolved because there is no difference between the antagonists. It indicates the absence of separation as much as absolute separation: *since it was impossible to choose between the twins, even where age was concerned*, it is left up to the gods, but the gods themselves only appear to make a decision, *a decision* which in itself was *indecisive* and only feeds the quarrel and makes it fiercer. Each of the brothers desires what the other desires, even when it is something that does not yet exist, the city of Rome. The rivalry is purely mimetic and is identical with the sacrificial crisis, which makes all the participants the same in the same conflicting desire, and which transforms them all, not just the two brothers, into twins by their own violence.

The translation I have quoted is not exactly inaccurate but it is vague and unsatisfactory. *It makes what is essential invisible.* The collective character of the murder of Remus, which is very precise in Livy's Latin text, is almost unnoticeable in the translation. The Latin "*in turba*," that is "in the crowd," becomes "in the scuffle." Michel Serres pointed out to me both the original Latin — *ibi in turba ictus Remus cecidit* — and the remarkable process by which the translation I have quoted is diminished and minimized. No doubt it will be pointed out that the word *scuffle* in the present context suggests many participants,

6. Ibid., pp. 6–7.

which is true. But the word *turba* has an almost technical meaning; a crowd that is *confused, perturbed,* and *disturbing*; it is the one word that recurs most often in the numerous accounts of collective murders contained in the first book of Livy. Its importance is such that its literal equivalent is essential in any translation of Livy's text. Its omission contributes just as effectively, if less spectacularly, to the elimination of collective murder as texts such as the myth of Baldr or the myth of the Curetes. At each different cultural period we can find the same phenomenon, the concealment of the original murder. The process continues today through the most diverse ideologies, such as classical humanism or the struggle against "Western ethnocentrism."

No doubt people will think I am fantasizing. Proof that this is not so can be found in the concept I have just discussed, that almost everyone assumes that there is no representation of collective murder in a myth like that of Romulus and Remus. It is in fact central to the myth and disappears gradually by a process of suffocation and strangulation, the true intellectual equivalent of what the patricians did to Romulus himself in one of the murders recorded in Plutarch. Michel Serres shows that there are several other murders which hover ever in the background, being pushed further and further away until the moment that has almost come to pass, when they disappear completely. At their first mention "true scholars" raise their eyebrows; the second puts you beyond the pale of "serious" researchers, who now claim that the religious phenomenon may not exist. You are considered a sort of intellectual adventurer, greedy for sensation and publicity. At the very best you are shamelessly exploiting collective murder, that sea serpent of mythological studies.

I would like to reiterate that Livy's relevance does not lie in his contribution of one more myth that portrays collective murder in his subversive versions of the death of Romulus. Even if it could be shown that all myths originally contained this representation, the demonstration would only be of secondary interest. The process that gradually eliminates the collective murder is much more interesting because it is too constant to be accidental.

Livy reveals methodically what can be called the elementary mythological drama: the (non)significance of twins, their mimetic rivalry, the resulting sacrificial crisis that ends in collective murder. All of this can, of course, be found in the great ancient writers and their classical imitators. By recognizing this common bond between Livy and Corneille, or between Euripides and Racine, we acknowledge evidence of centuries-long "censorship." This is to be admired and imitated in Livy, and even more so in the fact that he represented both the collective and the individual version of Remus's murder in the proper order of their diachronic evolution. In contrast to contemporary schools of criticism, which still adhere to a single synchronic order, the Roman historian perceives the existence of a *time* of elaboration which always moves in the same direction, with the same objective, the elimination of collective murder. The version without collective murder must be considered posterior to the version in which it still appears, as I have tried to show in the myths of Baldr and the Curetes. Mythological transformation moves in only one direction, toward the elimination of any traces of violence.

It is worth noting that a truly apocalyptic tradition has always existed in Rome. The violent destruction of the city was prophesied from the time of its violent origin. In his *History of Religious Ideas* Mircea Eliade speaks of the repercussions of the myth of Romulus and Remus in the Roman conscience:

The people will keep forever the terrifying memory of that first bloody sacrifice offered to the divinity of Rome. More than seven hundred years after the founding of Rome Horace writes of it in terms of an original sin which must inevitably bring about the loss of the city by driving its sons to kill each other. At every critical moment in its history, Rome agonizes over the weight of the curse it bears. It was neither at peace with men at its birth, nor with the gods. This religious worry will weigh heavily on its destiny.[7]

This tradition is interesting because it makes the people as a whole responsible for the original murder. It is rooted firmly in a collective version of the murder and, even though there is a touch of magic in the concept of Rome as the only city under this type of curse, nevertheless it expresses in its own way a truth independent of its style of expression. The foundation and structure of every community is based on violence that is and should have remained destructive at its very essence, but by some miracle the community has been able to *ward off* this violence which, for the time being, has become constructive and has achieved a means of reconciliation through some divinely bestowed reprieve.

7. Eliade, *History of Religious Ideas*, 2:109.

CHAPTER EIGHT
The Science of Myths

WE KNOW NOW to recognize in religious forms, ideas, and institutions in general the warped reflection of violent events that have been exceptionally "successful" in their collective repercussions. We can identify the commemoration in mythology of these same violent acts that are so successful that they force their perpetrators to reenact them. This memory inevitably develops as it is transmitted from generation to generation, but instead of rediscovering the secret of its original distortion it loses it over and over again, each time burying it a little deeper. As religion and cultures are formed and perpetuated, the violence is hidden. The discovery of their secret would provide what must be called a *scientific* solution to man's greatest enigma, the nature and origins of religion.

It is important not to confuse the reciprocal and ritualized extermination of "methodologies" with the totality of actual intelligence. This drama is no more distracting than storms at sea; they roll over the surface but leave the depths untouched. The more we become disturbed, the more real our agitation appears while the invisible escapes us. The pseudo-demystifiers can destroy each other without really weakening the critical principle which is the source for them all but which becomes less accurate. Recent doctrines have all evolved from one single process of decoding, the oldest to be invented in the Western world and the only truly lasting process. Precisely because it is uncontested, it goes unnoticed, like God himself. It has such a hold over us that it is confused with immediate perception. If attention was drawn to the process in action the observers would be astonished.

The reader has already recognized our old friend, the decoding of representations of persecution. It seems banal in the context of our history, but remove it from that context and it is an unknown quantity. Our ignorance is not like that of M. Jourdain, who speaks in prose without knowing it. The local banality of the procedure in question should not blind us to what is exceptional and even unique in an anthropological framework. No one outside of our culture has ever discovered this process; it can be found nowhere, and even for us there is something mysterious in the way we use it without ever examining it.

We speak of the process negatively today and use it to accuse each other of persecuting tendencies. It is contaminated by factions and ideologies. In order to reveal it in its pure form I have chosen illustrations from ancient texts that are free from interpretations subject to modern controversies. The demystification of a Guillaume de Machaut is universally acceptable. That was my starting point, and I shall always return to it to cut short the endless fuss over our textualized mimetic twins.

There is always an outcry, especially in such a troubled time as ours, against powerful evidence, but such quibbling is not in the least important intellectually. To go even further, it is possible that the revolt against the type of evidence I have described may grow in strength and we may once more be faced with the legions of Nuremberg or their equivalent. The historical consequences would be catastrophic, but the intellectual consequences would be nil. Cultural relativism and the critics of "ethnocentrism" have overlooked this. Whether we like it or not we must recognize it, and most of us do when forced to, but we do not like the obligation. We have a vague fear that it will take us further than we want.

Can we call this *truth* scientific? During the period when the term *science* was unhesitatingly applied to all that we were most sure of, many would have answered yes. Even today, many will say that only the scientific mind could have brought an end to witch-hunts. The cause of those witch-hunts was the belief in magic that was accompanied by persecution; the end of the witch-hunts had to be preceded by the end of belief in magic. It is significant that the first scientific revolution in the West coincides more or less with the definitive renunciation of witch-hunts. In the language of the ethnologists we would say a determined orientation toward natural causes gradually displaced man's immemorial preference for *significant causes on the level of social relations* which are also *the causes that are susceptible to corrective intervention,* in other words *victims.*

There is a close connection between science and the end of witch-hunts. Is it enough to justify our qualifying the interpretation that subverts the representation of persecution by revealing it as scientific? We have become sensitive in recent years about matters of science. Philosophers of science who are perhaps under the influence of the times are less and less appreciative of stable certainties. They would surely disapprove of an undertaking so free of risks and difficulties as the demystification of a Guillaume de Machaut. Admittedly, it is incongruous to invoke science in this case. So let's not use such an inflated term for such an ordinary affair. I am agreeable on this point, especially since in the light of it the necessarily scientific status of my undertaking becomes obvious. It is a question of interpreting texts by a process that no one has ever considered using for that purpose, an ancient process of decoding that has been very successful in its own domain of application and has been proven to be valid on a thousand occasions.

The real argument over my hypothesis has not even begun. I have limited myself to widening the angle of vision for a method of interpretation the validity of which is unchallenged. The real question is whether that enlargement is valid. Either I am right and I have really discovered something or I am wrong and I have wasted my time. The hypothesis that I have not invented but merely transposed only requires minor adaptations if it is to be applied to myths just as it was applied to Guillaume de Machaut. I could be right and I could be wrong, but I do not have to be fundamentally right in order for the only adjective that fits my hypothesis to be *scientific*.

The only reason for not applying the adjective *scientific* to the generally accepted reading of Guillaume de Machaut is not uncertainty but rather excessive certainty, the absence of risk, the lack of an alternative. As soon as our thesis of demystification is transposed to the domain of myth, its characters change. Mundane evidence gives way to adventure; the unknown reappears. There are numerous rival theories, and at least for the moment they seem "more serious" than mine. The day will come, however, when not to read the myth of Oedipus in the same way as Guillaume de Machaut does will seem as strange as it does to compare the two texts today. On that day the amazing disjunction we have noticed between the interpretation of a myth in its mythological context and of that same myth when it is transplanted to a historical context will disappear.

Then the demythification of mythology will no longer be a question of science just as it is no longer a question for Guillaume de Machaut today.

Earlier we expressed a certain repugnance for describing as scientific a hypothesis that was so free of risk and uncertainty. But a hypothesis that consists only of risks and uncertainties is equally unscientific. To earn the glorious title of scientific it must combine the maximum of actual uncertainty with the maximum of potential certainty. That is precisely the combination of my hypothesis. Researchers have decided too rapidly, on the basis of past failures, that this combination is only possible in domains that are quantifiable and subject to experimental verification. The fact that it is here, now, already realized, is proof to the contrary. My hypothesis has existed for centuries and, thanks to it, the transition from uncertainty to certainty in matters of demythification has already occurred once; it could therefore occur a second time.

We are uneasy in the recognition that this is so because we are unwilling to accept certainties; we tend to banish them to the obscure corners of our mind; just as, a hundred years ago, we used to banish uncertainties. We willingly forget that our demythification of sorcery and other superstitions related to persecution constitutes a certainty that cannot be shaken. If this certainty were tomorrow to encompass mythology, we would certainly not know all, but we would have some hard and probably definitive answers to some of the questions that research inevitably poses—or would pose had all hope of finding hard and definitive answers not been lost.

My demystification of Guillaume de Machaut can certainly not be considered "falsifiable" in the sense that Popper used the term. Does that mean I must renounce it? If even in this case certitude is not acceptable, if we hold absolutely to the great democracy of a never-true–never-false interpretation that is so popular these days for anything nonquantifiable, then that is inevitably the result. We must condemn in retrospect all those who brought an end to the witch trials. They were even more dogmatic than the witch-hunters and, like them, they believed they possessed the truth. Should we disillusion them? What right have these people to declare their interpretation to be the only right one when thousands of other interpreters, eminent witch-hunters, distinguished scholars, some of whom were even very progressive like Jean Bodin, had a completely different idea of the problem? What insufferable arrogance, what frightful intolerance, what shocking puritanism. Should we not let all the different interpretations blossom, witches and nonwitches, natural and magical causes, those that are susceptible to corrective intervention and those that never receive the correction they deserve.

By a slight change of context, without any real change of the essential, it is easy to see how ridiculous certain contemporary attitudes are, or at least as regards their application to these matters. Critical thought no doubt is in a state of extreme decadence, temporary it is to be hoped, but the sickness is no less severe since it considers itself the supreme refinement of the critical mind. If our ancestors had thought in the same mode as do today's masters, they would never have put an end to the witch trials. We should not be surprised, then, to see the recent most undeniable horrors doubted by people who are faced with an intelligentsia reduced to impotency by sterile exaggerations to which it falls prey and by the arguments that result from them. The self-destructive character of these theses is no longer perceptible or, if it is perceived, it seems only like a "positive" development.

CHAPTER NINE

The Key Words of the
Gospel Passion

THE PRECEDING ANALYSES force us to conclude that human culture is
predisposed to the permanent concealment of its origins in collective
violence. Such a definition of culture enables us to understand the successive stages of an entire culture as well as the transition from one stage
to the next by means of a crisis similar to those we have traced in myths
and to those we have traced in history during periods of frequent persecutions. During periods of crisis and widespread violence there is always the threat of subversive knowledge spreading, but that very
knowledge becomes one of the victims or quasi-victims of the convulsions of social disorder.

This model continues to be valid for our society; in fact it is even
more relevant, although it is clearly not enough to account for what we
call history, our history. Even if the process for decoding the persecutors' accounts of persecution, which is central to our history, is not expanded to include all of mythology, it nevertheless represents a major
defeat for cultural occultation that might rapidly become total. Either
culture is not as I have described it or the force of occultation sustaining
it must struggle against a counterforce in our universe that tends toward
the revelation of the immemorial lie.

We all know of the existence of this force of revelation, but instead
of recognizing it in my terms, most of us see it as the force of occultation.
This is the most serious misperception of our culture, and it will inevitably be dissipated by our recognition of the full effect in mythology of the
illusions of persecution, an attenuated version of which we are now able
to decipher at the heart of our history.

The Christian Bible, the combination of the Old and New Testaments, has provided that force of revelation. The Bible enables us to decipher what we have actually learned to identify in persecutors' representations of persecution. It teaches us to decode the whole of religion. The victory this time will be too decisive for the sustaining force to remain hidden. The Gospels will be seen as that universal force of revelation. For centuries the most respected scholars have declared that the Gospels are merely one myth among many, and have succeeded in convincing most people.

The Gospels do indeed center around the Passion of Christ, the same drama that is found in all world mythologies. I have tried to show that this is true of *all* myths. This drama is needed to give birth to new myths, to present the perspective of the persecutors. But this same drama is also needed to present the perspective of a victim dedicated to the rejection of the illusions of the persecutors. Thus the same drama is needed to give birth to the only text that can bring an end to all of mythology.

In order to accomplish the prodigious feat, that of forever destroying the credibility of mythological representation (and this feat is being accomplished right beneath our eyes), we must oppose the very real force of myth, real because it has always had mankind in its grip, with the even greater force of a true representation. The event portrayed must indeed be the same or the Gospels would not be able to discredit point by point all the characteristic illusions of mythologies that are also the illusions of the protagonists of the Passion.[1]

We are aware that the Gospels reject persecution. What we do not realize is that, by doing so, they release its mechanism and demolish the entire human religion and the resulting cultures: we fail to recognize the fruit of the persecutors' accounts of persecution in the symbolic forces surrounding us. But the very fact that these forms have a diminished hold, and their power of illusion is weakened, is due precisely to our increasing ability to identify the underlying scapegoat mechanisms. Once understood, the mechanisms can no longer operate; we believe less and less in the culpability of the victims they demand. Deprived of the food that sustains them, the institutions derived from these mechanisms collapse one after the other about us. Whether we know it or not, the Gospels are responsible for this collapse. Let us therefore try and prove it.

1. Girard, *Des choses cachées depuis la fondation du monde*, pp. 161–304.

In studying the Passion we are struck by the role played by quotations from the Old Testament, particularly from the Psalms. The early Christians took these references seriously, and the so-called allegorical or figural interpretation in the Middle Ages involved the expansion and appropriate amplification of this New Testament practice. Modern critics generally, and mistakenly, have no interest in this. They tend more to a rhetorical and strategic interpretation of the quotations. The Evangelists make many innovations with respect to theology. We could attribute to them the desire to make their innovations respectable by sheltering them as much as possible behind the prestige of the Bible. In order to gain acceptance for the extraordinary, endless exaltation of Jesus they place their writing under the protective shelter of texts that denoted authority.

The Gospels, admittedly, highlight portions of the Psalms almost to extreme, fragments seemingly of very little intrinsic interest and of such platitude that their significance does not seem to justify their presence. For example what should we conclude from John's (15:25) solemn reference in speaking of the condemnation of Jesus to the sentence: "They hated me for no reason" (Ps. 35:19)?[2] And the Evangelist insists gravely that the hostile forces are gathering for the Passion *to fulfill the words written in their Law*. The awkwardness of the stereotyped formula reinforces our suspicion. There is unquestionably a link between the Psalm and the way in which the Gospels report the death of Jesus, but the sentence is so banal, its application so obvious, that there is no need to emphasize it.

We have a similar impression when Luke has Jesus say: "These words of Scripture have to be fulfilled in me 'He let himself be taken for a criminal' " (Luke 22:37; Mark 15:28). This time the quotation is not from the Psalms but from chapter 53 of Isaiah. The profound thought that could inspire such references is not evident, and we fall back on the ordinary ulterior motives of our own universe.

These two short sentences are actually extremely interesting in themselves as well as in relation to the story of the Passion, but to understand this, we must understand that the control exercised by persecutors and their accounts of persecution over the whole of humanity are at stake in the Passion. These sentences, which are apparently too trite to

2. Biblical quotations are taken from *The Jerusalem Bible*, Reader's Edition (New York: Doubleday, 1968).

be taken seriously, express the denial of magic causality and stereotyped accusations. It is refusal of everything that is accepted blindly by persecuting crowds, such as the Thebans' unhesitating acceptance of Oedipus's responsibility for the plague, because he is incestuous; or the Egyptians' imprisonment of the unfortunate Joseph, on the strength of the gossip of a provincial Venus clinging to her prey. The Egyptians always behaved this way. We remain very Egyptian where mythology is concerned, especially Freud, who charges Egypt with the truth of Judaism. All the theories in vogue are pagan in their attachment to parricide, incest, etc., and in their blindness to the false character of stereotyped accusations. We are very far behind the Gospels and even Genesis.

The Passion crowd also accepts blindly the vague accusations made against Jesus. In their eyes Jesus becomes the cause that is susceptible to corrective intervention, the Crucifixion. All those who love magical thinking resort to it at the first sign of disorder in their world. Our two quotations highlight the continuity between the Passion crowd and the persecution crowds already stigmatized in the Psalms. Neither the Gospels nor the Psalms accept the cruel illusions of these cruel crowds. The two quotations stop short of any mythological interpretation. They truly eradicate the root, for the victim's guilt is the mainspring of the victim mechanism, and its apparent absence in the most developed of the myths, those that manipulate or eliminate the scene of this murder, has nothing in common with what is happening here. The uprooting in the Gospels bears the same relationship to the mythological conjuring tricks of a Baldr or the Curetes as the complete removal of a tumor to a village quack's "magnetic" tricks.

Persecutors always believe in the excellence of their cause, but in reality *they hate without a cause*. The absence of cause in the accusation (*ad causam*) is never seen by the persecutors. It is this illusion that must first be addressed if we are to release all the unfortunate from their invisible prison, from the dark underground in which they are stagnating but which they regard as the most magnificent of palaces.

The Old Testament provides an inexhaustible source of legitimate references to this extraordinary work of the Gospels, which is an account of persecution that has been abrogated, broken, and revoked. We should not wonder that the New Testament is dependent on the Old Testament and relies on it. Both are participating in the same enterprise. The initiative comes from the Old Testament, but is brought to fruition by the New Testament where it is accomplished decisively and definitively.

Particularly in the penitential Psalms we see the word shift from the persecutors to the victims, from those who are making history to those who are subjected to it. The victims not only raise their voices but are also vociferous even in the midst of their persecution. Their enemies surround them and prepare to strike them. Sometimes the latter retain the monstrous, animal appearance they had in mythology; these are the packs of dogs or herds of bulls, "strong beasts of Bashaan." Yet these texts are torn from mythology, as Raymond Schwager has clearly shown: they increasingly reject sacred ambivalence in order to restore the victim to his humanity and reveal the arbitrary nature of the violence that strikes him.[3]

The victim who speaks in the Psalms seems not in the least "moral," not evangelic enough for the good apostles of modern times. The sensibilities of our humanists are shocked. Usually, the unfortunate victim turns to hate those who hate him. The display of violence and resentment "so characteristic of the Old Testament" is deplored, and is seen as a particularly clear indication of the famous malice of the God of Israel. Ever since Nietzsche people have seen in the Psalms the invention of all the bad feeling infecting us, humiliation, and resentment. We are offered in contrast to the venomous Psalms the beautiful serenity of mythologies, particularly Greek and German. Strong in their righteousness, and convinced that their victim is truly guilty, persecutors have no reason to be troubled.

The victim of the Psalms is disturbing, it is true, and even annoying compared with an Oedipus who has the good taste to join in the wonderful classical harmony. See with what art and delicacy, at the given moment, he denounces himself. He brings to it the enthusiasm of the psychoanalytic patient on his couch or the old Bolshevist in the time of Stalin. Make no mistake, he provides a model for the supreme conformism of our time which is no different from the blustering of avantgardism. Our intellectuals are so eager for servitude that they formed their Stalinist cells before Stalinism was invented. How can we be surprised that they have waited fifty years or more before making discreet inquiries into the greatest persecutions in human history. Mythology is the very best school in the training of silence. We never hesitate between

---

3. *Brauchen wir einen Sündenbock?* (Munich: Kosel/KNO, 1978). See especially the second chapter on the Old Testament. See also Paul Beauchamp, *Psaumes nuit et jour* (Paris: Seuil, 1980).

the Bible and mythology. We are classicists first, romantics second, and primitives when necessary, modernists with a fury, neoprimitives when we are disgusted with modernism, gnostics always, but biblical never.

The causality of magic is one with mythology, so the importance of its denial cannot be exaggerated. The Gospels are certainly aware of this since the denial is repeated at every possible opportunity. They even put it in the mouth of Pilate, who says, after interrogating Jesus, "I find no case against this man." ["Je ne vois pas de *cause*."] Pilate has not yet been influenced by the crowd, and the judge in him, the incarnation of Roman law, of legal rationality, acknowledges the facts in a brief but significant moment.

But what is so extraordinary about the biblical rehabilitation of victims? Isn't it a common practice that dates right back to antiquity? Yes, but previously the victims were rehabilitated by one group in opposition to another. The faithful remain gathered around the rehabilitated victim and the flame of resistance is never extinguished. Truth is not allowed to submerge. That is what is false, with the result that the persecutors' accounts of persecution are never really compromised or threatened in mythology. Take the death of Socrates, for example. "True" philosophy never enters into it. It escapes the contagion of the scapegoat. There is always truth in the world; even though this is no longer so at the moment of Christ's death. Even his favorite disciples are speechless in the face of the crowd. They are literally absorbed by it. It is the Gospel of Peter that informs us that Peter, the leader of the apostles, denied his master in public. This betrayal is not anecdotal; it has nothing to do with the psychology of Peter. The fact that even the disciples cannot resist the effect of the scapegoat reveals the power exerted by the persecutors' account over man. To understand what is happening we must count the group of disciples among the forces that are united in condemning Christ, despite their usual disagreement. They are all forces capable of endowing the condemned person's death with significance. It is easy to enumerate them as they are always the same. They can all be found in the witch-hunts or in the great totalitarian regressions of the present day. First there are the religious leaders, then the politicians, and above all the crowd. They all participate in the action—at first separately, but gradually more and more in unison. Note that all these forces intervene in the order of their importance, beginning with the weakest and ending with the strongest. The conspiracy of religious leaders is of symbolic but little real importance. Herod plays an even smaller role. The only reason for Luke's inclusion of Herod in his account of the Passion is his fear of omitting any possible force that contributed to the sentencing of Jesus.

Pilate is the person with real power, but ahead of him is the crowd. Once mobilized, the crowd has absolute power, dragging institutions with it until they are forced to disintegrate. Clearly, this is an example of the unanimity of the generative collective murder of mythology. This crowd is the group in dissolution, the community is literally dispersed and cannot reform except at the expense of the victim, of the scapegoat. Everything is therefore at its most favorable for the persecutors' confident account of persecution. Yet this is not what is provided by the Gospels.

The Gospels attribute to Pilate the desire to resist the verdict of the crowd. Is this meant to make him more sympathetic and the Jewish authorities more antipathetic by contrast? This is what is claimed, and there are many who would explain everything in the New Testament in the most ignoble light. These are truly today's crowd, possibly the crowd of every day. Nevertheless they are wrong. Pilate in the end joins the mob of persecutors. There is no need to study the psychology of Pilate. Instead the total power of the crowd should be underscored to show that sovereign authority is forced to yield despite its impulse to resist. Pilate, however, has no real interest in the affair. Jesus is unimportant in his eyes. He is so insignificant a person that even if Pilate had few political instincts, he would not risk an uprising just to save him. Pilate's decision is too easy, actually, to illustrate clearly the subordination of the ruler to the crowd and the dominant role of the crowd at the moment of greatest excitement when the mechanism of the scapegoat is set in motion.

It seems to me that John introduces the character of the wife in order to make Pilate's decision less easy and more revealing. Warned by a dream, and more or less committed to the cause of Jesus, Pilate's wife urges her husband to resist the crowd. John wants to show Pilate torn between two influences, between two poles of mimetic attraction, on the one hand the wife who wants to save an innocent man and, on the other, the totally anonymous and impersonal crowd that is not even Roman. No one would be closer to Pilate than his wife, no one more closely linked to his existence. No one could exercise more influence on him than this wife who knows how to play on his religious fear. Yet the crowd wins out; nothing is more important than this victory, nothing more significant for the revelation of the mechanism that selects a victim. We shall see later that the Gospels present another victory similar to that of the crowd in yet another scene of collective murder, the beheading of John the Baptist.

We would be seriously mistaken if we thought that this crowd was composed only of representatives of the lower classes; it does not represent only the "popular masses"—the elite also form a part, and the Gospels cannot be accused of social condescension. To understand this crowd we should once more turn to quotations from the Old Testament, where we shall find the clearest commentary on the purpose of the Gospels.

In chapter 4 of the Acts of the Apostles, a book that is evangelical in character, Peter gathers his companions together in order to meditate on the Crucifixion. He quotes to them at length the Psalm that describes the pervasively hostile reception that the forces of the world reserve for the Messiah:

> Why this arrogance among the nations,
> these futile plots among the peoples?
> Kings on earth setting out to war,
> princes making an alliance,
> against the Lord and against his Anointed.

This is what has come true: in this very city Herod and Pontius Pilate *made an alliance* with the pagan *nations* and the peoples of Israel, against your holy servant Jesus whom you anointed, but only to bring about the very thing that you in your strength and your wisdom had predetermined should happen. (Acts 4:25–28)

Here, too, the modern reader questions the interest of the quotation. He does not understand and suspects some petty ulterior motive. Isn't it simply an effort to endow Jesus' ignoble death with nobility and provide a grandiose orchestration for the somewhat insignificant agony of an unimportant preacher from Galilee? A moment ago we were accusing the Gospels of scorn for the mob of persecutors, and now we suspect them of exalting the same crowd to increase their hero's prestige. Which is to be believed? This type of speculation is wrongheaded. Systematic suspicion in the face of the Gospels never yields interesting results. Instead we should return to the question that has guided our entire study. What in this text can be traced to a representation of persecution from the standpoint of persecutors and to its root in unanimous violence? All of this is categorically subverted at the very point of its greatest strength: the unanimity of the forces capable of providing the basis for such an account. Not only is there actual subversion but also a conscious desire to subvert the whole mythology of persecution and make the reader aware. With this recognition the relevance of the Psalms is immediately apparent.

The Psalm provides the list of all these forces. The conjunction, on the one hand, of the people's restlessness, *the rumbling of nations*, with kings and leaders, the constituted authorities, on the other, is essential. This conjunction is irresistible everywhere else but in the Passion of Christ. The fact that this formidable coalition is formed at a relatively low echelon and in a remote province of the Roman empire does not in any way reduce the importance of the Passion which consists in the failure of persecutors' representation of persecution and the exemplary force of that failure.

The coalition remains invincible on the level of brute force, but it is no less "vain" in the words of the Psalm because it is unsuccessful in imposing its viewpoint. It has no difficulty in putting Jesus to death but it does not prevail on the level of significance. The weakness of Holy Friday gives way in the disciples to the strength of Pentecost, and the memory of Jesus' death will be important in a far different way from what the rulers wanted. Its importance will not be immediately apparent in all its incredible newness, but it will gradually pervade all the converted, teaching them how to recognize the persecutors' accounts of persecution and reject them.

By putting Jesus to death the rulers fall into a trap since it is their own earlier secret, revealed in my quotations from the Old Testament and in many other passages, that is fully inscribed in the account of the Passion. The scapegoat mechanism becomes brilliantly apparent; it is advertised widely, and becomes the most talked-about and well-known news. Men will learn slowly, very slowly (for they are not very intelligent) to insert this knowledge into accounts of persecution.

Men will finally be liberated by means of this knowledge, which will help them first to demystify the quasi-mythologies of our own history and then, before long, to demolish all the myths of our universe whose falsehoods we defend not because we believe in them but because they protect us from the biblical revelation that will spring from the ashes of mythology and with which it has long been confused. The vain undertakings of people are even more the order of the day, but it is child's play for the Messiah to thwart them. The stronger the illusion the more ridiculous they will seem to us tomorrow.

The essential factor, though it is never perceived by theology or human sciences, is that the persecutors' perception of their persecution is finally defeated. In order to achieve the greatest effect that defeat must take place under the most difficult circumstances, in a situation that is the least conducive to truth and the most likely to produce a new mythology. This is why the Gospel text constantly insists on the irrationality ("without a cause") of the sentence passed against the just and at the same time on the absolute unity of the persecutors, of all those who believe or appear to believe in the existence and validity of the cause, the *ad causam*, the accusation, and who try to impose that belief on everyone.

It is a waste of time to examine, as certain modern commentators do, the unequal way in which the blame in the Gospels is attributed to the various protagonists of the Passion, since to do so indicates an essential misunderstanding of the real purpose of the account. Like the Heavenly Father, the Gospels have no favorites; their only interest is in the unanimity of the persecutors. All the schemes that are meant to reveal anti-Semitism, elitism, antiprogressiveness, and any other such crime that the Gospels could be accused of in the face of innocent humanity, its victim, are only of interest because their symbolism is so transparent. The authors of these schemes do not realize that they are interpreted by the text that they think has settled their case conclusively. Among the foolish undertakings of mankind, there is none more ridiculous than this.

There are a thousand ways to avoid understanding the message of the Gospels. When psychoanalysts and psychiatrists turn their attention to the Passion they readily discover in the unanimous circle of persecutors a reflection of the "characteristic paranoia of the early Christians," the traces of a "persecution complex." They are sure of this because it is based on the strongest authorities: Marxists, Nietzscheans, and Freudians for once all agree on this one point – that the Gospels are at fault. Yet this same type of interpretation never occurs to these same psychoanalysts when confronted with the witch-hunts. In this case it is not the victims they attack but their persecutors. The change of target is a relief. A mere glimpse of the reality of the persecution suffices to understand that the psychoanalytic theses are hateful and ridiculous when applied to real victims and real acts of collective violence. Persecution complexes certainly exist, and often most intensely in doctors' waiting rooms, but persecution also exists. The unanimity of the persecutors may only be a paranoic hallucination, especially in privileged modern Western society, but it is also a real phenomenon that occurs from time to time. Those who are obsessed with hallucination will never have the least hesitation in applying their principles. They always know a priori that outside of history there is only hallucination; there is no real victim.

The same stereotyped persecutors can be found everywhere, but they are not recognized. Once again it is the exterior casing, in this case historical, in the other religious, that determines the choice of interpretation, rather than the text under consideration. We find again that invisible line that crosses through our culture; underneath we admit the possibility of real acts of violence, above we are no longer willing to admit it and we fill the void created with all the pseudo-Nietzschean abstractions and their linguistic barriers. It becomes increasingly clear: after German idealism all the ups and downs of contemporary theory are no more than petty arguments meant to prevent the demystification of mythologies, new mechanisms for retarding the progress of biblical revelation.

WITHOUT USING OUR terminology, yet omitting none of the knowledge necessary to protect us from its insidious effects, the Gospels reveal the scapegoat mechanism everywhere, even within us. If I am right in this, then we should be able to trace in the Gospels everything that we have identified about the mechanism in the preceding pages, especially its *unconscious* nature. The persecutors would not allow themselves to be restricted to their accounts of persecution were it not for this unconsciousness which is identical with their sincere belief in the culpability of their victim. It is a prison whose walls cannot be seen, a servitude the more complete because it assumes freedom, a blindness that believes its perceptiveness.

Does the idea of the unconscious belong to the Gospels? The word does not appear, but modern readers will recognize it immediately if their minds are not paralyzed when confronted with the text and bound by the traditional Lilliputian threads of piety and antipiety. The sentence that defines the unconscious persecutor lies at the very heart of the Passion story in the Gospel of Luke: "Father, forgive them; they do not know what they are doing (Luke 23:34). Christians insist here on the goodness of Jesus. This would be fine were it not that their insistence eclipses the sentence's real meaning, which is scarcely ever recognized. The commentary on this sentence implies that the desire to forgive unpardonable executors forces Jesus to invent a somewhat trifling excuse for them that hardly conforms to the reality of the Passion.

Commentators who refuse to believe what this sentence says can only feel faint admiration for it, and their devotion imbues the text with the taint of their own hypocrisy. The most terrible distortion of the Gospels is our ability to project our own hypocrisy on them. In reality the Gospels never seek lame excuses; they never speak for the sake of speaking; sentimental verbiage has no place in them.

If we are to restore to this sentence its true savor we must recognize its almost technical role in the revelation of the scapegoat mechanism. It says something precise about the men gathered together by their scapegoat. *They do not know what they are doing.* That is why they must be pardoned. This is not dictated by a persecution complex or by the desire to remove from our sight the horror of real violence. In this passage we are given the first definition of the unconscious in human history, that from which all the others originate and develop in weaker form: the Freudians will push the dimension of persecution into the background and the Jungians will eliminate it altogether.

The Acts of the Apostles put the same idea into the mouth of Peter when he is addressing the crowds in Jerusalem, the same people that witnessed the Passion: "Now I know, brothers, that neither you nor your leaders had any idea what you were really doing." The considerable interest of this sentence lies in the fact that it once more draws our attention to the two categories of forces, the crowd and the leaders, both of whom are equally unconscious. It is an implicit rejection of the falsely Christian idea that made the Passion a unique event *because of its evil dimension* since its uniqueness lies in its dimension of revelation. If we accept the first idea we are making a fetish of violence and reverting to a variation of mythological paganism.

CHAPTER TEN

That Only One Man Should Die

ONLY THE ACTUAL formulation of the process by which a victim pays for others in some way is still missing. The most explicit sentence in this regard in the Gospels is the one that John puts in the mouth of the High Priest Caiaphas during the debate that ends in the decision to put Jesus to death. It articulates unequivocally everything that I have mentioned:

Then the chief priests and Pharisees called a meeting. "Here is this man working all these signs," they said, "and what action are we taking? If we let him go on in this way everybody will believe in him, and the Romans will come and destroy the Holy Place and our nation." One of them, Caiaphas, the high priest that year, said, "You don't seem to have grasped the situation at all; you fail to see that it is better for one man to die for the people, than for the whole nation to be destroyed." He did not speak in his own person, it was as high priest that he made this prophecy that Jesus was to die for the nation—and not for the nation only, but to gather together in unity the scattered children of God. From that day they were determined to kill him. (John 11:47–53)

The reason for the council is the crisis caused by Jesus' excessive popularity. But this is but the temporary form of a greater crisis in the entire Jewish society which ends, less than half a century later, in the complete destruction of the state of Israel. The existence of a debate already indicates that a decision is impossible. The indecisive debate reflects the crisis that it endeavors to decide. Because it gets nowhere Caiaphas interrupts somewhat impatiently and abruptly: "Ye know nothing at all," he says. Listening to Caiaphas, all the leaders say: "But this is true; it is better for one man to perish and for the nation to survive. How come I didn't think of that?" No doubt they had thought of it, but only the boldest of the leaders, the most convinced and decisive, could express the thought explicitly.

Caiaphas is stating the same political reason we have given for the scapegoat: to limit violence as much as possible but to turn to it, if necessary, as a last resort to avoid an even greater violence. Caiaphas is the incarnation of politics at its best, not its worst. No one has ever been a better politician.

There are nevertheless all sorts of risks attached to violence; by taking them on Caiaphas proves himself a leader. The others rely on him. They adopt him as their model; they imitate his serene certainty. Listening to Caiaphas, they no longer doubt. If the entire nation is sure to perish then it obviously would be better for one man to die for all the others, especially since he increases the imminence of the danger by refusing to keep quiet.

Caiaphas's statement triggers to a certain extent the effect of the scapegoat it defines. It not only reassures his listeners, it galvanizes them into action; it "mobilizes" them in the sense that we speak of mobilizing the military, or the "militants" who must be *mobilized*. What is at work? The formation of the famous group in fusion that Jean-Paul Sartre dreamed of, without of course ever saying that it will produce nothing but victims.

For the statement to have such an effect it has to be understood in a superficial and mythic way. The political reason defined above remains mythic because it is based on what is still hidden in the political interpretation within the "victimage" mechanism, the same thing that controls the council of Caiaphas as it controls our world. The scapegoat effect is clearly very weakened just as it is weakened in modern history. That is why the political reason is always contested by its victims and denounced as *persecution* even by those who would unwittingly resort to it should they find themselves in a position similar to Caiaphas's. The political reason is offered because the mechanism is worn out and its transcendent qualities are replaced by the justification of social utility. The political myth permits the appearance of enough of the truthful aspects of the process to give many people today the illusion that the generalized political reading contains the sort of complete revelation of "victimage" mechanisms and their justification that has sometimes been attributed to me.

For the sentence to be truly revealing it must be understood not in the political sense but in the evangelic sense, in the context of everything I have identified and everything that can be identified. Then we can recognize the brilliant definition of the mechanism revealed in the Passion story, in all the Gospels, and in the entire Bible. The scapegoat that takes shape under our eyes is the same as at the origin of Judaic sacrifices. Caiaphas is the perfect sacrificer who puts victims to death to save those who live. By reminding us of this John emphasizes that every real cultural *decision* has a sacrificial character (*decidere*, remember, is to cut the victim's throat) that refers back to an unrevealed effect of the scapegoat, the sacred type of representation of persecution.

The High Priest's decision provides the definitive revelation of sacrifice and its origin. It is expressed without either the speaker or the listeners being aware. Not only do Caiaphas and his listeners not know what they are doing, they do not know what they are saying. They must therefore be forgiven. It is all the more necessary because our political realities are usually more sordid than theirs; only our language is more hypocritical. We avoid speaking like Caiaphas because we have a clearer, though still imperfect, understanding of the meaning of his words. This is proof that revelation is making its way among us. But we would have no idea of this from reading either New Testament studies, religious history, ethnology, or political science. The experts see none of what we have been discussing. Everyone shares this knowledge except for them; the disciplines I have mentioned will have nothing to do with it. Everything seems to be done to neutralize and contain true intuition rather than cultivate it. This is always the case at the beginning of great revolutions. Resistance to knowledge of the scapegoat mechanism will prevent the upheaval. It is merely one more sign of its proximity.

If we are truly to understand the sentence in John and gain the most benefit from its revelation within the evangelic context, we must not isolate it from that context. Understanding no longer depends on merely justifying the mechanism; it is meant to increase our resistance to the temptation of the victimization, to the representations of persecution that surround it, and to the mimetic consequences that favor it. It is the inverse of the effect on those who heard it first. Both effects can be observed today which is one of the signs that our history, for better or for worse, is inseparable from the revelation of the Gospels.

FROM THE anthropological perspective the essential characteristic of the revelation is the crisis it provokes in every representation of persecution from the standpoint of the persecutor. There is nothing unique about the persecution in the story of the Passion. The coalition of all the worldly powers is not unique. This same coalition is found at the origin of all myths. What is astonishing about the Gospels is that the unanimity is not emphasized in order to bow before, or submit to, its verdict as in all the mythological, political, and even philosophical texts, but to denounce its total mistake, its perfect example of nontruth.

This is what constitutes the unparalleled radicalism of the revelation. To understand it we must briefly evoke, in contrast, the political thought of the modern Western world. The forces of this world are clearly divided into two nonsymmetrical groups, on the one hand the constituted authorities and, on the other, the crowd. The former usually get the better of the latter, but in times of crisis the reverse is true. Not only does the crowd get the upper hand but it also becomes a kind of melting pot in which even authorities that seem unshakable eventually collapse. This process of fusion assures the reformation of the authorities through the mediation of the scapegoat, or in other words the sacred. The theory of mimesis throws light on a process that political science and the natural sciences have been unable to penetrate.

The crowd is so powerful that the most surprising results can be achieved without even assembling the entire community. The constituted authorities give in to them and yield up the victims demanded by their caprice, just as Pilate gives up Jesus or Herod John the Baptist. Thus the authorities swell the crowd with their number and are absorbed by them. In understanding the Passion we come to understand the temporary removal of any difference not only between Caiaphas and Pilate, or Judas and Peter, but between those who cry out or allow others to cry out: "Crucify him!"

No matter whether "conservative" or "revolutionary," modern political thought criticizes only one category of powers, either the crowd or the established rulers. For them, it is a necessity to give systematic support to the other. It is this choice that classifies them either "conservative" or "revolutionary." The continuing fascination of the *Social Contract* is owing not to the truths it may contain but to the dizzying oscillation it maintains between these two forces. Instead of resolutely choosing one and holding to that choice, like the rational members of all parties, Rousseau wanted to reconcile the irreconcilable; his work is somewhat like the disturbance of a real revolution, incompatible with the great principles it expresses.

Those who are conservative try to consolidate the constituted authorities, the institutions that embody the continuation of a religious, cultural, political, and judicial tradition. They are susceptible to criticism for their excessive bias toward the established powers. They are equally susceptible to threats of violence from the crowd. For the revolutionaries the reverse is true. They systematically criticize institutions and shamelessly revere the violence of the crowd. The revolutionary historians of the French and Russian revolutions mythologize all the crimes. Any serious research into the crowd is considered reactionary by them. They do not welcome illumination in these areas. It is a fact that "victimage" mechanisms need obscurity if they are to "change the world." Nonetheless the great revolutionary writers provide explicit confirmation of the symbolic role of real violence, Saint-Just on the death of the king for example.

For the very reason that revolutionaries resort openly to violence, the desired effects are no longer produced. The mystery has been exposed. The foundation of violence was not effective and could only be maintained by terror. Some of this is true of the French Revolution compared with Anglo-American democracy; it is even more valid for the Marxist revolutions. Modern political thought cannot dispense with morals, but it cannot become purely moral without ceasing to be political. Another ingredient must therefore be mixed with morals. If we really tried to identify what this is we would inevitably end up with formulas like Caiaphas's: "It is better that this man or those die so that the community may survive."

Different schools of political thought no less than competing schools of criticism are based on partial and biased adaptations of the Gospel revelation. Our world is full of Christian heresies, i.e., divisions and portions. If the revelation is to be used as a weapon of divisive power in mimetic rivalry it must first be divided. As long as it remains intact it will be a force for peace, and only if it is fragmented can it be used in the service of war. Broken into pieces it provides the opposing doubles with weapons that are vastly superior to what would be available in its absence. This is the reason for the endless dispute over the remains of the body of the text, and why today the revelation itself is held responsible for the evil usage that has been made of it. The apocalyptic chapter of Matthew sums up the whole process in one startling sentence: "Wherever the corpse is, there will the vultures gather" (Matt. 24:28).

The Gospels constantly reveal what the texts of historical persecutors, and especially mythological persecutors, hide from us: the knowledge that their victim is a scapegoat, in the sense that we describe Guillaume de Machaut's Jews as scapegoats. The expression scapegoat is not actually used, but the Gospels have a perfect substitute in *the lamb of God*. Like "scapegoat," it implies the substitution of one victim for all the others but replaces all the distasteful and loathsome connotations of the goat with the positive associations of the lamb. It indicates more clearly the innocence of this victim, the injustice of the condemnation, and the causelessness of the hatred of which it is the object.

Thus everything is completely explicit. Jesus is constantly compared with and compares himself with all the scapegoats of the Old Testament, all the prophets that were assassinated or persecuted by their communities: Abel, Joseph, Moses, the Servant of Yaweh, and so on. Whether he is chosen by others or self-appointed, his role as a despised victim, inasmuch as he is innocent inspires the designation. He is the stone rejected by the builders that will become the cornerstone. He is also the millstone of scandal that will bring down even the wisest because of his ambiguous role which is easily confused with the old-style gods. Everything down to the title of king contains a reference to the "victimary" character of sacred royalty. Those who demand an unequivocal sign should be content with the *sign of Jonah*.

What is the sign of Jonah? The reference to the whale, in Matthew's text, is not very revealing; Luke's silence and that of all the exegetes is preferable. But nothing prevents us from trying to provide a better answer than Matthew to the question that was probably left unanswered by Jesus himself. In the very first lines we are given the information. During a storm Jonah is chosen by lot to be the victim thrown overboard by the sailors to save their ship in distress. The sign of Jonah is yet another sign of the collective victim.

WE THEREFORE HAVE two types of text that are related to the "scapegoat." Although they all concern victims, one group—mythological texts and those of Guillaume de Machaut, for example—does not mention that the victim is a scapegoat and forces us to articulate that fact instead. The other group—the Gospels—tells us explicitly that the victim is a scapegoat. I am not being particularly perceptive in calling Jesus a scapegoat since the text already makes that point as explicitly as possible by calling him the Lamb of God, the stone rejected by the builders, the one who suffers for everyone, and, especially, in presenting the distortion of persecution as distortion, *that which must not be believed,* in other words.

I am interpreting Guillaume de Machaut, however. When I exclaim at the end of his text: "The Jews are scapegoats," I am stating something that does not appear in the text and that contradicts the sense intended by the author. The latter is not presenting a distortion from his persecutor's viewpoint but *what he believes* to be the bare truth. The scapegoat released to us by the text is a scapegoat both *in* and *for* the text. The scapegoat that we must disengage from the text for ourselves is the scapegoat *of* the text. He cannot appear in the text though he controls all its themes; he is never mentioned as such. He cannot become the theme of that text that he *shapes.* This is not a theme but a mechanism for giving *structure.*

I have promised to be as simple as possible, and the contrast between theme and structure may seem abstract and to some readers may smack of jargon. It is, however, indispensable. If it is to become clear it must be applied to the problem confronting us. The comment on Guillaume's text "The Jews are scapegoats" summarizes the correct *interpretation* of this text. In the place of the author's uncritical presentation of persecution we substitute an interpretation that puts the Jews in the same place as Jesus in the story of the Passion. They are not culpable; they are victims of a hatred without cause. The entire crowd and in some cases the authorities are in agreement to the contrary, but this unanimity does not impress us. The persecutors know not what they are doing.

When we engage in this type of decoding, we are all involved, without knowing it, in structuralism at its best. Structural criticism is older than we think, and I shall locate its origin as far back as possible in order to use undeniable and unquestioned examples. It is enough to identify the scapegoat in the case of Guillaume de Machaut because here the term articulates the hidden structural principle that is the source of all themes. It provides the basis for the stereotypes of persecution presented from the false perspective of an author who is incapable of recognizing in the Jews described by him the *scapegoats* that we identify, in the same way as the Gospels identify Jesus as a scapegoat.

It would be absurd to assimilate the two types of texts, Guillaume de Machaut and the Gospels, under the pretext that they are both dealing with a certain connection with the "scapegoat." They describe the same event in such different ways that it would be stupid to confuse them. The first tells us that the victim is guilty. Because it reflects the scapegoat mechanism that binds it to an uncritical representation of persecution, we ourselves are engaged in the criticism. The second precedes us in that same criticism since it proclaims the innocence of the victim.

It is important to understand why this potential confusion is stupid and wrong. We would be equally wrong if we did not distinguish, for example, between the anti-Semitism of Guillaume and the denunciation of this same Guillaume by a modern historian, on the pretext that the two texts, that of Guillaume and that of the historian, both have a close yet ill-defined relationship with *the scapegoat mechanism*. Such a confusion would really be the height of the grotesque and of intellectual perversity.

Before invoking the scapegoat in connection with a text we must first ask whether we are dealing with a scapegoat *of* the text (the hidden structural principle) or a scapegoat *in* the text (the clearly visible theme). Only in the first case can the text be defined as one of persecution, entirely subjected to the representation of persecution from the standpoint of the persecutor. This text is controlled by the effect of a scapegoat it does not acknowledge. In the second case, on the contrary, the text acknowledges the scapegoat effect which does not control it. Not only is this text no longer a persecution text, but it even reveals the truth of the persecution.

It is absurd to pretend that Guillaume de Machaut's text has nothing to do with the scapegoat structure because it does not mention it. A text in which there is little mention of the scapegoat effect is more likely to be dominated by it, since it is less capable of identifying its controlling principle. In this case, and only in this case, the text is written entirely as a function of the illusion of a victim and his false culpability, the magic causality. We are not so foolish as to expect the explicit mention of the scapegoat or his equivalent in texts written from the perspective of the persecutor. If the decoding of representations of persecution by the persecutors must wait for the perpetrators of violence to be so good as to acknowledge their role in destroying scapegoats, then we can expect a long wait. I am happy enough that they leave indirect but fairly transparent signs of their persecutions, fairly transparent, of course, but requiring interpretation. Why would myths be any different? Why would the same stereotypes of persecution or their visible concealment not constitute also the indirect signs of the structure of persecution, of the scapegoat *effect*.

We reserve the structural usage of scapegoat for the world around us, going back as far as the Middle Ages. As soon as we move from historical to mythological and religious texts, we literally *forget* this usage, no matter how banal, and substitute a kind of ritual scapegoat not in the biblical sense, which might lead somewhere, but in the sense of Frazer and his disciples, who bury us in an uninteresting impasse. Rites are indeed mysterious actions, particularly for those who practice them, but they are deliberate and intentional. Cultures cannot practice their rites unconsciously. Rites are the *themes* and *motifs* at the heart of the vast cultural text. By interpreting the expression *scapegoat* in the ritual sense only and making a generalization of it, Frazer has done a grave injustice to ethnology. He conceals the most interesting meaning of the expression, which appeared at the beginning of the modern era and which never indicated any kind of rite or theme, or cultural motif, but rather identified the unconscious mechanism for the representation and acts of persecution, the scapegoat mechanism.

By inventing scapegoat rites, because he, too, did not understand the origin of all the rites in the *mechanism* of the scapegoat, Frazer has annoyingly short-circuited the opposition between them and structure, typical of the science of his time. He did not perceive that the popular and common expression that comes to our lips in reading the text of Guillaume de Machaut is infinitely more rich, interesting, and promising than all the *themes* and all the *motifs* contained in the encyclopedia he was compiling which was purely thematic and inevitably tainted. Frazer turned straight to Leviticus for a Hebrew rite to head the list of a whole nonexistent category of ritual without ever questioning the connection between religion in general and the type of phenomenon alluded to when we say that an individual or a minority group acts as "scapegoat" for the majority. He did not understand that there was something essential in this phenomenon for the understanding of the scapegoat; he did not see that it extended into our own time. He only saw an ignorant superstition that religious disbelief and positivism have served to remove. He perceived in Christianity the remains of and even the ultimate triumph of that superstition.

As soon as we turn our thoughts today from the historical to the mythological we still irresistibly slip from the structural scapegoat into the pathetic commonplace of theme and motif invented by Frazer and his disciples. But if that group of intellectuals had not been there to do the work, others would have taken their place. The work was three-quarters done when they began it. We should not compound the original error by imagining that this, too, is an easy error to correct. There is something fundamental at stake. Judging from the persistence of misunderstandings, the aversion to the structural usage of the scapegoat in mythology and religion goes far beyond the field of ethnology. It is part of the general cultural schizophrenia. We refuse to apply the same criteria used in reading history to the interpretation of mythology and religion.

It is significant that the Cambridge ethnologists looked everywhere for the scapegoat *rite* which they felt should correspond to the myth of Oedipus. They sensed that there was a close relationship between Oedipus and the "scapegoat," and they were right, but they could not understand the nature of that relationship. The current positivism prevented them from seeing anything but themes and motifs. The concept of a structural principle that is *absent* from the text it structures would have seemed epistemologically incomprehensible to them. It is the same for most scholars, and I am not even sure that I can make myself understood, despite my reference in the interpretation of Guillaume de Machaut, accepted unhesitatingly by everyone, to a scapegoat *that cannot be found in the text.*

Other knowledgeable readers since Frazer, among them Marie Delcourt and, more recently, Jean-Pierre Vernant, have again sensed that myth has "something to do" with the scapegoat. One would have to be very blind and deaf indeed not to perceive the stereotypes of persecution that are so conspicuous and make myth the most glaring example of all witchcraft trials. But no one will ever resolve this poor enigma without having recourse to the structural usage of the scapegoat that is the universal key to the persecutor's representation of persecution. As soon as it is a question of myth, especially that of Oedipus which is all the more strengthened by the psychoanalytic, tragic, aesthetic, and humanist qualities of the sacred in that it is actually quite transparent, the idea of the scapegoat inevitably falls into the rut of theme and motif. The spontaneous structuralism of demystified persecution disappears, not to be found again.

Even Jean-Pierre Vernant, despite his "structuralism," treats myth like a flat surface covered with themes and motifs, among which is the scapegoat or *pharmakos*. Vernant uses the Greek name, probably to avoid being criticized for ethnocentrism by his colleagues.[1] Admittedly, *pharmakos* is a *theme* or *motif* in Greek culture, but traditional philologists are quick to note that this theme never exactly occurs in the myth of Oedipus, and if it appears at all in the tragedy its appearance is problematic; it is there because Sophocles, like Jean-Pierre Vernant himself, "suspects something". I think Sophocles' suspicion goes quite far, though it cannot be expressed directly within the framework of the tragedy, which forbids the author to modify in any way the story he is recounting. *Aristoteles dixit*. No doubt Sophocles is responsible for whatever is exemplary in the portrayal of the stereotypes of persecution in *Oedipus Rex*. He transforms the myth into a trial; he draws the stereotypical accusation out of the process of mimetic rivalry and strews his text with suggestions either of a king who is suffering alone for all his people or of one man, Oedipus himself, who alone is responsible instead of the *collective* murderers of Laius. In fact the author insists that Laius fell at the hands of many murderers. He shows that Oedipus counts on this fact to clear himself but then Sophocles mysteriously refrains from answering the questions he himself has posed.[2] Certainly, Sophocles suspects something, but he never goes as far in revealing the structural principle of the scapegoat as the Gospels or even the Prophets. Greek culture forbids it. The myth does not burst apart in his hands and show its inner workings. The trap closes on Oedipus, and the interpreters are caught in the same trap, including Jean-Pierre Vernant, who sees only theme and never states the real problem, the representation of the myth as a whole and the system of persecution which has been shaken by the tragedy but not really subverted or made to appear false as in the Gospels.

What no one ever recognizes is that Oedipus could not be both incestuous son and parricide and at the same time *pharmakos*. When we speak of *pharmakos* we mean an innocent victim in the contaminated Judaic and Christian sense. This is still not the same as the ethnocentric sense since for Jews and Christians to speak of the *pharmakos* or scapegoat as innocent is a *truth* we can only deny at the expense of the demystification of Guillaume de Machaut and the denial of magical

---

1. Jean-Pierre Vernant, *Mythe et tragédie en Grèce ancienne* (Paris: La Decouverte, 1972), pp. 99–131.
2. Sandor Goodhart, "Oedipus and Laius' Many Murderers," *Diacritics* (March 1978): 55–71.

thought. Either Oedipus is a scapegoat and not guilty of parricide and incest, or he is guilty and is not, at least for the Greeks, the innocent scapegoat that Jean-Pierre Vernant modestly calls *pharmakos*.

That the tragedy seems to move in conflicting directions is indicative of its internal struggle; it can neither adhere to the myth nor reject it in the way the Prophets, the Psalms, and the Gospels reject it. It is this internal contradiction which tears it apart, violently, rather than the impossible coexistence of the guilty son and the innocent scapegoat in the false aesthetic harmony of humanist beatitudes, that gives the tragedy its beauty.

By speaking of *pharmakos* rather than scapegoat, Jean-Pierre Vernant hopes to escape the blame of those of his colleagues who are not in the least sensitive to the aura of the victim released by the myth. But why try to satisfy people with so little sensitivity? Jean-Pierre Vernant is himself too sensitive for this and is almost as suspect in this as I am. It never occurs to anyone to substitute *pharmakos* for scapegoat in the case of Guillaume de Machaut. Even if Guillaume de Machaut had written in Greek, which in a way is what he is doing when he replaces plague with *epydimie*, I do not think we would consider that his attitude toward the innocent who were persecuted was in any way influenced by a *pharmakos* effect. We would still talk about scapegoats. The day we understand the source of the myth of Oedipus, the genetic and structural mechanism that marks this myth, we shall have to admit that *Oedipus is a scapegoat*. The distance is not great between this expression and Jean-Pierre Vernant's *pharmakos*, but strong prejudices prevent many from crossing it. Jean-Pierre Vernant diverges from the myth as much in speaking of *pharmakos* as I do in speaking of *scapegoat*. But unlike Jean-Pierre Vernant, I have not the slightest hesitation; I can completely justify this divergence. I diverge neither more nor less from the myth than the positivist philologists themselves do from Guillaume de Machaut when they read him the way we all do. Why do our learned positivists find acceptable in relation to Guillaume de Machaut what they absolutely forbid in the name of textual accuracy in the case of Oedipus and his myth? They cannot answer but I can answer for them. They understand Guillaume de Machaut and do not understand the myth of Oedipus; they do not understand what they hold most dear because they make a fetish of the great texts needed by Western humanism to justify itself before the Bible and the Gospels. The same is true of those who are violently opposed to ethnocentrism and share another form of the same illusion. Why do they not condemn the mention of scapegoat in relation to Guillaume de Machaut as ethnocentric?

If I risk boring my readers by returning to Guillaume it is not because of its intrinsic interest, but because our interpretation of him clearly diverges from the text by the very fact that it is radically structural. It is based on a principle that never appears in the text; it is nonetheless legitimately untouchable, truly indestructible. Since I never do more with the texts I am discussing than this interpretation does with this text, it provides me with a marvelous counterproof, the quickest, most intelligible, and surest means of sweeping away all the false ideas that are so abundant today, not only in the areas of mythology and religion but also in everything that involves interpretation. It reveals the deliquescence hidden beneath the radical pretensions of present-day nihilism. The pernicious idea that there is no truth anywhere, and especially not in the texts we interpret, is triumphant everywhere. Against this notion we must brandish the truth we have all extracted unhesitatingly from Guillaume de Machaut and the witch trials. We must ask the nihilists whether they renounce this truth, too, and whether they see all the accounts as the same, whether from the perspective of the persecutors or the victim.

CHAPTER ELEVEN

The Beheading of
Saint John the Baptist

CHRISTIANS AND anti-Christians are alike in their conception of originality. The romantics taught us that to be original is not to say the same thing as anyone else; always to be creating new schools or new fashions; to practice innovation like today's bureaucrats and idealists in a world that is not even capable of creating new labels and alternates constantly between "modern" and "new" for want of being able to imagine a third alternative.

This concept of originality dominates the argument over the Gospels. For the Gospels and, subsequently, Christianity to be truly original, their subject matter must be different from that of all the other religions. But it is not. For centuries ethnologists and historians of religion have been demonstrating this; it is the source of their entire knowledge. See how primitive the Gospels are, we are told in a hundred different ways by all the most fashionable scholars. Look at that collective punishment in its fine setting, as in very primitive myths, look at this business of a scapegoat. How curious! In the case of the so-called ethnological myths there is never any question of violence. One is not supposed to label myths and religions primitive and certainly not more or less savage. This "ethnocentric problematic" can have no relevance. Yet, as soon as the Gospels appear on the scene, it becomes possible again and even commendable to use such terms.

I hasten to adopt this way of looking at things and applaud with both hands the words of the ethnologists. They are right; the Gospels are talking about the same event as the myths. They are talking about the original murder that is found at the heart of all mythology, and they are right about the most primitive myths resembling the Gospels most closely, since they are generally explicit in their mention of the murder. More developed myths, if they have not transfigured that murder, have carefully erased it.

If the Gospels talk about the same event as the myths then they cannot fail to be mythic, according to the ethnologists, who have overlooked something. One can talk about the same murder without talking about it in the same way. One can talk about it as murderers talk or one can talk about it not as any ordinary victim talks but as does this incomparable victim that is the Christ of the Gospels. One can call him an incomparable victim without any sentimental piety or suspect emotion. He is incomparable in that he never succumbs in any way, at any point, to the perspective of the persecutor—neither in a positive way, by openly agreeing with his executioners, nor in a negative way, by taking a position of vengeance, which is none other than the inverse reproduction of the original representation of persecution, its mimetic repetition.

This total absence of positive or negative complicity with violence is what is needed for a complete revelation of its system of representation and the system of every representation apart from the Gospels themselves. This is true originality; it is a return to the origin, a return that revokes the origin as it reveals it. The constant repetition of the origin that characterizes the false originality of innovations is based on the concealment and camouflage of that origin.

Christians have failed to understand the true originality of the Gospels. They subscribe to their adversaries' concept. They believe that the Gospels cannot be original unless they are talking about something utterly remote from myths. They are therefore resigned to the Gospels not being original. They espouse a vague syncretism, and their personal beliefs are far behind Voltaire's. Or else they try in vain to prove exactly the opposite of the ethnologists, but always within the same frame of reference. They waste their efforts trying to show that the Passion is radically new in every respect. They tend to see in the trial of Jesus, in the crowd's intervention, in the Crucifixion, an incomparable event in itself, as a world event, whereas the Gospels say that Jesus is in the same position as all past, present, and future victims. Theologians see in this only more or less metaphysical and mystical metaphors. They do not read the Gospels literally, and they tend to make a fetish of the Passion. Unwittingly, they play the game of their adversaries and of all mythology. They once more make sacred the violence that has been divested of its sacred character by the Gospel text. The proof that this is unnecessary is that there is a second example of collective murder in this same Gospel text. The details are different, but it is identical to the Passion in the mechanisms it employs and in the relationships among the participants.

I refer to the murder of John the Baptist. My analysis is based on the account given by Mark. Although it is not lengthy, this text brings into astonishing focus the mimetic desires, followed by mimetic rivalries, that result in the final scapegoat effect. The text cannot be treated merely as a reflection or double of the Passion. The differences are too great to be able to conclude that the two accounts are from the same source or that one is the faded replica of the other. The similarities are better explained by the identical structure of the events portrayed and by an absolute control, in each case, of a single concept of the individual and collective relationships which comprises these two events, the mimetic concept.

The murder of John the Baptist provides a sort of counterproof to the analysis I have given of the Passion. It allows us to verify the systematic character of evangelical thought on the subject of collective murder and its role in the genesis of non-Christian religion.

Herod wanted to take Herodias, the wife of his own brother, as his second wife. The union was condemned by the prophet, whom Herod imprisoned apparently as much to protect him as to punish him for his audacity. Herodias demanded his head relentlessly. Herod did not want to give in. Herodias, however, prevailed by having her daughter dance for Herod and his guests at a banquet. At her mother's instruction and with the encouragement of the guests, the daughter demands the head of John the Baptist, which Herod dare not refuse (Mark 6:17–28).

Let us begin at the beginning:

Now it was this same Herod who had sent to have John arrested, and had him chained up in prison because of Herodias, his brother Philip's wife whom he had married. For John had told Herod, "It is against the law for you to have your brother's wife."

It is not on the strict legality of the marriage that the prophet places emphasis. In the sentence: *It is against the law for you to have your brother's wife*, the verb *exein*, to have, does not have a legal connotation. Freudian-structuralist dogma favors a type of interpretation that does not fit the Gospels. We should not introduce a petty legalism where it never existed on the pretext of thrashing it. The spirit and letter of the

Gospel text are opposed to it. What is the real question? Sibling rivalry. The brothers are condemned to rivalry by their very proximity; they fight over the same heritage, the same crown, the same wife. It all begins as in a myth with a story of enemy brothers. Do they have the same desires because they are alike or are they alike because they have the same desires? Is it the relationship in the myths that determines the twin desires, or do the twin desires determine a likeness that is defined as brotherly?

In our text both propositions seem true at the same time. Herod and his brother constitute both the symbol of the desire that interests Mark and a real historical example of the effects of that desire. Herod really had a brother; he really took his wife, Herodias, from him. We know from Joseph that the pleasure of supplanting his brother cost Herod some serious repercussions; they are not mentioned in our text but they are totally in the style of mimetic complications and, therefore, in the spirit of prophetic injunction. Herod had a first wife whom he had to repudiate, and the father of the abandoned wife decided to punish his son-in-law's inconstancy by inflicting a stinging defeat on him.

To have Herodias, to carry her off, is forbidden to Herod not by virtue of some formal rule but because his possession can only be at the expense of a dispossessed brother. The prophet warns his royal listener against the evil effects of mimetic desire. There is no illusion in the Gospels about the possibility of arbitration between the brothers. This warning should be compared with a very short but revealing text in the Gospel of Luke:

A man in the crowd said to him, "Master, tell my brother to give me a share of our inheritance." "My friend," he replied, "who appointed me your judge, or the arbitrator of your claims?" (Luke 12:13–14)

The brothers are divided over the indivisible heritage. Jesus declares himself incompetent. The formula: "*Who appointed me your judge, or the arbitrator of your claims?*" recalls a sentence from the beginning of Exodus. Moses intervenes for the first time between an Egyptian and a Hebrew. He kills the Egyptian, who is mistreating the Hebrew. He intervenes a second time between two Hebrews and is asked: "*And who appointed you to be prince over us, and judge? Do you intend to kill me as you killed the Egyptian?*" It is striking that Jesus for his part repeats not what Moses says but what the Hebrew says when he challenges Moses' authority. Jesus suggests that the question calls for no more of an answer on his part than in Moses' case when it was asked. No one has made him, Jesus, nor will make him, the judge of his fellow men to decide their disputes.

Does this mean that Jesus is protesting the idea that he is charged with a divine mission as Moses was eventually? Certainly not, but Jesus suggests that his mission is very different from that of Moses. The time for a national liberator and legislator is past. It is no longer possible to separate the enemy brothers by a controlled violence that would put an end to their violence. The Hebrew's challenge, which reminds Moses of his murder the day before, is henceforth universally valid. No longer is any distinction possible between legitimate and illegitimate violence. There are only enemy brothers, and they can only be warned against their mimetic desire in the hope that they will renounce it. This is what John does, and his warning recalls the preaching of the Kingdom of God in the career of Jesus.

Except for the prophet, there are only enemy brothers and mimetic twins in the text: the mother and daughter, Herod and his brother, Herod and Herodias. The latter two names even suggest the twin quality, phonetically and they are constantly repeated, one after the other, in the beginning of our text, where the name of the dancer is not mentioned, no doubt because it has nothing to serve as an echo; it adds nothing to the relationship of mimetic effects.

The brother, or rather half-brother, with whom Herod disputes Herodias, was not called Philip, as Mark mistakenly stated, but he too was called Herod; he had the same name as his brother. Herodias finds herself caught between two Herods. If Mark had known he probably would have played on this homonymy. The historical reality is even better than the text.

On the fringe of our text John's warning indicates the type of relationship that controls the whole narrative and ends convulsively in the murder of the prophet. Desire festers and becomes overwrought because Herod does not heed the prophetic warning, and everyone follows his example. All the incidents and details of the text illustrate the successive moments of this desire, each of them produced by the demented logic of a higher bid nourished by the failure of the previous moments.

The proof that Herod desires above all to triumph over his brother is that, once possessed, Herodias loses all direct influence over her husband. She cannot get from him the death of an insignificant prophet. To achieve her ends Herodias must by means of her daughter establish a triangular configuration, similar to that which established her influence over Herod, by making her a prize for the enemy brothers. Mimetic desire is extinguished in one place only to reappear a little further away in an even more virulent form.

Herodias feels herself denied and obliterated by the words of John. This is true for her not as a human being but as a mimetic prize. She herself is too consumed by mimeticism to be able to realize the distinction. By shielding the prophet from Herodias's vengeance Herod is conforming to the laws of desire; he is verifying the prophetic announcement, and the abandoned woman's hatred is redoubled. Attracted by John because rejected by him, the desire becomes the desire of destruction; it glides immediately toward violence.

By imitating my brother's desire, I desire what he desires; we mutually prevent each other from satisfying our common desire. As resistance grows on both sides, so desire becomes strengthened; the model becomes increasingly obstructive and the obstacle becomes increasingly the model, so that ultimately the desire is only interested in that which opposes it. It is only taken with the obstacles created by itself. John the Baptist is that obstacle; inflexible, inaccessible to all attempts at corruption, it is that which fascinates Herod and, even more so, Herodias. Herodias is always the coming into being of Herod's desire.

As mimeticism becomes more exacerbated it increases its dual power of attraction and repulsion and communicates itself as hatred more rapidly from one individual to another. The sequel provides an extraordinary illustration of this law:

When the daughter of this same Herodias came in and danced, she delighted Herod and his guests; so the king said to the girl, "Ask me anything you like and I will give it you." And he swore her an oath, "I will give you anything you ask, even half my kingdom." She went out and said to her mother, "What shall I ask for?" She replied, "The head of John the Baptist." The girl hurried straight back to the king and made her request, "I want you to give me John the Baptist's head, here and now, on a dish." (Mark 6:22–26)

Something very odd happens after Herod's offer, or rather, nothing happens. Instead of mentioning the precious or foolish things that young people are supposed to desire, Salome remains silent. Neither Mark nor Matthew gives a name to the dancer. We call her Salome because the historian Josephus speaks of a daughter of Herodias by that name. Salome has no desire to formulate. This human being has no desire of her own; men are strangers to their desires; children don't know how to desire and must be taught. Herod does not suggest anything to Salome because he offers her everything and anything. That is why Salome leaves him and goes to ask her mother what she should desire.

But does the mother really communicate her desire to her daughter? Perhaps Salome is merely a passive intermediary, a good child who obediently carries out her mother's terrible errands. She is much more than that, as can be seen from her haste as soon as her mother has spoken. Her uncertainty disappears and she changes entirely. Such attentive readers as le père Lagrange have remarked on the difference in her appearance, but they have not understood its significance:

The girl hurried straight back to the king and made her request, "I want you to give me John the Baptist's head, here and now, on a dish."

Hurried, straight back, here and now. It is not unintentional that a text that normally gives so few details provides so many signs of impatience and feverishness. Salome is worried that the king might be sobered by the end of the dance and her departure and might go back on his promise. And it is her desire that is worrying her; her mother's desire has become her own. The fact that Salome's desire is entirely patterned after another desire does nothing to lessen its intensity. On the contrary, the imitation is even more frenetic than the original.

Herodias's daughter is a child. The Greek word that describes her is not *kore*, young woman, but the diminutive *korasion*, little girl, as the Jerusalem Bible correctly translates it. We must forget the concept of Salome as a professional seducer. The genius of the Gospel text has nothing in common with Flaubert's courtesan, the dance of the seven veils, and other Orientalia. Although she is childish or, rather, because she is a child, Salome changes immediately from innocence to the convulsion of mimetic violence. A more luminous sequence cannot be imagined. First the daughter's silence in response to the extravagant offer of the king, then the mother's answer, the mother's desire, and, finally, the daughter's adoption of that desire, the daughter's desire. The child asks the adult not to fulfill some desire of hers but to provide her *with the desire she is lacking.* This is a revelation of imitation as pure essence of desire, which is too unfamiliar to be understood. It fits neither our philosophical ideas of imitation nor our psychoanalytic theories of desire.

There is to be sure something schematic in this revelation, achieved at the expense of psychological realism. No matter how rapidly one person can be infected by another's desire, it is hard to imagine that a mother's brief answer to her daughter's question would be enough. All the commentators had trouble with this schematic. Matthew was the first to reject it. Between Herod's offer and Salome's response the whole exchange between mother and daughter is omitted. Matthew recognized its awkwardness but not its genius, or else he considered its expression too elliptic to be retained. He says simply that the daughter is "prompted" by her mother, which is a correct interpretation of what happens in Mark, but deprives us of the striking spectacle of a Salome suddenly transformed, mimetically, into a second Herodias.

After "appropriating" her mother's desire, the daughter is indistinguishable from her. The two women take turns playing the same role with Herod. Our unshakable cult of desire prevents us from recognizing the process of uniformization; it "scandalizes" our accepted notions. Modern interpreters are equally divided between those who celebrate only Herodias and those who celebrate only Salome. Each of them, interchangeably, becomes the heroine of the most intense desire that is for them totally unique, spontaneous, liberated, and liberating. The force and simplicity of Mark's text, in contrast, show all this to be false. It completely avoids the vulgarity (in the literal sense) of the analytical tools created by psychoanalysis, sociology, ethnology, and the history of religion.

By dividing themselves between Herodias and Salome modern critics with their cult of desire are quietly reestablishing the truth that their cult is meant to deny, the knowledge that desire, instead of creating individuals, as it becomes increasingly mimetic, makes those it possesses more easily interchangeable and capable of substitution as its intensity increases.

Before speaking of the dance we should explore a notion that prevades our text without ever being mentioned explicitly: the notion of scandal or the stumbling block. Derived from *skadzein*, which means to limp, *skandalon* designates the obstacle that both attracts and repels at the same time. The initial encounter with the stumbling block is so fascinating that one must always return to it, and each return becomes more fascinating.[1]

I recognize in scandal a rigorous definition of the mimetic process.

---

1. Girard, *Des choses cachées depuis la fondation du monde*, pp. 438–53.

The modern sense only recaptures a glimmer of the evangelical meaning. Desire clearly understands that, in desiring what another desires, it makes a rival and an obstacle of this model. It would be wise to give up, but if desire were wise it would not be desire. Finding only obstacles in its path, it incorporates them in its vision of the desirable and brings them into the foreground; it can no longer desire without them and cultivates them avidly. Thus it becomes full of hatred for the obstacle, and allows itself to be scandalized. This is the evolution revealed in the transition from Herod to Herodias and then to Salome.

To Herodias, John the Baptist is a scandal because he speaks the truth, and there is no worse enemy of desire than truth. That is how it can make a scandal of this truth; the truth itself becomes scandalous, and that is scandal at its worst. Herod and Herodias keep the truth captive; they make it a kind of prize and compromise it in the dance of their desire. Happy are those, Jesus says, for whom I am not a cause of scandal. Scandal in the end always succeeds in investing and incorporating what has most successfully eluded it, what should be most foreign to it. Prophesy is one example and childhood another. My interpretation of Salome reveals her as a child victim of scandal. Jesus' words on scandal and childhood can be applied to her:

"Anyone who welcomes a little child like this in my name welcomes me. But anyone who is an obstacle to bring down one of these little ones who have faith in me would be better drowned in the depths of the sea with a great millstone around his neck." (Matt. 18:5–7)

The child inevitably chooses the closest adult as model. If he only encounters people who are already scandalized and too devoured by desire to be open, inevitably he will model his behavior on theirs; he will become a mimetic replica of them and a grotesque caricature.

Herodias uses her own child to circumvent Herod and obtain his consent to the death of the innocent man. How could Salome not be scandalized? In an effort to protect herself from scandal the child sinks deeper by making her mother's appalling desire her own. In the previous quotation the drowning person with a millstone around his neck is a figure of scandal. Like other metaphors it suggests a natural mechanism of self-destruction rather than supernatural intervention. By becoming a part of the vicious circle of scandal, men forge the destiny they deserve. Desire is a noose that each one ties around his own neck; it is tightened at each tug of the scandalized. The physical equivalent of this process, the treadmill turned by mules, is less terrible than the process itself. Hanging is another equivalent; by hanging himself, Judas inflicts the punishment that prolongs his own evil, the scandal to which he is prey, the mimetic jealousy that devours him.

Men create their own hell and help one another descend into it. Perdition is an equitable exchange because it results from reciprocal evil desires and evil behavior. The only innocent victims are children on whom scandal is imposed from the outside without any participation on their part. Fortunately, all men were once children.

Scandal and the dance are in opposition. Scandal is what prevents us from dancing. To enjoy the dance is to identify with the dancer and escape the scandal that holds us a prisoner of Mallarmé's ice or Sartre's *visqueux*. If dance were merely a spectacle in the modern sense, a simple image of the freedom we dream of, its effects would only be imaginary or symbolic in the shallowest sense of modern aestheticism. But dance has a different power. It exacerbates desire, rather than suppressing it. What prevents us from dancing is not just the physical but the dreadful intertwining of our desires which keep us tied to the ground, and the *other* of desire always seems responsible for this misfortune; we are all like Herodias, obsessed with some John the Baptist. Even when the knots of desire are very individual and each has his own model obstacle, still the mechanism is identical; this identity makes substitutions possible. Dance accelerates the mimetic process. It involves all the guests at the banquet in the dance, converging all the desires on the one object, the head on the platter, the head of John the Baptist on Salome's platter.

John the Baptist is first the scandal of Herodias and then becomes the scandal of Salome, who, through her artistic power, transmits the scandal to all the spectators. She gathers all the desires together and directs them toward the victim chosen for her by Herodias. The inextricable knot of desire must be loosened at the end of the dance, and this requires the death of the victim, who, for the time being, incarnates that desire, for mimetic reasons (no matter how remote), reasons that are almost always insignificant, except, perhaps, here and in the case of Jesus when the just denunciation of this desire unleashes the fatal mechanism.

To say that the dance pleases not only Herod but also all his guests is to say that they are all possessed by Salome's desire. In the head of John the Baptist they do not really identify what the dancer claims, or scandal in general—the philosophical concept of scandal, which does not exist—but each one sees his own scandal, the object of his desire and hatred. The collective "yes!" to the beheading should not be interpreted as merely a polite gesture of acquiescence. The guests are all under Salome's spell. Mimeticism again. The power of the dance resembles that of the shaman who leads his patients to think that he has extracted the harmful substance from their bodies. They were possessed by something that chained them and the dance frees them. The dancer can make the lame dance because her dance exorcises the demon that possesses them. She enables them to exchange all that wearies and torments them for the head of John the Baptist. She not only reveals the demon that possesses them but she also carries out the act of vengeance of which they dream. By espousing the violent desire of Salome, all the guests feel as if they are satisfying their own desire. Everyone shares the same frenzy toward the model obstacle, and they all willingly mistake the object because the proposed object feeds their appetite for violence. It is not Hegelian negativity or the impersonal death of the philosophers that guarantees the symbolic quality of the prophet's head, but the mimetic contagion of collective murder.

There is a popular legend in which Salome dies in the course of a dance on ice. The dancer slips and, as she falls, her neck hits a sharp piece of ice, which beheads her.[2] Even though in the Gospel text the dancer keeps her balance perfectly and, as a result, obtains the head that she desires, yet here in the end she fails and pays for her failure with her own head. This retribution seems to be carried out without an intermediary; it is vengeance without avengers. But we have in the ice, the mirror or reflection, an image of the *others*, the spectators, and the ground is wonderfully slippery, suitable for the most spectacular performance. Her admirers urge the dancer to defy the laws of gravity in increasingly daring fashion, but in an instant they can become a fatal trap, witness and cause of the fall from which the artist does not recover.

If the dancer does not control the desires, the public immediately turns on her, there is no one else to become the sacrificial victim. Like a lion-tamer, the master of ritual unleashes monsters that will devour him unless he remains in control through constantly renewed efforts. The legend is separated from the Gospel by its dimension of vengeance,

2. Charles J. Ellicott, *Ellicott's Bible Commentary*, ed. Donald Bowdle (Grand Rapids, Mich.: Zondervan, 1971), p. 715.

but it confirms that the connection exists in the popular mind between John's murder, the dance and the scandal, the loss of balance that is the opposite of the successful dance. In short it verifies the mimetic reading, I might even add for the pleasure of my critics, the *simplism, systematism,* and *dogmatism* of this reading, in that it leaves no stone unturned in a prodigious shortcut but not without re-creating the myth that Mark removed since it replaces the other, the double, the scandalous rival, explicit in the evangelical text, with one of its most common mythic symbols: ice, the mirror.

Scandal is the unobtainable that desire wishes to obtain, the absolutely unavailable that it wants absolutely at its disposition. Because it is lighter, more portable and manageable, the head becomes a better representation once it is severed from the body, especially when placed on a dish. The thin plate of metal slipped under John's head stresses the icy cruelty of the dancer. It transforms the head into an accessory of the dance but, above all, it conjures up the material expression of the ultimate nightmare of desire. We can recognize a certain similarity with the primitive obsession with an antagonist's head that was demanded by ritual, the head of a member of a neighboring tribe, for example, that was locked into a relationship of mimetic rivalry with the murderers. In primitive tribes these heads are sometimes embalmed, a process that shrinks them and turns them into a kind of trinket. This refinement parallels the horrible desire of Salome.

Tradition recognizes Salome as a great artist, and powerful traditions are never established without reason. But what is that reason? The dance is never described. There is nothing original about Salome's desire since it is copied from Herodias. Even the words belong to Herodias. Salome adds only one thing, the idea of the dish. "I want you to give me the head of John the Baptist on a dish." Herodias had mentioned the head but not the dish. The dish is the only new element and the only detail that truly belongs to Salome. If a textual reason for the prestige of Salome is needed, that is where it must be found. There is no other justification. Unquestionably, everything rests on that dish. That is the most famous part of the scene in Mark. That is what is remembered when all else is forgotten. We cannot ignore the fact that in modern times we identify "culture" by such signs as these. The idea is scandalous, striking; its very coarseness contributes to its subtlety—it is the idea of a decadent artist.

But is it really an *original* idea in the modern sense of *novelty*? On closer examination its apparent originality again dissolves into *mimesis*. When Herodias gives her daughter the answer: "The head of John the Baptist," she is not thinking of decapitation. In French as in Greek, to ask for someone's head is to demand his death. The part is taken for the whole. Herodias's answer does not refer to a precise method of execution. The text has already mentioned the desire of Herodias in neutral terms that do not suggest any fixation with her enemy's head: "As for Herodias, she was furious with him and wanted to kill him." One cannot conclude from this that she wanted to hold his head in her hands, that she desired the physical object. Even in countries where beheading is customary, to demand someone's head must be understood rhetorically, whereas Salome takes it literally. She does not do so intentionally. Only an adult can make such distinctions. This head is the most wonderful day of her life.

The beheading of John the Baptist is one thing; holding his head in her hands is something else. Salome wonders what she can do with it. A freshly beheaded head needs to be put somewhere, and the practical solution is to put it on a platter. This idea is no more than a common-sense reaction. Salome takes the words too-literally to convey the message accurately. A too-literal interpretation results in a misinterpretation through a lack of understanding. The inaccuracy of the copy is a result of an excessive concern for accuracy. What appears to be most creative in the role of Salome is really what is most mechanical and hypnotic in the submission to the chosen model.

All great aesthetic ideas are the same—narrowly, obsessively *imitative*. Traditionally, art is only spoken of in terms of *mimesis*. The passion with which we deny this is suspect, since art has rightly withdrawn from our world. By discouraging imitation we are not eliminating it but forcing it into the ridiculous fads and ideologies that make up our contemporary attempts at innovation. Our desire for originality ends in insignificant efforts. Instead of renouncing the notion of *mimesis* we should expand it to include desire or, perhaps, desire should be expanded to mimesis. By separating *mimesis* from desire philosophy has deformed them both, and we remain prisoners of this mutilation that perpetuates all the false dichotomies of modern culture; between the aesthetic, for example, the mythical, and the historical.

The text says nothing about the actual dance; it only says: "and danced." Yet it must say something in order to exert the fascination it has always exerted over Western art. Salome dancing was already portrayed on Romanesque capitals, and her portrayal has continued since then in an increasingly diabolic and scandalous form as the world sinks deeper into its own scandal.

The space meant for "description" in modern texts is usurped by the antecedents and consequences of the dance. It all reflects back to the significant moments of a single mimetic game. Thus *mimesis* occupies the space, not in the sense of a realistic copying of objects but, rather, in the relationships controlled by mimetic rivalries. The acceleration of this vortex produces the "victimage" mechanism that brings about its end.

All the mimetic effects are pertinent in relation to the dance; they are already effects of dance but they are not gratuitous, they are not there for "aesthetic reasons." It is the relationships among the participants that interest Mark. The dancer and the dance are reciprocally generative. The infernal progress of the mimetic rivalries, the becoming *similar* of all the characters, the progress of the sacrificial crisis toward its denouement in a victim are all part of Salome's dance. It must be this way: art is never other than the reproduction of this crisis or denouement in a more or less concealed form. Everything begins with symmetrical confrontations that are ultimately resolved in the rounds of the victims.

The text in its entirety has something in common with the dance. As it follows the mimetic effects carefully and as simply as possible, it must go back and forth between one character and another, designing a kind of ballet in which each dancer comes forward in turn before disappearing once more into the group to play his role in the sinister final apotheosis. But the existence of a calculating intelligence will certainly be noted. Herod still protects John, but Herodias, like a spider in its web, waits for a suitable occasion:

An opportunity came on Herod's birthday when he gave a banquet for the nobles of his court, for his army officers and for the leading figures in Galilee.

The suitable occasion, Herod's birthday, has a ritual character; it is a feast that recurs every year; festive, or ritual, activities take place on the occasion; the community is assembled around a banquet; the spectacle of dance at the end of the banquet also has a ritual character. All the institutions that Herodias puts to use against John are ritual by nature.

Like the conspiracy of the priests in the Passion story, Herodias's plot plays only a secondary role: it contributes somewhat to the acceleration by moving in the direction of desire and *mimesis* like ritual itself.

An inferior, too differentiated, understanding imagines that Herodias is manipulating all the desires, which is what Herodias herself thinks. A superior, more mimetic, and less differentiated understanding perceives that Herodias herself is being manipulated by her desire. All the activities mentioned by the text are also found in ritual and usually culminate in a sacrificial immolation. John's murder occupies the place and moment of sacrifice. All the textual elements could therefore be read in a strictly ritual key, but such a reading would have no explanatory value. According to some bygone ethnologists, the ritual aspects clarify a text such as ours. In fact they increase the mystery because of a lack of understanding of the rites and the reason for their existence. It often happens in the human sciences that explanatory value is given to the most opaque details precisely because of their opaqueness. Anything that provides no hold for the interpreter feels like a smooth rock; and with no crack where doubt may be insinuated, its very obscurity is taken for clarity.

Far from neglecting the ritual and institutional aspects of the text, by using desire to interpret them I am creating the only framework that makes ritual intelligible. It not only resembles the final stages of the mimetic crisis that are resolved spontaneously by the scapegoat mechanism, but it is also a complete replica of the crises from which it cannot be distinguished. This replication is perfectly feasible because, as we have seen, ritual is the mimetic repetition of an original mimetic crisis. Because there is nothing original about the ritual dimension except its concealed origin it fits smoothly into the history of desire outlined in our text. It is totally *mimesis*, imitation, the scrupulous repetition of the crisis. The rite does not provide any real solution, it merely recopies the solution that occurred spontaneously. There is therefore no structural difference between the rite itself and the spontaneous, natural course of the mimetic crisis.

Instead of curbing or interrupting the mimetic play of desires, ritual activity fosters and channels it in the direction of designated victims. Each time the faithful feel themselves threatened by authentic mimetic discord they engage in it voluntarily; they mimic their own conflicts and use their own wiles to bring about a sacrificial resolution that will achieve agreement at the victim's expense.

Our reading is thus confirmed; ritual and the arts it inspires are mimetic by nature and function mimetically; they do not have a verifiable specificity. Does this mean that there is no difference between them and the spontaneous crisis or Herodias's complicated maneuver? Am I confusing all these things? Certainly not. Authentic rites are different from authentic disorder by virtue of the unanimous opposition to the victim that is then perpetuated under the aegis of a victim mythically restored and made sacred.

Rite is the reenactment of mimetic crises in a spirit of voluntary religious and social collaboration, a reenactment in order to reactivate the scapegoat mechanism for the benefit of society rather than for the detriment of the victim who is perpetually sacrificed. For this reason, in the diachronic evolution of rites the disorders that precede and necessitate the sacrifice are invariably attenuated whereas the festive and convivial aspects increase in importance.

Even the most weakened ritual institutions are inclined toward sacrifice. A crowd stuffed with food and drink wants something extraordinary, a spectacle of eroticism or violence, preferably both at the same time. Herodias knows enough about ritual to use its power in the promotion of her murderous scheme. She inverts and perverts the ritual function because the victim's death interests her more than the community's reconciliation. The symbols of the authentic ritual function are still present in our text, but in purely vestigial form.

Herodias mobilizes the ritual forces and directs them knowingly toward the victim of her hate. By perverting the rite she restores *mimesis* to its former virulence and redirects sacrifice back to its murderous origins. She reveals the scandal at the heart of every religious sacrificial institution, playing a role similar to that of Caiaphas in the Passion. Herodias in herself is not important. She is only an instrument of the revelation and reveals its "paradoxical" nature by the use of ritual that is revealing in its perversity. It is John's opposition to her marriage with Herod—"*It is against the law for you to have your brother's wife*"—that turns Herodias against the prophet. But, in principle, ritual mystification always involves this occultation of mimetic desire by means of the scapegoat. Herodias and Caiaphas could be defined as living allegories of the rite that is forced to return to its nonritual origins, the undisguised murder, by the power of the revelation that forces it out of its religious and cultural hiding places.

I speak of Mark's text as if he were always telling the truth, and, in effect, he is. Certain aspects, however, strike the reader as legendary. They are vaguely reminiscent of a black fairy-tale with an unhappy ending. There is something of this in the relationship of Salome with her mother, in the mixture of horror and childish submission. There is also something of it in the excessive character of the exorbitant offer of recompense to the dancer. Herod does not have a kingdom to divide. To tell the truth, he was not a king but a tetrarch, and his very limited powers were totally dependent on Roman goodwill.

Commentators look for literary sources. In the book of Esther, King Ahasuerus makes an offer to the heroine that is similar to Herod's (Esther 5:6). Both Mark and Matthew could have been influenced by this text. But the theme of an exorbitant offer is so common in legends that it could have been in the minds of Mark and Matthew without reference to any particular text. It would be more interesting to study the significance of this theme. In folktales the hero, when put to the test or performing some feat, often unexpectedly shows some unappreciated quality. The ruler who sets the test is all the more astounded by the hero's success because he has been impervious to his charm for so long. He then makes him an exorbitant offer: his kingdom or, what amounts to the same thing, his only daughter. If the offer is accepted it transforms one who has nothing into one who possesses everything and vice versa. If a king's person is inseparable from his possessions and his kingdom, then the donor is literally giving his being to the receiver. By dispossessing himself, the donor makes the receiver another self. He gives him everything that makes him what he is, and he keeps nothing for himself. If the offer only concerns half the kingdom, as here, the sense basically remains the same. A Salome who possessed half of Herod would be the same as the other half, Herod himself. There would only be one person interchangeable between the two people.

Despite his riches and titles the donor is in an inferior position. An offer to a dancer to dispossess us is the same as asking her to possess us. The exorbitant offer is the fascinated spectator's response. It expresses the strongest desire of all, the desire to be possessed. Disoriented by this desire, the subject tries to become a part of the orbit of the sun that dazzles him, and he literally becomes a "satellite."

Possession in this context must be understood in the technical sense of the trance practiced in certain cults. Like Jean-Michel Oughourlian, we must recognize a mimetic manifestation too intense for the perspective of *alienation*, which has been valuable enough, until now, to remain relevant. Alienation implies the vigilance of a self, a subject that is not completely obliterated by this experience and thus experiences it as alienation or slavery. As for the possessed, the invasion by this other, the mimetic model is so total that neither person nor thing can resist it and the perspective becomes inverted. There is no longer a self to be alienated; there is only the other, and the other is at home and there to stay.[3]

The language of the offer is both that of an oath and that of incantatory prayer. It is the language of extreme mimesis. Salome becomes the deity invoked by Herod when he repeats the same words and offers the same formulas:

"Ask me anything you like and I will give it you." And he swore her an oath, "I will give you anything you ask, even half my kingdom."

The person making the offer always has an object or, rather, a person to whom he is particularly attached and whom he wants to keep. Unfortunately, when he formulates his offer, he does not mention this person. He may have actually forgotten him in the frenzy of his desire, or he may fear that his generosity would seem diminished by excluding anything at all that he possessed. Perhaps he does not mention this object for fear of making it desirable. For whatever reason, the spirit of the trance triumphs and the offer is made without any restriction. It would not seem to matter. Compared with the immense riches in the balance, one person could not be considered to have enough value to be chosen in preference to all else.

And yet that is always what happens. Invariably the demand is directed toward that one insignificant being who should not be of interest to anyone inasmuch as no one has mentioned him. Can we lay the blame on destiny, fate, the narrator's perversity, Freud's unconscious? No, there is a simple and perfect explanation: mimetic desire. What makes the object valuable is not its true price but the desires that are already focused on it. Desire need not be pointed out to become visible. Mimetic desires hide their objects from us, since they themselves are hidden, but they cannot hide anything from each other. They seem to defy all the rules of probability by making people either blind or too clairvoyant.

Herod thinks he has concealed his interest in John by throwing him into prison. But Herodias has understood the situation perfectly. The prophet makes much more noise and attracts much more attention from the depths of the prison where the king thought he had hidden him.

3. See Jean-Michel Oughourlian, *Un Mime nommé désir* (Paris: Grasset, 1982).

Mimetic desire is most capable of tying the great knots of traditional drama, which is why real tragedies so closely resemble daily life, if only we knew how to find ourselves in them, or conversely, lose ourselves completely.

An exorbitant offer always receives an apparently modest answer that costs more to satisfy than all the kingdoms of the universe. The value of the demand cannot be measured against worldly things. It is essential to understand that we are dealing with a *sacrifice*. The demand represents the hardest sacrifice for the one who must give up a cherished being. The one who claims the victim is a kind of idol, a Salome, a half-monstrous divinity. The freedom, well-being, and life of the abandoned person are involved. Above all, the demand involves the spiritual integrity of all those concerned. Herod's integrity is already compromised and is destroyed as the prophet is destroyed by the collective murder. The text is therefore written in opposition to sacrifice, as are all the great legends, such as the story of Faust or Don Juan, which contain variations on the theme of the exorbitant offer and the sacrificial demand.

Thus the few modern myths are not real myths because they do not accept the final sacrifice without reservation as do real myths. Instead of reflecting the vision of persecution, they refuse this form of sacrifice and denounce it as an abomination. In this they are influenced by the Gospels.

We always want to eliminate the essential from these legends because it disturbs us. The notion of sacrifice irritates us; we see it as the remains of piety that must be immediately eradicated. We ridicule the idea of the immortal soul claimed by Mephistopheles, and are contemptuous of the Commander's statue and his *festin de pierre*. We do not recognize in this stumbling block our last communal meal. Modern society's last link to religion is found in the idea of scandal so patiently cultivated by scholars. Yet here we remove all flavor from it by our banal treatment.

By removing all traces of sacrifice, the one concept that is worth the effort of investigation, since it controls everything, modern authors transform Faust and Don Juan into merely an imaginary consumerism of women and riches. Notice that this does not prevent them from endlessly criticizing our so-called consumer society, no doubt because it is not purely imaginary and because it has the advantage of supplying what is demanded of it.

The essential in our text is the obvious connection between collective mimeticism, the murder of John the Baptist, and the state of trance brought about by the dance. The dance is identified with the pleasure of the text, of Herod and of the guests. "When the daughter of this same Herodias came in and danced, she delighted Herod and his guests." This pleasure must be interpreted in a stronger sense than Freud's pleasure principle; it has the effect of a spell. When the possessed person abandons himself to the mimetic model, its genius takes possession of him and "rides" him, as is often said in such cases; it begins to dance with him.

Submerged in mimeticism the subject loses awareness of self and purpose. Instead of rivaling the model he is transformed into a harmless marionette; all opposition is abolished and the contradiction of desire dissolves. But where now is the obstacle that was barring the way and pinning him down? The monster must be lurking somewhere; for the experience to be complete the monster must be found and destroyed. At this moment there is always an appetite for sacrifice that requires appeasement, a scapegoat to destroy, or a victim to behead. At this moment of greatest intensity sacrificial mimeticism reigns supreme. For this reason truly profound texts always reach this point.

Mimeticism, at this point, absorbs all the dimensions that might compete with it at a less intense level—sexuality, ambition, psychology, sociology, and ritual itself. This does not mean that by taking the forefront mimeticism removes or "reduces" these other dimensions. They are all implicit in the mimetic analysis and can all become explicit in the same way as the dimension of ritual.

The benefactor never anticipates the demand to be made. He is painfully surprised but incapable of resisting. On learning that the dancer's demand is for the head of John "the king was deeply distressed but, thinking of the oaths he had sworn and of his guests he was reluctant to break his word to her." Herod's desire is to save John. His desire belongs to an earlier stage of the mimetic process. Herod wants to protect John's life whereas Salome wants to destroy it. The desire becomes more murderous as it progresses and affects more individuals such as the crowd of guests. It is this lowest desire that triumphs. Herod does not have the courage to say no to his guests, whose number and prestige intimidate him. In other words he is controlled by mimesis. The guests comprise all the elite of Herod's world. A little earlier in the text Mark took care to enumerate them by categories: "the nobles of his court, his army officers and the leading figures in Galilee." He is trying to suggest to us their enormous potential for mimetic influence; similarly, the Passion story enumerates all the forces of this world that form a coalition against the Messiah. The crowd and the rulers join and meld. It is the crowd that provides the supplement of mimetic energy necessary for Herod's decision. The same energy motivates our text, and it is clearly mimetic in nature.

If Mark describes this in detail, he does so not for the pleasure of telling the story but to clarify the decision to remove the prophet's head. The guests all react identically. At the supreme stage of mimetic crisis they provide the type of crowd that alone can intervene decisively. When the crowd is unanimously murderous the decision always rests with it. Subjected to such formidable pressure Herod can only ratify *nolens volens* the decision of the crowd, just as Pilate does a little later. By yielding to this pressure he loses himself in the crowd; he is no more than the least of its members.

There is no need to look for a *psychology* of the principal characters either. There is no need to believe that John and Jesus are dead because they fell into the hands of particularly malevolent schemers or particularly weak rulers. All of human weakness when faced with the temptation of scapegoats must be revealed and branded. The prophet dies because he has revealed the truth of desire to people who do not want to listen to him. No one ever wants to listen. But the truth he proffers is not sufficient reason for his murder: it is one more, and the most ironic, preferential sign for the selection of a victim. It does not contradict the very problematic character of the mimetic choice that is vividly illustrated by the *delay* in the choice of victim until after the dance.

The lengthy deferral of the choice allows Mark to illustrate both the alpha and omega of desire, its mimetic beginning and its equally mimetic conclusion with a victim. The "What shall I ask?" of Salome indicates that, at that moment, Herodias or anyone else could designate anyone at all. The ultimate designation does not prevent the victim from being passionately adopted at first by Salome and then by all the guests. At this stage even the most resolute of tyrants can no longer effectively resist.

The fact that mimeticism inevitably becomes unanimous is what interests the Gospels. The unanimous mimeticism of the scapegoat is the true ruler of human society. One person's beheading can sometimes cause universal agitation and sometimes calm it. How can that be? The convergence on John's head is only a mimetic illusion, but its unanimous character achieves a real calm from the moment when the actual reason has been lost in the widespread agitation. The diffusion of mimeticism at the height of its intensity guarantees the absence of any real object for the desire. Beyond a certain threshold hate exists without cause. It no longer has need of cause or pretext; there remain only intertwined desires, buttressed against one another. If these desires are divided and set in opposition as they focus on an object they wish to preserve—alive, in order to monopolize it, as in Herod's case, when he imprisons the prophet—then by becoming purely destructive these same desires may be reconciled. This is the terrible paradox of human desires. They can never be reconciled in the preservation of their object but only through its destruction; they can only find agreement at the expense of a victim. "And immediately the king sent a soldier of the guard and gave the orders to bring his head. He went and beheaded him in the prison, and brought his head on a dish, and gave it to the girl; and the girl gave it to her mother."

Whoever reproaches men for their desire is a living scandal for them, the only thing in their opinion that keeps them from being happy. We think no differently today. Being alive, the prophet disturbed all their relations, and, in his death, he facilitates them by becoming this inert and docile object that is circulated on Salome's platter; the guests offer it to one another like the food or drink at Herod's banquet. It becomes the astonishing spectacle that both prevents us from doing what must not be done and incites us to do what it is fitting to do, it is the sacrificial beginning of all such exchanges. The truth of all religious institutions can be found clearly in this text, the truth of myths, rituals, and interdicts. But the text itself does not carry out what it reveals; it sees nothing divine in the mimeticism that gathers men together. It has infinite respect for the victim but is careful not to make him divine.

What interests me most about a murder like John's is its fundamentally religious, rather than cultural, force. I want to show how Mark's text makes explicit reference to this religious force. This is perhaps what is most extraordinary about it. The passage I am thinking of comes not at the end of the story but before it. The account is presented as a kind of *flashback*. Herod is impressed by Jesus' growing reputation:

Meanwhile King Herod had heard about him, since by now his name was well-known. Some were saying, "John the Baptist has risen from the dead, and that is why miraculous powers are at work in him." Others said, "He is Elijah;" others again, "He is a prophet, like the prophets we used to have." (Mark 6:14–16)

Of all the rumored hypotheses, Herod chose the first, according to which Jesus was the resurrected John the Baptist. The text suggests the reason for his choice: Herod thinks that John the Baptist is resurrected because of the role he himself played in his violent death. Persecutors cannot believe in the definitive death of their victims. The resurrection and consecration of the victims are above all phenomena of persecution, the perspective of the persecutors themselves on the violence in which they have participated.

The Gospels of Mark and Matthew do not take the resurrection of John the Baptist seriously, and they do not intend for us to take it seriously either. But they ultimately reveal a process of consecration strangely similar to that which constitutes the main object of the Gospel text, the Resurrection of Jesus and the proclamation of his divinity. The Gospels are quite aware of the resemblances, but feel no discomfort; they have not the slightest doubt. Modern believers scarcely comment on the false resurrection of John the Baptist because, in their eyes, it is insufficiently distinguished from that of Jesus himself; if there is no reason to believe in the resurrection of John, then there is no reason to believe in that of Jesus.

For the Gospels, the difference is obvious. The type of resurrection we are talking about is imposed on the mystified persecutors by their own persecution. Christ's resurrection, on the contrary, succeeds in freeing us of these illusions and superstitions. The Paschal resurrection can only really triumph in the ruins of all other religions based on collective murder.

The false resurrection of John certainly has the sense that I have given it, for it is mentioned a second time in a context that leaves no doubt.

When Jesus came to the region of Caesarea Philippi he put this question to his disciples, "Who do people say the Son of Man is?" And they said, "Some say he is John the Baptist, some Elijah, and others Jeremiah or one of the prophets." "But you," he said, "who do you say I am?" Then Simon Peter spoke up, "You are the Christ," he said, "the Son of the living God." Jesus replied, "Simon son of Jonah, you are a happy man! Because it was not flesh and blood that revealed this to you but my Father in heaven. So I now say to you: You are Peter and on this rock I will build my Church. And the gates of the underworld can never hold out against it. (Matt. 16:13–18)

At the time of this profession of faith John the Baptist is already dead. All the personages that the crowd identified in Jesus are already dead. This means that the crowd believes all to be resurrected in the person of Jesus. Thus it is a belief similar to that of Herod, an imaginary belief in the Resurrection. Luke makes it even more explicit: Jesus, he writes, is believed to be one of the ancient prophets *resurrected*.

The reference to the *powers of death* (or the gates of Hades) seems to me to be significant. It indicates more than just that evil shall not overcome good. In it can be recognized an allusion to the religion of violence, which can only be a religion of the dead and of death. The words of Heraclitus come to mind: *Dionysus is the same as Hades*.

Children recognize the difference between the two religions because violence makes them afraid and Jesus does not make them afraid, but the wise and clever cannot see the difference. They knowledgeably compare themes and, because they find the same themes everywhere, even if they believe themselves to be structuralists, they fail to recognize the real structural difference. They do not see the difference between the hidden scapegoat that John the Baptist represents for those who are ready to worship him after killing him, and the revealed and revealing scapegoat that is the Jesus of the Passion.

Peter recognizes the difference, but this does not prevent his several lapses into the mimetic behavior of all mankind. The extraordinary solemnity of Jesus in this passage shows that the difference Peter perceives will not be seen by all men. The Gospels insist, in fact, on the paradox of faith in the resurrection of Jesus, which, for someone not informed by that faith, is viewed with the same extreme skepticism as apparently very similar phenomena.

CHAPTER TWELVE

Peter's Denial

JESUS QUOTES THE prophet Zechariah to his disciples in order to describe for them what the effect of the Passion will be: "I shall strike the shepherd and the sheep will be scattered" (Zech. 13:7; Mark 14:27). The dispersal takes place immediately after his arrest. The only one not to run away is Peter. He follows the procession at a distance and makes his way into the courtyard of the High Priest while Jesus is being brutally interrogated inside the palace. He manages to enter the courtyard through the auspices of someone familiar with the place, "another disciple" who joined him. The "other disciple" is not mentioned by name but is meant without a doubt to be the apostle John.

Mark tells us that Peter had followed Jesus at a distance, "right into the courtyard of the high priest; and he was sitting with the guards, and warming himself at the fire" (Mark 14:54). Nothing is more natural than this fire on a March evening in Jerusalem. "Now the servants and officers had made a charcoal fire, because it was cold, and they were standing and warming themselves; Peter also was with them, standing and warming himself" (John 18:18).

Peter is already doing what the others are doing, and for the same reasons. He is imitating the others, but there is nothing remarkable about this. It is cold and everyone is huddled around the fire. Peter joins them. At first we are not aware of what should be noticed. Yet the concrete details are all the more significant in a text that provides so few. Three of the four Gospels mention this fire. There must be a reason for this, and we should try to discover it in Mark's text, which is considered the most *primitive*.

While Peter is standing below in the courtyard one of the maids of the high priest arrives. Seeing Peter warming himself, she looks into his face and says:

"You too.were with Jesus, the man from Nazareth." But he denied it. "I do not know, I do not understand, what you are talking about," he said. And he went out into the forecourt. The servant girl saw him and again started telling the bystanders, "This fellow is one of them." But again he denied it. A little later the bystanders themselves said to Peter, "You are one of them for sure! Why, you are a Galilean." But he started calling down curses on himself and swearing, "I do not know the man you speak of." At that moment the cock crew for the second time, and Peter recalled how Jesus had said to him, "Before the cock crows twice, you will have disowned me three times." And he burst into tears. (Mark 14:66–72)

At first we think that Peter is a brazen liar. Peter's denial has forced him to that lie, but there is no such thing as a pure and simple lie, and this one, on second thought, is not that simple. What is actually being asked of Peter? He is being asked to admit that *he was with Jesus*. But since the recent arrest there are no longer disciples or community surrounding Jesus. Neither Peter nor anyone else is truly with Jesus any longer. As we know, existentialists recognize in "the being with" an important modality of being. Martin Heidegger calls it the *Mitsein*, which may be literally translated *the being with*.

Jesus' arrest seems to have destroyed any possible future *being with Jesus*, and Peter seems to have lost all memory of *having been*. He answers as if in a dream, like a man who does not really know where he is: *"I do not know, I do not understand, what you are talking about."* He may well not have understood. He is dispossessed and destitute, reduced to a vegetablelike existence, controlled by elemental reflexes. He feels cold and turns to the fire. Elbowing one's way to the fire and stretching hands toward it with the others is to act like one of them, as if one belongs with them. The simplest gestures have their logic, and that logic is as much sociological as biological, the more powerful because it is situated far beneath the level of consciousness.

All Peter wants is to warm himself with the others but, deprived of his *being with* by the collapse of his universe, he cannot warm himself without wanting obscurely the being that is shining there, in this fire, and the being that is indicated silently by all the eyes staring at him, by all the hands stretched toward the fire.

A fire in the night is much more than a source of heat and light. As soon as it is lit, people arrange themselves in a circle around it; they are no longer a mere crowd, each one alone with himself, they have become a community. Hands and faces are turned toward the fire and in turn are lit by it; it is like a god's benevolent response to a prayer addressed to him. Because everyone is facing the fire, they cannot avoid seeing each other; they can exchange looks and words; a place for communion and communication is established. Because of the fire vague new ways of *being with* become possible. For Peter, *the being with* is re-created but in a different place and with different partners.

Mark, Luke, and John mention this fire a second time, at the moment when, in Mark and Luke, the servant girl appears for the first time. The impression is that it is Peter's presence around the fire rather than in the courtyard that provokes her interference. *"She saw Peter warming himself there, stared at him and said, 'You too were with Jesus, the man from Nazareth.'"* Peter perhaps had pushed his way to the front, and there he was right by the fire, in full light, where everyone could see him. Peter, as always, has gone too far too fast. The fire enabled the servant girl to recognize him in the dark, but that is not its chief role. The servant does not fully understand what scandalizes her in Peter's attitude and forces her to speak to him so insolently, but the fire, in Mark, is certainly there for a purpose. The companion of the Nazarene is behaving as if he were among his own, as if he belonged around this fire. Without the fire the servant girl would not have been so indignant with Peter. The fire is much more than an ordinary background. The *being with* cannot become universal without losing its own value. That is why it is based on exclusions. The servant speaks only of the *being with Jesus*, but there is a second *being with* around the fire; this is what interests the servant girl, because it is hers; she knows how to defend its integrity; that is why she refuses Peter the right to warm himself by the fire.

John makes the servant girl the porter, the guardian of the entrance. She is the one who allows Peter to enter the courtyard on the recommendation of the other disciple. The servant girl in fact plays the role of guardian. The idea in itself is excellent, but it forces the evangelist to maintain that Peter is recognized straight off, before he even approaches the fire. So it is no longer by the light of this fire that the servant recognizes the intruder; it is no longer the intimate and ritual character of the scene that rouses her indignation. Moreover, in John, Peter is questioned a third time not by the whole band of servants but by an individual who is presented as a relative of the man whose ear Peter cut off (in a useless effort to defend Jesus by violence, at the time of arrest). John prefers the traditional interpretation that recognizes only one motive in Peter's denial: fear. Although fear, of course, should not be entirely excluded, it should not be considered to play a decisive role, and careful study of the four versions—not even John's—does not support such an interpretation, despite first appearances. If Peter were truly afraid for his life, as most commentators suggest, he would never have gone into the courtyard, especially if he had already been recognized. He would have felt threatened and left immediately.

On the summons of the servant girl the circle loses its fraternal character. Peter wants to hide himself from sight but the crowd presses around him. He stays too close to the center, and the servant can follow him easily with her eyes as he retreats to the entranceway. Once there, he hesitates and waits for the sequence of events. His conduct is not that of a man who is afraid. Peter moves away from the light and the heat because he senses obscurely what the servant is trying to do, but he does not leave. That is why she can repeat her accusation. She is trying not to terrorize Peter but to embarrass him and to make him go away.

Seeing that Peter is not about to leave, the servant becomes involved and repeats her news a second time. She announces that Peter belongs to the group of disciples: "This man is one of them." The first time she said it directly to Peter, but she intended it for the people around him, those who were warming themselves at the fire, members of the community threatened by the invasion of a stranger. She wanted to mobilize them against the intrusion. The second time she speaks directly to them, and achieves the result she wants; the whole group turns on Peter: "*You are one of them for sure!*" Your *being with* is not here, it is with the Nazarene. In the exchange that follows it is Peter who raises his voice and begins "*calling down curses on himself and swearing.*" If he were afraid for his life, or even for his freedom, he would have spoken less forcefully.

The superiority of Mark's text lies in the fact that he makes the same servant girl speak twice running, instead of putting the words in the mouths of others. His servant girl is more prominent. She shows initiative and stirs up the group. We would say today that she shows leadership qualities. But we should always be wary of psychologizing; it is not the servant's personality that interests Mark but rather the way in which she unleashes the group mechanism, the way she brings collective mimeticism into play.

As I pointed out, the first time she is trying to stir up a group made sluggish by the late hour and the heat of the fire. She wants them to follow her example, and when they do not, she is the first to follow it. Her lesson has no effect, so she repeats it a second time. Leaders know that they must treat those who follow them like children; they must always inspire imitation. The second example reinforces the effect of the first, and this time it works. All the bystanders repeat together: "*You are one of them for sure! Why, you are a Galilean.*"

The mimeticism is not characteristic only of Mark; the denial scene is completely mimetic in all four Gospels, but in Mark the mechanism for releasing the mimeticism is more clearly defined, from the beginning, in the role of the fire and in that of the servant girl. Only Mark makes the servant repeat herself twice in order to prime the mimetic mechanism. She sets herself up as a model and, to make that model more effective, she is the first to imitate it; she emphasizes her own role of model and details mimetically what she expects from her companions.

The students repeat what their mistress tells them. The very words of the servant are repeated but with something extra which reveals wonderfully what is at work in the denial scene: *for you are a Galilean.* Illuminated in the first place by the fire, then revealed by his face, Peter is finally identified by his accent. Matthew, as he does so often, puts on the finishing touches by making Peter's persecutors say: "your accent gives you away." All those who are legitimately warming themselves around the fire are from Jerusalem. That is where they are from. Peter has only spoken twice, and each time only a few words, but it is enough for his listeners to know without a doubt that he is a stranger, a scorned provincial, a Galilean. The person with the accent, any accent, is always the person who *is not from here.* Language is the surest indicator of the *being with.* This is why Heidegger and his colleagues attach such importance to the linguistic dimension of being. The specificity of national or even regional language is fundamental. Everywhere it is said that the essential, in a text or even in a language, that which gives it its value, is untranslatable. The Gospels are seen as inessential because they are written in a cosmopolitan, debased Greek that is deprived of literary prestige. Moreover, they are perfectly translatable, and it is easy to forget what language one is reading them in provided one knows it, whether it is the original Greek, vulgar Latin, French, German, English, or Spanish. When one knows the Gospels, translating them into an unknown language is an excellent way of penetrating the intimacy of that language with as little loss as possible. The Gospels are all things to all people; they have no accent because they are all accents.

Peter is an adult, and he cannot change the way he speaks. He is unable to imitate precisely the accent of the capital. Possession of the desired *being with* is not just saying the same things as everyone else but saying them the same way. The slightest nuance of intonation can betray one. Language is a treacherous servant – or a too faithful one – that always reveals the true identity one tries to conceal.

A mimetic rivalry is unleashed between Peter and his interlocutors and at stake is the *being with* that dances in the flames. Peter tries desperately to "integrate himself," to prove the excellence of his imitation, but his antagonists turn unhesitatingly toward those aspects of cultural mimeticism that cannot be imitated, such as language buried in the unconscious regions of the psyche.

The more deeply rooted, "authentic," and ineradicable is the belonging, the more it is based on idioms that seem profound but are perhaps insignificant, idiocies in both the French and the Greek sense of *idion*, meaning "one's own." The more something becomes our own, the more in fact we belong to it; which does not mean that it is particularly "inexhaustible." In addition to language there is sexuality. John indicates that the servant girl is young, and this may be a significant detail.

We are all possessed of language and sex. Of course, but why always mention it in the tone of the possessed. Maybe we can do better. Peter understands clearly that he cannot deceive the world, and when he denies his master so fiercely, it is not to convince anyone but to sever the bonds that unite him to Jesus and to form others with those around him: *"But he started calling down curses on himself and swearing, 'I do not know the man you speak of.' "*

This is a truly religious bond – *religare*, to bind – and therefore Peter has recourse to curses – like Herod in his exorbitant offer to Salome. His violence and angry gestures are aimed not at Peter's interlocutors but at Jesus himself. Peter makes Jesus his victim in order to stop being the sort of lesser victim that first the servant girl and then the whole group make him. What the crowd does to Peter he would like in turn to do to them but cannot. He is not strong enough to triumph through vengeance. So he tries to conciliate his enemies by allying himself with them against Jesus, by treating Jesus as they want and in front of them, exactly as they themselves treat him. In the eyes of these loyal servants Jesus must be a good-for-nothing since he has been arrested and questioned brutally. The best way to make friends in a hostile world is to espouse the enmities and adopt the others' enemies. What is said to these others, on such occasion, varies very little: "We are all of the same clan, we form one and the same group inasmuch as we have the same scapegoat."

No doubt there is fear at the origin of the denial, but there is also shame. Like Peter's arrogance somewhat earlier, shame is a mimetic sentiment, in fact the most mimetic of sentiments. To experience it I must look at myself through the eyes of whoever makes me feel ashamed. This requires intense imagination, which is the same as servile imitation. Imagine and imitate are in fact one and the same term. Peter is ashamed of this Jesus whom all the world despises, ashamed of the model he chose, and therefore ashamed of himself.

His desire to be accepted is intensified by the obstacles in the way. Peter is therefore ready to pay very dearly for the admission denied him by the servant and her friends, but the intensity of his desire is completely local and temporary, roused by the excitement of the game. This is one of those small acts of cowardice that everyone commits and no one remembers. We should not be surprised at Peter's petty betrayal of his master; we all do the same thing. What is astonishing is that the sacrificial structure of persecution remains intact in the denial scene and is transcribed as a whole just as accurately as in the murder of John the Baptist or in the Passion story.

Certain words of Matthew must be interpreted in the light of this structural identity; their legal significance is merely their appearance. What Jesus is really saying to people is the structural equivalent of all persecution behavior:

"You have learned how it was said to our ancestors: *You must not kill*; and if anyone does kill he must answer for it before the court. But I say this to you: anyone who is angry with his brother will answer for it before the court; if a man calls his brother 'Fool' he will answer for it before the Sanhedrin; and if a man calls him 'Renegade' he will answer for it in hell fire." (Matt. 5:21–22)

The best way not to be crucified, in the final analysis, is to do as everyone else and join in the crucifixion. The denial therefore is one episode of the Passion, a kind of eddy, a brief swirl in the vast current of mimeticism of the victim that carries everyone toward Golgotha.

The formidable power of the text is confirmed immediately in that its true significance cannot be ignored without repercussion, without reproducing the structure of denial itself. More often than not this ends in a "psychology of the prince of the Apostles." Determining someone's psychology is always to a certain degree a trial. Peter's ends in acquittal diluted with blame. Peter is not completely at fault, nor is he completely absolved. He cannot be counted on. He is changeable, impulsive, somewhat weak in character. In other words he is like Pilate, and Pilate is somewhat like Herod, who resembles anyone at all. Nothing is more monotonous or simplistic in the last analysis than this mimetic psychology of the Gospels. It may not be a psychology at all. From a distance it takes on the infinite variety of the world that is so amusing, engaging, and enriching. Close up, the same elements can be recognized in our own lives and are, to tell the truth, scarcely amusing.

Around the fire the usual religion, which is inevitably mixed with sacrifices, surfaces, in defense of language and the *lares*, the purity of the familial cult. Peter is naturally attracted by all this, just as we presumably are, since we reproach the biblical god for depriving us of it. Out of wickedness, we say. It takes real wickedness to reveal the dimension of persecution in this immemorial religion which still holds us under its sway by indescribable bonds. The Gospel is not gentle with persecutors, who are ashamed like ourselves. It unearths even in our most ordinary behavior today, around the fire, the ancient gesture of the Aztec sacrificers and witch-hunters as they forced their victims into the flames.

Like all deserters, Peter demonstrates the sincerity of his conversion by blaming his old friends. We understand the moral implications of the denial, we must also understand the anthropological dimension. With his oaths and curses, Peter is inviting those who surround him to form a *conjuration*. Any group of men bound by oath forms the *conjuration*, but the term is applied most readily when the group unanimously adopts as their goal the death or loss of a prominent person. The word is equally applied to rites of demonic expulsion and to magical practices intended to counter magic.

The experience of innumerable rites of initiation consists of an act of violence, putting an animal to death, or sometimes even a man recognized as the adversary of the whole group. To achieve that belonging the initiate must transform the adversary into a victim. Peter resorts to oaths or religious formulas to endow his denial with its initiatory force among his persecutors.

If we are to interpret the denial accurately, we must take into account all that has gone before in the synoptics, especially in the two scenes in which it is directly prepared and indicated. These are the two chief announcements of the Passion by Jesus himself. The first time, Peter does not want to understand: "Heaven preserve you, Lord, this must not happen to you." His reaction is the same as that of all the disciples. Inevitable at the beginning the ideology of success dominates this little world. They argue over the best places in the Kingdom of God. They are mobilized for the good cause. The whole community is in the grasp of mimetic desire and so is blind to the true nature of the revelation. Jesus is seen above all as the miracle worker, the great leader, the political chief.

The faith of the disciples is clothed in triumphant messianism. It is nonetheless real for all this. Peter has shown us this, but a part of him is still weighing the adventure he is about to experience in terms of worldly success. What is the sense of a commitment that only ends in failure, suffering, or death?

On this occasion Peter is severely reprimanded: "Get behind me, Satan! You are an obstacle in my path"; [*you scandalize me*] (Matt. 16:23). When it is proved to Peter that he is wrong, he immediately changes direction and begins to run in the opposite direction at the same speed as before. At the second announcement of the Passion, only a few hours before the arrest, Peter does not react in the least as he did the first time. "*You will all lose faith in me this night*"[*be scandalized*]. Jesus said to them:

At this, Peter said, "Though all lose faith in you, I will never lose faith." Jesus answered him, "I tell you solemnly, this very night before the cock crows, you will have disowned me three times." Peter said to him, "Even if I have to die with you, I will never disown you." And all the disciples said the same. (Matt. 26:33–36)

Peter's apparent conviction becomes one with the intensity of his mimeticism. The "argument" has been reversed since the first announcement, but the basis has not changed. It is the same with all the disciples, who always repeat what Peter says, since they are as mimetic as he. They imitate Jesus through the intermediary of Peter.

Jesus perceives that this zeal is heavy with the desertion that will follow. He understands that his worldly prestige will collapse with his arrest and he will no longer be the sort of model for his disciples that he has been until now. Every mimetic incitement comes from an individual or group that is hostile to his person or his message. The disciples, and particularly Peter, are too easily influenced not to be influenced yet again. The text of the Gospel has shown this in the passages I have discussed. The fact that the model is Jesus himself is unimportant so long as it is imitated out of a conquering greed which is always basically identical with the alienation of desire.

Peter's first about-face, admittedly, is not in itself blameworthy, but it is not exempt from mimetic desire, and Jesus clearly sees this. He sees in it the promise of another about-face, which can only take the form of a denial, given the catastrophe that is about to occur. Thus the denial can be rationally predicted. In foreseeing it as he does, Jesus is only outlining for the immediate future the consequences of what he has observed. Jesus, in other words, makes the same analysis as we do: he compares Peter's successive reactions to the announcement of the Passion in order to deduce his probable betrayal. The proof of this is that the prophesy of his denial is a direct answer to the second mimetic exhibition of Peter's, and the reader draws on the same details as Jesus does to form his opinion. If we understand mimetic desire we cannot fail to draw the same conclusions. We are therefore led to believe that the character called Jesus understands this desire in the sense that we understand it. This understanding reveals the rationality of the link between the elements of the sequence formed by the two announcements of the Passion, the prophesy of the denial, and the denial itself.

From Jesus' perspective mimetic desire is unquestionably involved, since he resorts to the term that designates this desire, *scandal*, every time he describes Peter's reactions, including the denial: *You will all scandalize yourselves because of me this night*. And you will be scandalized all the more surely because you are already victims of scandal. Your certainty that you are not, your illusion of invulnerability, says much of your real condition and the future that is building. The myth of individual difference that Peter is defending here when he says *I myself* is itself mimetic. Peter feels he is the most authentic of all the disciples, the most capable of being the true emulator of Jesus, the only one really to possess the ontological model.

By rivaling each other in their theatrical show of affection the evil sisters in *King Lear* persuade their father that they love him passionately. The poor man imagines their rivalry is fed by genuine affection, when the reverse is true. Pure rivalry produces a phantom affection. Jesus is never cynical, nor is he ever taken in by this kind of illusion. Without confusing Peter with one of the twins from Lear, we should nevertheless recognize in him the puppet of a similar desire, which, because he is unaware of it, possesses him. He perceives the truth only later, after the denial, when he weeps bitterly at the thought of his master and the prophesy.

In the great scene where Peter and the disciples display a false eagerness for the Passion, the Gospels suggest a satire of a certain religious fervor which must be recognized as specifically "Christian." The disciples invent a new religious language, the language of the Passion. They renounce the ideology of happiness and success but create a very similar ideology of suffering and failure, a new social and mimetic mechanism that functions exactly like the former exultation.

All the forms of adherence that men in groups can give to an enterprise are declared unworthy of Jesus. These attitudes are seen over and over again during the course of the history of Christianity, especially in our day. The new manners of the disciples are reminiscent of the triumphant anti-exultation of certain current Christian movements, their very clerical anticlericalism. The fact that these sorts of attitudes are stigmatized in the Gospels indicates that Christian inspiration at its greatest has no connection with its psychological and sociological by-products.

THE ONE MIRACLE in the message of the denial is the same as the science of desire seen in the words of Jesus. Because that science was not fully understood in the Gospels, it took the form of a miracle in the narrow sense. "this very night, before the cock crows, you will have disowned me three times. Such miraculous precision in the prophetic announcement eclipses the higher rationality revealed by textual analysis. There are, however, too many details that contribute to that rationality to ignore it. The convergence of the content of the narratives with the theory of *skandalon*—the theory of mimetic desire—cannot be fortuitous. We are forced therefore to question whether the authors of the Gospels fully understood the scope of this desire which is revealed in their texts.

The extraordinary importance given to the cock, first by the Gospels and later by the whole of posterity, suggests a lack of total comprehension. This relative lack of understanding transforms the cock into a sort of animal fetish around which a certain "miracle" is crystallized.

In the Jerusalem of that time, we are told, the first and second cock-crows indicated simply certain hours of the night. Thus originally the reference to the cock may have had nothing to do with a real animal crowing. In his Latin translation, Jerome makes this cock crow one more time than in the original Greek. One of the two times the cock crows is not mentioned and, on his own initiative, the translator corrects what seems to him to be an inadmissible, scandalous omission. The other three evangelists probably felt that Mark had given too much importance to the cock. To put the cock in its place they make it crow only once but do not dare omit it altogether. John finally mentions it, although he leaves out any mention of the entire prophesy of the denial, without which the cock has no reason for being.

There is no reason to treat a prediction that has a perfectly reasonable explanation as miraculous unless, of course, one fails to perceive the mimetic reasons for the denial and its antecedents in Peter's behavior. Why would an author make into a miracle a prediction that can be rationally explained? The most likely explanation is that he probably did not understand that rationality, or understand it fully. This is what I think happened in the story of the denial. The writer perceived but could not identify a continuity underlying the apparent discontinuities in Peter's conduct. He saw the importance of the concept of scandal but could not master its application and was satisfied with repeating word for word what he understood from Jesus himself or the primary intermediary. The writer also did not understand the role of the cock, which was less serious. But the two examples of incomprehension combine naturally in the one outcome of the miracle of the cock. Both instances correspond so well in their lack of clarity that, ultimately, each seems to explain the other in a supernatural fashion. The tangible yet inexplicable cock polarizes the diffuse, unaccountable quality of the whole scene. Men tend to see a miracle in everything they don't understand. One apparently mysterious but concrete detail is enough to bring about a mythological crystallization. Thus the cock becomes a kind of fetish.

Inevitably, my analysis is speculative. But there are indications in the Gospels that encourage such speculation. Jesus is critical of the disciples' excessive taste for miracles and of their inability to understand the teaching imparted to them. These are the two weaknesses or, rather, two faces of the one weakness that must be identified if we are to understand the inclusion of a kind of miracle in a scene that has no need of one. The superfluous presence of the miracle detracts from the denial scene because it pushes into the background that wonderful comprehension of human behavior to be found in the text. The miracle fosters intellectual and even spiritual laziness among believers and nonbelievers alike.

The text of the Gospels was developed in the environment of the early disciples. Even after the clarification of the Pentecostal experience, the first and second generations of Christians were aware of their own shortcomings, which had been pointed out by Jesus himself. The texts do not emphasize the unintelligibility of the revelation, even for the most alert, in order to humiliate the first disciples or diminish them in any way in the eyes of posterity. They do so in order to suggest the distance separating Jesus and his spirit from those who were the first to receive his message and transmit it to us. We cannot afford to ignore this indication when we interpret the Gospels, some two thousand years later, in a world that has no more natural intelligence than in the time of Jesus but is nonetheless capable for the first time of hearing certain aspects of his doctrine because they have slowly penetrated over the course of centuries. These are obviously not the aspects that occur to us when we think of "Christianity" or even "the Gospels," but they are extremely necessary if we are to have a better understanding of such texts as the denial scene.

If I am right and the evangelists did not understand clearly the rationality of the denial and the prophesy Jesus made, then our text is astonishing in that it relates simultaneously both the miracle imposed on the scene by writers who did not understand its logic and the details that permit us today to trace that logic. The Gospels put into our hands all the parts of a document they are not quite capable of interpreting since they substitute an irrational interpretation for the rational one we extract from the same details. I am forever aware that we can say nothing about Jesus that does not come from the Gospels.

Our text adds a miraculous explanation to a scene that is better understood without the aid of this miracle. The writers of the Gospels, therefore, despite their inability to understand, must have put together and transcribed the pieces of the document with a remarkable accuracy. If I am right, their inadequacy on certain particular points is compensated for by an extraordinary fidelity on all other points.

At first sight, this combination of qualities and defects seems hard to reconcile, but a moment's reflection is enough to convince us that it is not only likely but also probable, for the very reason that the writing of the Gospels was influenced by the very same mimeticism that was the subject of Jesus' endless reproaches to his disciples, the same mimeticism that we see in their behavior. It is normal that with the best will in the world they did not fully understand its function since they had not yet freed themselves from it.

If my reading is accurate, the mythical crystallization around the cock derives from a phenomenon of mimetic exacerbation similar to the examples given us in the Gospels. In the murder of John the Baptist, for example, the motif of the head on the platter results from a too-literal imitation. For absolute fidelity, the passage from one individual to another, or the translation from one language to another, demands a certain distance. The transcriber who is too absorbed in his model and therefore too close to him reproduces all the details with an admirable accuracy but is subject to occasional lapses that are truly mythological. The powerful mimetic attention or extreme concentration on the victim-model results in the primitive custom of making the victim sacred, the scapegoat whose innocence is not recognized becomes divine.

The strengths and weaknesses of the Gospel witness can be found in a particularly precise and clear form in the treatment of the concept that is crucial for the mimetic reading: scandal. The most interesting uses of *skandalon* and *scandalidzein* are all attributed to Jesus himself, and they appear as fragments gathered in a somewhat arbitrary fashion. Important sentences do not always follow in a logical sequence, and their order is frequently different from one Gospel to another. Scholars have shown that this order can be determined by the presence in a phrase of a single word which is then followed by another sentence, only because the same word appears in it. This gives an impression of sentences learned by heart and joined together by mnemonic means.

In order to understand the value of scandal in explaining, therefore, all these sentences must be reorganized. They must be treated like pieces of a puzzle which is the mimetic theory itself, once the correct arrangement has been found. This is what I tried to show in *Des choses cachées*...

We are therefore dealing with an extraordinarily coherent unity that was never perceived by the exegetes because its components are muddled, and sometimes a little deformed, due to the authors' lack of control. When left to themselves these authors tell us vaguely that *Jesus knows what is in man*, but they explain this knowledge poorly. They have all the details in their hands, but these are disorganized and contaminated with miracles because the authors have only partial control over them.

There is an irreducible supernatural dimension to the Gospels that I do not wish to deny or denigrate. But because of this we should not refuse the means of comprehension now available to us which can only

decrease the role of the miraculous if they are truly means of comprehension. The miraculous by definition is the unintelligible; it is not
therefore the true work of the spirit according to the Gospel meaning.
There is a greater miracle than the narrowly defined miracle and that is
something becoming intelligible that was not so – mythological obscurity becoming transparent.

Confronted with the text of the Gospels, proponents and opponents
alike only want to see the miracle and unequivocally condemn even the
most legitimate effort to show that its role may be exaggerated. But
rational suspicion is in no way contrary to the Gospels which themselves
warn us against abuse of the miraculous. The rationality I am disclosing, the mimeticism of human relations, is too systematic in principle,
too complex in its effects, and too visibly present, both in the "theoretical" passages on scandal and in the accounts entirely controlled by it, to
be there by accident. Nevertheless this rationality was not completely
devised or created by those who put it there. If they had understood it
fully they would not have interposed between their readers and the
scenes we have just read the coarse presence of the miraculous cock.

Under these circumstances the Gospels cannot be the product of a
work that was purely within the effervescent milieu of the early Christians. At the text's origin there must have been someone outside the
group, a higher intelligence that controlled the disciples and inspired
their writings. As we succeed in reconstituting the mimetic theory in a
kind of coming and going between the narratives and the theoretical
passages, the words attributed to Jesus, we are disclosing the traces of
that intelligence, not the reflections of the disciples.

The Gospel writers are the necessary intermediaries between ourselves and him whom they call Jesus. But in the example of Peter's
denial, and in all of its antecedents, their insufficiency becomes a positive quality. It increases the credibility and power of the witness. The
failure of the Gospel writers to understand certain things, together with
their extreme accuracy in most cases, makes them somewhat passive intermediaries. Through their relative lack of comprehension we cannot
help but think that we can attain directly a level of comprehension
greater than theirs. We have the impression therefore of a communication without intermediaries. We gain this privilege not through an intrinsically superior intelligence but as the result of two thousand years
of a history slowly fashioned by the Gospels themselves.

There is no need for this history to unfold according to the principles of conduct articulated by Jesus; it need not become a utopia before making accessible to us aspects of the Gospel text that were not accessible to the first disciples. It is sufficient that there has been a gradual but continual growth of awareness of the representation of persecutions by persecutors which continues to grow without, unfortunately, preventing us from engaging in persecution ourselves.

In those passages that suddenly become clear, the Gospel text is somewhat like a password communicated by go-betweens who are not included in the secret. Those of us who receive the password are all the more grateful because the messenger's ignorance guarantees the authenticity of the message. We have the joyous certainty that nothing essential can have been falsified. My image is not a good one, however, for if a sign is to become a password it is sufficient to modify its sense by a conventional decision, whereas here there is a whole collection of signs, formerly inert and colorless, that suddenly catch fire and shine with intelligence, without any preliminary convention. A festival of light is lit around us to celebrate the resurrection of a meaning that we did not even know was dead.

CHAPTER THIRTEEN

The Demons of Gerasa

THE GOSPELS REVEAL all kinds of human relationships that at first seem incomprehensible and fundamentally irrational. These can and must ultimately be reduced to a single unifying factor: mimeticism. Mimeticism is the original source of all man's troubles, desires, and rivalries, his tragic and grotesque misunderstandings, the source of all disorder and therefore equally of all order through the mediation of scapegoats. These victims are the spontaneous agents of reconciliation, since, in the final paroxysm of mimeticism, they unite in opposition to themselves those who were organized in opposition to each other by the effects of a previous weaker mimeticism.

These are the underlying dynamics of all mythological and religious beginnings, dynamics that other religions succeed in concealing from themselves and from us by suppressing or disguising collective murders and minimizing or eliminating the stereotypes of persecution in a hundred different ways. The Gospels, on the other hand, expose these same dynamics with an unequaled severity and strength.

Peter's denial, the murder of John the Baptist, and, above all, the Passion itself, the true heart and center of this revelation, delineate the lines of force with an almost didactic insistence. It is a question of forcing people who from time immemorial have been imprisoned by mythological representations of persecution to accept certain decisive truths that would prevent them from making their own victims sacred and thereby free them.

Each of the Gospel stories reveals a religious origin that must remain hidden if mythology and ritual are to be the result. This origin is based on the unanimous belief in the victim's guilt, a belief that the

Gospels destroy forever. There is no common ground between what happens in the Gospels and what happens in myths, particularly the more developed myths. Later religions diminish, minimize, soften, and even totally eliminate sacred guilt as well as any trace of violence; but these are minor dissimulations and bear no relation to the system of representing persecution. This system collapses in the world of the Gospels. There is no longer any question of softening or sublimation. Rather, a return to truth is made possible by a process which, in our lack of understanding, we consider primitive simply because it reproduces the violent origin once more, this time in order to reveal it and thus make it inoperative.

The texts we have just read are all examples of this process. They correspond perfectly to the way in which Jesus himself, and after him Paul in the Epistles, defines the effect of disintegration that the Crucifixion had on the forces of this world. The Passion reveals the scapegoat mechanism, i.e., that which should remain invisible if these forces are to maintain themselves. By revealing that mechanism and the surrounding mimeticism, the Gospels set in motion the only textual mechanism that can put an end to humanity's imprisonment in the system of mythological representation based on the false transcendence of a victim who is made sacred because of the unanimous verdict of guilt.

This transcendence is mentioned directly in the Gospels and the New Testament. It is even given many names, but the main one is Satan, who would not be considered simultaneously *murderer from the beginning, father of lies, and prince of this world* were he not identified with the false transcendence of violence. Nor is it by chance that, of all Satan's faults, envy and jealousy are the most in evidence. Satan could be said to incarnate mimetic desire were that desire not, by definition, disincarnate. It empties all people, all things, and all texts of their substance.

When the false transcendence is envisaged in its fundamental unity, the Gospels call it the devil or Satan, but when it is envisaged in its multiplicity then the mention is always of demons or demonic forces. The word *demon* can obviously be a synonym for Satan, but it is mostly applied to inferior forms of the "power of this world," to the degraded manifestations that we would call psychopathological. By the very fact that transcendence appears in multiple and fragmented form, it loses its strength and dissolves into pure mimetic disorder. Thus, unlike Satan, who is seen as principle of both order and disorder, the demonic forces are invoked at times when disorder predominates.

Since the Gospels give to these "forces" names that come from religious tradition and magic belief they would still appear to recognize them as autonomous, spiritual entities, endowed with individual personality. On every page of the Gospels we see demons speaking, questioning Jesus, begging him to leave them in peace. In the great temptation-in-the-desert scene Satan appears *in person* to seduce the Son of God with false promises and divert him from his mission.

Far from destroying magic superstitions and vulgar forms of religious beliefs the Gospels seem to reintroduce this type of belief in a particularly pernicious form. The witch-hunters of the late Middle Ages, after all, based the justification for their activities on the demonology and satanism of the Gospels. For many people, especially today, the swarms of demons "obscure the luminous aspect of the Gospels," and Jesus' miraculous cures are hard to distinguish from the traditional exorcisms of primitive societies. None of the miracles appears in my commentaries so far. Some critics have remarked on this and suggested, naturally, that I am avoiding an encounter that would not support my thesis; by choosing my texts with extreme care in order to avoid all the others, I confer a false probability on perspectives that are too contrary to good sense to be taken seriously.

In order to provide as conclusive a proof as possible I will once more refer to Mark. Of the four evangelists Mark is most fond of miracles, devotes the most time to them, and presents them in the fashion that is most contrary to modern sensibility. Perhaps the most spectacular of all the miraculous cures to be found in Mark is the episode of the *demons of Gerasa*. The text is long enough and contains enough concrete details to provide commentators with a grasp that is lacking in the shorter episodes.

Gerasa is one of those texts that is always alluded to with terms such as "wild," "primitive," "backward," "superstitious," and all the typical adjectives which positivists apply to religion in general, no matter what the origin, but which, because they are considered too pejorative for the non-Christian religions, will in the future be reserved for Christianity. My analysis will focus on Mark, but I will refer to Luke and Matthew each time their version provides interesting variants. After crossing the sea of Galilee, Jesus lands on the west bank, in heathen territory, in the country of Decapolis:

And no sooner had he left the boat than a man with an unclean spirit came out from the tombs toward him. The man lived in the tombs and no one could secure him any more, even with a chain; because he had often been secured with fetters and chains but had snapped the chains and broken the fetters, and no one had the strength to control him. All night and all day, among the tombs and in the mountains, he would howl and gash himself with stones. Catching sight of Jesus from a distance, he ran up and fell at his feet and shouted at the top of his voice, "What do you want with me, Jesus, son of the Most High God? Swear by God you will not torture me!"– For Jesus had been saying to him, "Come out of the man, unclean spirit." "What is your name?" Jesus asked. "My name is legion," he answered, "for there are many of us." And he begged him earnestly not to send them out of the district. Now there was there on the mountainside a great herd of pigs feeding, and the unclean spirits begged him, "Send us to the pigs, let us go into them." So he gave them leave. With that, the unclean spirits came out and went into the pigs, and the herd of about two thousand pigs charged down the cliff into the lake, and there they were drowned. The swineherds ran off and told their story in the town and in the country around about; and the people came to see what had really happened. They came to Jesus and saw the demoniac sitting there, clothed and in his full senses—the very man who had had the legion in him before—and they were afraid. And those who had witnessed it reported what had happened to the demoniac and what had become of the pigs. Then they began to implore Jesus to leave the neighborhood. (Mark 5:1–17)

The possessed lived among the tombs. This fact impressed Mark, and he repeats it three times. The wretched man, night and day, was always among the tombs. He comes out of the tombs to meet Jesus. He is freer than any other man since he has broken all the chains, despised all rules, and even, according to Luke, wears no clothes, yet he is possessed, a prisoner of his own madness. This man is a living corpse. His state can be recognized as one of the phenomena of the mimetic crisis that leads to the loss of differentiation and to persecution. There is no longer any difference between life and death, freedom and captivity. Yet existence in the tombs, far from human habitation, is not a permanent phenomenon, the result of a single and definitive break between the possessed and the community. Mark's text suggests that the Gerasenes and their demoniac have been settled for some time in a sort of cyclical pathology. Luke gives it even greater emphasis when he presents the possessed as a *man from the town* and tell us that a demon *had driven him into the wilds* only during his bad spells. Demonic possession abolishes a difference between life within and without the city, a difference that is not unimportant since it is mentioned again later in the text.

Luke's description implies intermittent spells, with periods of remission, during which the sick man returns to the city. "It was a devil that had seized on him a great many times, and then they used to secure him with chains and fetters to restrain him, but he would always break the fastenings, and the devil would drive him out into the wilds" (Luke 8:29–30). The Gerasenes and their demoniac periodically repeat the same crisis in more or less the same fashion. When the men of the city suspect that another departure is at hand, they try to prevent it by binding their fellow citizen with chains and fetters. They do this to *restrain him*, we are told. Why do they want to *restrain him?* The reason seems quite clear. Curing a sick man requires removal of the symptoms of his sickness. In this case the chief symptom is the wandering in the mountains and the tombs. This is what the Gerasenes are trying to prevent with their chains. The sickness is so terrible they have no hesitation in resorting to violence. But clearly this is not the best method: each time their victim overcomes every effort to hold him back. Recourse to violence only increases his desire for solitude and the strength of that desire, so that the unfortunate man becomes truly indomitable. "And no one had the strength to subdue him," Mark tells us.

The repetitive character of these phenomena is somewhat ritualistic. All the actors know exactly what is going to happen in each episode and behave appropriately so that in fact everything happens as it did before. It is difficult to believe that the Gerasenes cannot find chains and fetters strong enough to hold their prisoner. Perhaps they are ashamed of their violence and do not exert the energy needed to make it effective. Whatever the reason, they seem to behave like sick men whose every action fosters rather than decreases the disease. All rituals tend to be transformed into theatrical performances in which the actors play their parts with all the more exuberance for having played them *so many times before*. This does not mean that the participants do not experience real suffering. The drama would not be as effective as it obviously is if there were not moments of real suffering for the city and its surroundings, in other words for the community. The Gerasenes are consternated at the idea of their being deprived of the suffering. They must gain some enjoyment from this drama and even feel the need of it since they beg Jesus to leave immediately and stop interfering in their affairs. Their request is paradoxical, given that Jesus had just succeeded, without any violence, in obtaining the result which they had professed to be aiming at with their chains and fetters but which, in reality, they did not want at all: the complete cure of the possessed man. In this episode, as always, Jesus' presence reveals the truth of the hidden desires. Simeon's prophesy is once more confirmed. "You see this child: he is destined...to be a sign that is rejected...so that the secret thoughts of many may be laid bare."

But what is the meaning of this drama, what is its role on the symbolic plane? The sick man runs among the tombs and on the mountains, Mark tells us, always crying out and *bruising himself with stones*. In Jean Starobinski's remarkable commentary on this text he gives a perfect definition for this strange conduct: *autolapidation*.[1] But why would anyone want to stone himself? Why would one be obsessed with stoning? When the possessed breaks his bonds and escapes from the community he must expect to be pursued by those who tried to chain him. Such may actually be the case. He is fleeing from the stones that his pursuers may be throwing at him. The unfortunate Job was followed and stoned by the inhabitants of his village. Nothing similar is mentioned in the story of Gerasa. Perhaps because he never does become the object of stoning, the demoniac wounds himself with stones. In mythical fashion he maintains the peril with which he believes himself to be threatened.

Has he been the object of real threats, has he survived an aborted attempt at stoning like the adulterous woman in the Gospel of John, or is it, in this case, a purely imaginary fear, a simple *phantasm*? If it is a phantasm then I must ask the psychoanalyst whether the phantasm is the same among societies that practice stoning as among those that do not. Perhaps the possessed said to his fellow citizens: "Look, there's no need to treat me the way you wish, there's no need to stone me; I will carry out your sentence on myself. The punishment I will inflict on myself will be far more horrible than any you would dream of inflicting on me."

Notice the mimetic character of this behavior. As if he is trying to avoid being expelled and stoned in reality, the possessed brings about his own expulsion and stoning; he provides a spectacular mime of all the stages of punishment that Middle Eastern societies inflict on criminals whom they consider completely defiled and irredeemable. First, the man is hunted, then stoned, and finally he is killed; this is why the possessed lived among the tombs. The Gerasenes must have some understanding of why they are reproached or they would not respond as they do. Their mitigated violence is an ineffective protest. Their answer is: "No, we do not want to stone you because we want *to keep you* near us.

1. Jean Starobinski, "La Démoniaque de Gérasa," in *Analyse structurale et exégèse biblique* (Neuchatel: LABOR FIDES, 1971), pp. 63–94.

No ostracism hangs over you." Unfortunately, like anyone who feels wrongfully yet feasibly accused, the Gerasenes protest violently, they protest their good faith with violence, thereby reinforcing the terror of the possessed. Proof of their awareness of their own contradiction lies in the fact that the chains are never strong enough to convince their victim of their good intentions toward him.

The violence of the Gerasenes is hardly reassuring for the possessed. Reciprocally, the violence of the possessed disturbs the Gerasenes. As always, each one tries to end violence with a violence that should be definitive but instead perpetuates the circularity of the process. A symmetry can be seen in all these extremes, the self-laceration and the running among the tombs on the one hand, the grandiloquent chains on the other. There is a sort of conspiracy between the victim and his torturers to keep the balance in the game because it is obviously necessary to keep the balance of the Gerasene community.

The possessed does violence to himself as a reproach to the Gerasenes for their violence. The Gerasenes return his reproach with a violence that reinforces his own and somehow verifies the accusation and counteraccusation that circulate endlessly within the system. The possessed imitates these Gerasenes who stone their victims, but the Gerasenes in return imitate the possessed. A mirror relationship of doubles links the persecutors who are persecuted and the persecuted who persecutes. This is an example of the reciprocal relationship of mimetic rivalry. It is not a relationship of the stoned with those who stone him, but it is almost the same thing since, on the one hand, there is a violent parody of stoning and, on the other, the no-less-violent denial. This is a variant of violent expulsion that has the same aim as the other variants, including stoning.

If I am mistaken in my identification of mimetic doubles in the context of the demons of Gerasa, the mistake is not mine alone. It is shared in at least one of the Gospels, Matthew, when there is mention at the end of the miracle of a significant variant. Matthew substitutes for the single demoniac in Mark and Luke two identical possessed beings and has them speak for themselves instead of the demon – two demons – who are supposed to possess them. There is nothing to suggest a source different from Mark's. Rather it is an attempt to explicate (I wanted to say demystify) the demonic theme in general. In texts like the Gerasa text Matthew is often different from Mark, either in his suppression of a detail he considers worthless or in the explanatory twist he gives to the

themes he retains, so that they are both the themes and his own explica-
tion. We saw one example in the murder of John the Baptist. Matthew
substitutes the expression "prompted by her mother" for the exchange of
questions and answers which, in Mark, suggests somewhat enigmati-
cally the mimetic transmission of desire between mother and daughter.

Matthew is doing much the same thing here but much more auda-
ciously. He wants to suggest what we ourselves have learned during our
readings. Possession is not an individual phenomenon; it is the result of
aggravated mimeticism. There are always at least two beings who possess each other reciprocally, each is the other's scandal, his model-
obstacle. Each is the other's demon; that is why in the first part of Matthew's account the demons are not distinct from those they possess:

> When he reached the country of the Gadarenes on the other side, two
> demoniacs came toward him out of the tombs—creatures so fierce that no one
> could pass that way. They stood there shouting, "What do you want with us,
> Son of God? Have you come here to torture us before the time?" (Matt. 8:28)

The proof that Matthew considers the possession to be a function
of the mimeticism of doubles and of the stumbling block lies in the fact
that what he adds can be found neither in Mark's nor in Luke's text:
those that came to meet Jesus, he tells us, were "so fierce that no one
could pass that way." In other words these are essentially people who bar
the way, like Peter with Jesus when he advised against the Passion.
These are people who are each other's and their neighbors' scandal.
Scandal is always contagious; those who are scandalized are likely to
communicate their desire to you, or, in other words, drag you along their
same path so that they become your model-obstacle and in turn scandalize you. Every reference in the Gospels to the way that is barred, the in-
surmountable obstacle, the stone too heavy to be raised, is an allusion to
the whole concomitant system of scandal.

In order to explain possession through the mimeticism of scandal,
Matthew turns to the minimal mimetic relationship, to what might be
called its basic unit. He endeavors to return to the source of the evil.
This movement is not generally understood since it reverses the mythological practice of today's psychology and psychoanalysis. The latter in-
teriorize the double; they have need of an imaginary demon within
consciousness or the unconscious. Matthew exteriorizes the demon in a
real mimetic relationship between two real individuals.

Matthew improves the account of the miracle on this one major point or, rather, he prepares an analysis of it. He teaches us that duality cannot help but be present at the very outset of mimetic play. What is interesting is that, precisely because he introduces duality at the very beginning of his account, this writer then finds himself in difficulty in trying to introduce the multiplicity that is indispensable for the unfolding of the miracle. He has to eliminate Mark's key sentence: "My name is Legion; for there are many of us" which contributes so much to the fame of the text with its strange transition from singular to plural. This break is again found in the following sentence, which repeats indirectly the sequel to the proposals the demon is supposed to have made to Jesus: "and he begged him earnestly not to send them out of the district."

Nowhere in Matthew, or in Luke who is closer to Mark, do we find the one essential detail that the demon is actually many although he speaks as a single person, and, in a way, is only one person. By not including the crowd of demons Matthew loses the justification for the drowning of the herd of swine, yet he retains that action. In fact, he ultimately loses more than he gains. He seems to be aware of his failure and cuts the miracle short. Like all Mark's strokes of genius, such as Salome's question to her mother: "What shall I ask?", this juxtaposition of singular and plural in the same sentence may seem like a clumsy inclusion that has been eliminated by Luke who is generally more skillful and correct than Mark in his manipulation of the language. "'Legion,' he said – because many devils had gone into him. And these pleaded with him not to order them to depart into the Abyss" (Luke 8:30–31).

In his commentary on Mark, Jean Starobinski clearly shows the negative connotations of the word *Legion*. It indicates "the warlike mob, the hostile troop, the occupying army, the Roman invader, and perhaps even those who crucified Christ."[2] The critic rightly observes the important role played by the crowd not only in the history of the demoniac but also in the immediately preceding and succeeding texts. The healing in itself is portrayed as a single combat between Jesus and the demon, but before and after there is always a crowd around Jesus. First there was the crowd of Galileans whom the disciples sent away in order to get into the boat with Jesus. As soon as he returns the crowd is there again. At Gerasa there is not only the crowd of demons and the crowd of swine but there are also the Gerasenes who came running to him in crowds from the city and the country. Quoting Kierkegaard, "the mob

2. Ibid.

is the lie," Starobinski notes that evil in the Gospels is always on the side of plurality and the crowd.

There is, nevertheless, a remarkable difference between the behavior of the Galileans and the behavior of the Gerasenes. Like the crowds in Jerusalem, the Galileans are not afraid of miracles. They could turn against the thaumaturge in an instant, but for the moment they cling to him as a savior. The sick gather from all quarters. In Jewish territory everyone is greedy for miracles and signs, wanting either to benefit personally or to have others benefit, or quite simply to be a spectator and participate in the unusual event as in a play that is more extraordinary than enlightening.

The Gerasenes have a different reaction. When they see the demoniac "sitting there, clothed and in his full senses, the very man who had the legion in him before," they are afraid. They have the herdsmen explain to them "what had happened to the demoniac and what had become of the pigs." Instead of calming their fears and arousing their enthusiasm or at least their curiosity, the account increases their anxiety. The inhabitants demand Jesus' departure. And Jesus gives them that satisfaction without saying a word. The man he has cured wants to follow him, but he urges him to remain with his own people. He embarks in silence to return to Jewish territory.

There has been no sermon or any real exchange, not even a hostile one, with these people. We are given the impression that the entire local population demands his departure and that these Gerasenes arrive in an orderly fashion, unlike the flock without a shepherd that rouses Jesus' pity. The community is differentiated, since the inhabitants from the country can be distinguished from the inhabitants from the city. They ask for information calmly and make a thoughtful decision, which they then present to Jesus when they ask him to depart. They do not respond to the miracle with either hysterical adulation or passionate hate, but without hesitation they determine not to accept it. They want nothing to do with Jesus and what he represents.

The Gerasenes are not upset at the disappearance of their herd for mercenary reasons. Clearly, the drowning of their pigs disturbs them less than the drowning of their demons. If this is to be understood, it must be recognized that the attachment of the Gerasenes to their demons has its counterpart in the demons' attachment to the Gerasenes. Legion was not too fearful provided he was permitted to remain in his country. "And he begged him earnestly not to send them out of the district." Since the demons cannot survive without a living habitation they need to possess someone else, preferably a human being but, if not, then an animal, in this case the herd of swine. The reasonable request shows that the demons have no illusions. They ask as a favor the right to enter these loathsome animals: so they are obviously in a difficult position. They know they are dealing with someone powerful. They decide they are more likely to be tolerated if they are content with less. It is essential for them not to be *completely and definitively* expelled.

The reciprocal bond between the demons and the Gerasenes reproduces on a different level the relationship between the possessed and these same Gerasenes observed in our analysis. They cannot do without him or he without them. This conjunction of both ritual and cyclical pathology is not peculiar. As it degenerates ritual loses its precision. The expulsion is not permanent or absolute, and the scapegoat— the possessed—returns to the city between crises. Everything blends, nothing ever ends. The rite tends to relapse into its original state; the relationships of mimetic doubles provoke the crisis of indifferentiation. Physical violence gives way to the violence of psychopathological relationships that is not fatal but is never resolved or ended. The total lack of differentiation is never reached. There remains enough difference between the voluntary exile and the Gerasenes who refuse to expel him, enough real drama in each repetition to achieve a certain catharsis. A total disintegration is in process but has not yet taken place. The Gerasene society is therefore still somewhat structured, more so than the crowds from Galilee or Jerusalem. There are still differences within the system, between city and country for example, and these are manifested by the calmly negative reaction to Jesus' therapeutic success.

This society is not exactly in splendid shape; in fact it is quite disintegrated but not quite desperate, and the Gerasenes are able to preserve their fragile status quo. They still form a community in the accepted sense. As far as we can tell this system is perpetuated, for better or worse, by very degenerate sacrificial procedures that are nevertheless precious and irreplaceable since they have apparently reached the limit.

All the commentators say that Jesus heals the possessed by the classical methods of the shamans. For example, in this passage, he makes the impure spirit name himself, thereby acquiring over him the power that is so often associated in primitive societies with the manipulation of proper names. There is nothing very exceptional in this, and it is not what the text is trying to suggest to us. If there were nothing extraordinary in what Jesus did, there would have been no reason for the Gera-senes to be afraid. They certainly had their own healers who worked with the same methods critics attribute to Jesus. If Jesus were just another more successful *medicine man*, these good people would have been delighted rather than afraid. They would have begged Jesus to stay instead of going away.

Can the Gerasenes' fear be accounted for by rhetorical exaggeration? Is it lacking in substance and intended merely to make the Messiah's prowess more impressive? I do not think so. The destruction of the herd of pigs possessed by the demons is described in the same way in all three Gospels. "And the herd...charged down the cliff into the lake." The steep bank appears also in Matthew and Luke; therefore the pigs had to have been on a kind of promontory. Mark and Luke are aware of this, and to prepare the way for the cliff they place the animals *on a mountain*. Matthew does not mention a mountain but he does retain the cliff—which means it was the cliff that caught the attention of the evangelists. It increased the height of the fall. The further the pigs fell, the more striking the scene. But the Gospels are not concerned with the pic-turesque, and it is not for the visual effect that they all speak of a cliff. A functional reason could be urged. The distance covered in free fall be-fore hitting the surface of the lake guaranteed the definitive disappear-ance of the herd of pigs. There is no risk that they may escape, they will not swim back to the bank. All this is true; the cliff is necessitated by the realistic economy of the scene, but the Gospels were not particularly concerned with the realism either. There is something else much more essential.

Those who are used to reading mythological and religious texts will or should recognize immediately this theme of the cliff. Just like ston-ing, falling from a high cliff has collective, ritual, and penal connota-tions. This was a widespread practice among both ancient and primitive societies. It is a kind of sacrificial immolation that is distinct from the later practice of beheading. Rome had its Tarpeian rock. In the Greek universe the ritual *Pharmakos* was periodically put to death in the same way, especially in Marseille. The unfortunate man was made to throw himself into the sea from such a height that death was inevitable.

Two of the great ritualistic methods of execution figure explicitly in our text: stoning and falling from a high cliff. There are resemblances. All the members of the community can and should throw stones at the victim. All the members of the community can and should advance on the condemned person together and force him to the edge of the cliff so that there is no alternative but death. The resemblances are not limited to the collective nature of the execution. Everyone participates in the destruction of the anathema but no one enters into direct physical contact with him. No one risks contamination. The group alone is responsible. Individuals share the same degree of innocence and responsibility. It can be said that this is equally true of all other traditional forms of execution, especially any form of exposure, of which crucifixion is one variant. The superstitious fear of physical contact with the victim should not blind us to the fact that these techniques of execution resolve an essential problem for societies with weak or nonexistent judicial systems, societies still impregnated with the spirit of private revenge so that they were frequently exposed to the threat of endless violence at the heart of the community.

These methods of execution do not feed the appetite for vengeance since they eliminate any difference in individual roles. The persecutors all behave in the same way. Anyone who dreams of vengeance must take it from the whole collectivity. It is as if the power of the state, nonexistent in this type of society, comes into temporary but nevertheless real rather than symbolic existence in these violent forms of unanimity.

These collective modes of capital execution correspond so closely to the defined need that at first it is difficult to imagine that they occur spontaneously in human communities. So well adapted are they to their purpose it seems impossible that they were not conceived prior to their realization. This is always either the modern illusion of functionalism that believes that need creates the means or the ancient illusion of religious traditions that always point to a kind of primordial legislator, a being of superhuman wisdom and authority who endowed the community with all its basic institutions.

In reality things happen differently. It is absurd to think that such a problem is first posed in theory before it is resolved in practice. But as long as one does not accept that the solution might precede the problem or consider what type of solution might precede the problem, then the absurdity cannot be avoided. Obviously, this is one of the spontaneous effects of a scapegoat. In a crisis of mimetic conflict, the polarization on a single victim can become so powerful that all members of the group are forced to participate in his murder. This type of collective violence automatically prefigures the unanimous forms of execution that are egalitarian and performed at a distance, as we have noted.

This does not mean that the great primordial legislators claimed by so many religious traditions never existed. Primitive traditions, especially those that resemble each other, should always be taken seriously. Great legislators existed, but they never promulgated legislation *in their lifetimes*. It is obvious that they are identical with scapegoats whose murder is scrupulously imitated, repeated, and perfected in ritual because of its effects on reconciliation. The effect is real because this murder already resembles the type of execution that is derived from it and that reproduces the same effect of putting an end to vengeance. It would therefore seem to be derived from greater than human wisdom and can only be attributed to the sacred scapegoat, like all institutions whose origin lies in the mechanism of a victim. The supreme legislator is the very essence of a scapegoat who has been made sacred.

Moses is one example of the scapegoat-legislator. His stammer is the sign of a victim. We find traces in him of mythical guilt: the murder of the Egyptian, the transgression that causes him to be forbidden entrance into the Promised Land, his responsibility for the ten plagues of Egypt which are diseases that remove all differences. All the stereotypes of persecution are present except collective murder, which can be found on the fringe of official tradition, just as for Romulus. Freud was not wrong when he took seriously this hint of collective murder.

But, to return to the demons of Gerasa, is it reasonable to take into consideration the stoning and the cliff-top execution when interpreting this text? The context invites us to associate these two forms of execution. Stoning appears frequently in the Gospels and in the Acts: the adulterous woman saved by Jesus; Stephen, the first martyr; even the Passion is preceded by several attempts at stoning. There is also a significant attempt to push Jesus off a cliff that failed. The scene takes place in Nazareth. Jesus is received poorly in the city of his childhood; he cannot accomplish miracles there. His preaching in the synagogue scandalizes his listeners. He leaves without any disturbance, except in Luke, where the following happens:

When they heard this everyone in the synagogue was enraged. They sprang to their feet and hustled him out of the town; and they took him up to the brow of the hill their town was built on, intending to throw him down the cliff, but he slipped through the crowd and walked away. (Luke 4:28–30)

This episode should be seen as a preliminary sketch and therefore an announcement of the Passion. Its presence indicates that Luke, and certainly the other evangelists, considered falling from a cliff-top and stoning as equivalents of the Crucifixion. They understood what made such an equivalence interesting. All forms of collective murder have the same significance, and that significance is revealed by Jesus in his Passion. It is this revelation that is important, not the location of a particular cliff-top. If you listen to people who know Nazareth, the town and its immediate surroundings do not fit the role Luke gives them. There is no cliff.

Unfortunately, critics who have noticed this geographic inaccuracy were never curious enough to discover why Luke endowed the town of Nazareth with a nonexistent cliff. The Gospels are too interested in the diverse forms of collective death to be interested in the topography of Nazareth. Their real concern is with the demon's self-lapidation and the fall of the herd of pigs *from the cliff*. But in these cases it is not the scapegoat who goes over the cliff, neither is it a single victim nor a small number of victims, but a whole crowd of demons, two thousand swine possessed by demons. Normal relationships are reversed. The crowd should remain on top of the cliff and the victim fall over; instead, in this case, the crowd plunges and the victim is saved.

The miracle of Gerasa reverses the universal schema of violence fundamental to all societies of the world. The inversion appears in certain myths but not with the same characters; it always ends in the restoration of the system that had been destroyed or in the establishment of a new system. In this case the result is quite different. The drowning of the swine has a definitive character; it is an event without a future, except for the person cured by the miracle. This text suggests a difference not of degree but of nature between Jesus' miracle and the usual healings. This difference of nature corresponds in actuality to a whole group of concordant details. Modern critics have failed to notice them. The fantastic aspects of the miracle seem too gratuitous to attract attention for very long. The request the demons make of Jesus, their disorderly withdrawal into the swine, and the downfall of the latter all seem like familiar old stories; whereas in fact the treatment of these themes is extraordinary. It corresponds strictly to what is demanded at this point by the revelation of the victim's mimeticism, even though the whole style remains demonological.

If need be, the demons will tolerate being expelled provided they are not expelled *from their country*. This would seem to mean that ordinary exorcisms are always only local displacements, exchanges, and substitutions which can always be produced within a structure without causing any appreciable change or compromising the continuation of the whole society. Traditional cures have a real but limited action to the degree that they only improve the condition of individual X at the expense of another individual, Y, or vice versa. In the language of demonology, this means that the demons of X have left him to take possession of Y. The healers modify certain mimetic relationships, but their little manipulations do not compromise the balance of the system, which remains unchanged. The system remains and should be defined as a system not of men only but of men and their demons.

This total system is threatened by the cure of the possessed and the concomitant drowning of the Legion. Because the Gerasenes suspect this they are uneasy. The demons have an even clearer understanding. They appear more lucid than the humans in this case which does not prevent them from being blind in other areas and easy to deceive. These themes are far richer in meaning than people have supposed. The qualities attributed to the demons correspond strictly to the true characteristics of this strange reality they are made to incarnate in the Gospels, the mimetic *disincarnation*. As desire becomes more frantic and demonic, it becomes more aware of its own laws, but this awareness does not prevent enslavement. Great writers appreciate this paradox and display it in their work. Dostoyevsky borrowed from the demons of Gerasa not only the title for his novel *The Demons* but also the system of relationships between characters and the dynamics of the abyss that sweeps the system away.

The demons try to "negotiate" with Jesus, as they do with the local healers. They deal as equal to equal with those whose power or lack of power is scarcely different from their own. The negotiation with Jesus is more apparent than real. This traveler is not initiated in any local cult; he is not sent by anyone in the community. He does not need to make concessions in order for the demons to leave the possessed. The permission he gives them to possess the swine has no consequence because it has no lasting effect. It is enough for Jesus to appear somewhere to put a stop to demons and challenge the inevitably demonic order of all society. Demons cannot exist in his presence. They become extremely agitated, have short periods of convulsion, and then tend to disintegrate completely. This inevitable course of events is indicated by the miracle's moment of crisis.

In every great defeat the finest maneuvers become the perfect in-

THE DEMONS OF GERASA   181

strument for the downfall. Our text succeeds in conferring that double significance on the bargaining between the miracle worker and the demons. The theme is borrowed from the practices of the shamans and other healers, but here it is merely a vehicle for the meanings that transcend it. The only hope of the demons in the presence of Jesus is to remain on the edges of the universe where they formerly held sway in its most evil-smelling corners. The demons turn to him willingly for shelter from the abyss that threatens them. Panic-stricken, they decide in haste, and for lack of a better choice, they *become pigs*. This is strangely similar to what happens everywhere. Even becoming pigs, like Ulysses' companions, the demons cannot survive. Drowning is final perdition. It realizes the worst fears of the supernatural herd, *expulsion from their own country*. This is Mark's remarkable expression; it takes note of the social nature of the game, of the demoniac's role in what some call the "symbolic." Luke's text is also instructive. In showing us the demons begging Jesus not to send them forever *into the abyss*, he clearly articulates the definitive annihilation of the demoniac that is the major significance of the text and explains the reaction of the Gerasenes themselves. These unfortunate people fear that their precarious balance depends on the demoniac, on the activities they share periodically and on the kind of local celebrity their possessed citizen had become.

There is nothing in the possession that does not result from frantic mimeticism. Hence the variant in Matthew that substitutes two possessed beings that are indistinguishable, and therefore mimetic, for the solitary demoniac of the other two Gospels. Mark's text expresses basically the same thing, less obviously but therefore more essentially, by presenting his single person possessed by a demon that is both one and multiple, both singular and plural. This implies that the possessed is possessed not by only one other, as Matthew suggests, but by all the others inasmuch as they are both one and many, or in other words inasmuch as they form a society in the human sense of the term. This is also the demonic sense, if one prefers, in that it is a society based on the collective expulsion. This is precisely what the possessed is imitating. The demons are in the image of the human group; they are the *imago* of this group because they are its *imitatio*. Like the society of the Gerasenes at the end of our text, the society of demons at the beginning possesses a structure, a kind of organization; it is the unity of the multiple: "My name is Legion; for there are many of us." Just as one voice is raised at the end to speak in the name of all the Gerasenes, one voice is raised at the beginning to speak in the name of all the demons. These two voices say the same thing. Since all coexistence between Jesus and the demons is impossible, to beg him not to chase away the demons, when one is a demon is the same as begging him to depart, if one is from Gerasa.

The essential proof of my thesis that the demons and Gerasenes are identical is the behavior of the possessed insofar as he is the possessed of these demons. The Gerasenes stone their victims and the demons force theirs to stone themselves, which amounts to the same thing. This archetypal possessed mimics the most basic social practice that literally engenders society by transforming mimetic multiplicity in its most atomized form into the strongest social unity which is the unanimity of the original murder. In describing the unity of the multiple, the Legion symbolizes the social principle itself, the type of organization that rests not on the final expulsion of the demons but on the sort of equivocal and mitigated expulsions that are illustrated by our possessed, expulsions which ultimately end in the coexistence of men and demons.

I have said that Legion symbolizes the multiple unity of society and that is true, but in the rightly famous sentence "My name is Legion; for there are many of us," it symbolizes that unity in the process of disintegration since it is the inverse of social development that prevails. The singular is irresistibly transformed into a plural, within the same single sentence; it marks the falling back of unity into mimetic multiplicity which is the first disintegrating effect of Jesus' presence. This is almost like modern art. *Je est un autre*, says Matthew. *Je* is all the others, says Mark.

It is legitimate to identify the herd of pigs with the crowd of lynchers since the reference is explicit in at least one Gospel, that of Matthew. I am referring to a very significant aphorism that appears not far from the account of Gerasa. "Do not throw your pearls in front of pigs or they may trample them and then turn on you and tear you to pieces" (Matt. 7:6).

Yet in the account of Gerasa the lynchers experience the treatment "normally" reserved for the victim. They are not stoned like the possessed, but they go over the steep bank, which amounts to the same thing. If we are to recognize how revolutionary this inversion is we must transport it to classical Greek or Roman antiquity, which is more respected than the Judaic world of the Bible. Imagine the *Pharmakos* forcing the inhabitants of a Greek city, philosophers and mathematicians alike, over a precipice. Instead of the outcast being toppled from the height of the Tarpeian rock it is the majestic consuls, virtuous Cato, solemn juriconsults, the procurators of Judea, and all the rest of the *senatus populusque romanus*. All of them disappear into the abyss while the ex-victim, "clothed and in his full senses" calmly observes from above the astounding sight.

The miracle's conclusion satisfies a certain appetite for revenge, but can it be justified within the framework of my hypothesis? Does the element of revenge compromise my thesis that the spirit of revenge is absent in the Gospels? What is the force that drives the pigs into the sea of Galilee if not our desire to see them fall or the violence of Jesus himself? What can motivate a whole herd of pigs to destroy themselves without being forced by someone? The answer is obvious. It is the crowd mentality, that which makes the herd precisely a herd—in other words, the irresistible tendency to mimeticism. One pig accidentally falling into the sea, or the convulsions provoked by the demonic invasion, is enough to cause a stupid panic in which all the others follow. The frantic following fits well with the proverbial stubbornness of the species. Beyond a certain mimetic threshold, the same that defined possession earlier, the whole herd immediately repeats any conduct that seems out of the ordinary, like fashions in modern society.

If just one animal were to stumble, accidentally, it would immediately start a new fashion of rushing headlong—*the plunge into the abyss*—which would carry the last little pig eagerly away. The slightest mimetic incitement can agitate a close-knit crowd. The weaker the purpose, the more futile and fatal, then the more mysterious it will appear and the more desire it will inspire. All the swine are scandalized and have therefore lost their balance. They are bound to be interested and even electrified by a sudden, more radical, loss of balance. Everyone is groping for that beautiful gesture, the gesture *that cannot be undone*. They rush headlong after the "bold innovator."

Whenever Jesus speaks he usually puts the mimeticism of the scandalized in the place of the works of the devil. If we do the same thing in this context the mystery evaporates. These pigs are truly possessed in that they are mimeticized up to their ears. We should not look in manuals of demonology for references other than those in the Gospels. We should turn instead to a more joyful, deeper literature. The suicidal demons of Gerasa are Panurge's supersheep who do not even need a Dindenneau to throw themselves into the sea. There is always a mimetic answer to the questions posed in our text, and that answer is always the best.

CHAPTER FOURTEEN

Satan Divided against Himself

TEXTUAL ANALYSIS REVEALS nothing about the miraculous cures them-selves.[1] It can only have bearing on the language describing them. The Gospels speak the language of their universe. They therefore seem to make of Jesus a healer among healers, while at the same time protesting that the Messiah is very different. The text of Gerasa justifies this by describing the destruction of all the demons and their universe, that same universe which has provided the evangelists with the language to describe the demons and their expulsion. The central subject, then, is an expulsion, *the* expulsion that will rid the universe forever of its demons and the demoniac.

In a few passages in the Gospels, Jesus himself uses the language of demonology and expulsion. The most significant of these is a debate with a hostile audience. The text is crucial and appears in all three synoptic Gospels. Here it is in Matthew's version which is the richest. Jesus has just cured someone possessed. The crowd is full of admiration but there are members of the religious elite present—the "Pharisees" in Matthew, the "scribes" in Mark—and they are suspicious of this cure.

All the people were astounded and said, "Can this be the Son of David?" But when the Pharisees heard this they said, "The man casts out devils only through Beelzebul, the prince of devils." Knowing what was in their minds he said to them. "Every kingdom divided against itself is heading for ruin: and no town, no household divided against itself can stand. Now if Satan casts out Satan, he

---

1. On miracles and the meaning of miraculous cures, see Xavier Léon-Dufour, *Etudes d'Evangile* (Paris: Seuil, 1965). See also, by the same author, *Face à la mort, Jésus et Paul* (Paris: Seuil, 1979), especially on the sacrificial reading of the Passion.

is divided against himself; so how can his kingdom stand? And if it is through Beelzebul that I cast out devils, through whom do your own experts cast them out? Let them be your judges, then. But if it is through the spirit of God that I cast devils out, then know that the kingdom of God has overtaken you. (Matthew 12:23–28)

It is impossible to understand this text in one reading. The immediate reading leads into a deeper reading on another level. On initial reading we recognize in the first sentence only an unarguable but commonplace principle that retains the wisdom of nations. English turns it into a kind of maxim: *Every kingdom divided against itself. . .shall not stand.*

The next sentence at first glance seems to apply this principle: "and if Satan casts out Satan, he is divided against himself; so how can his kingdom stand?" Jesus does not answer, but the answer is obvious. If it is divided against itself, the kingdom of Satan will not stand. If the Pharisees are truly hostile to Satan, they should not reproach Jesus for casting out Satan by Satan; even if they are right, what Jesus has just done will contribute to Satan's final destruction.

But here is a different supposition and a different question: "And if it is through Beelzebul that I cast out devils, through whom do your own experts cast them out?" If my action is prompted by the devil, what about yours and your disciples', your spiritual sons? Jesus returns his critics' accusation to them: it is they who cast out demons *by means of Satan*, and he claims for himself a radically different way of expulsion, casting out by the Spirit of God: "But if it is through the spirit of God that I cast devils out, then know that the Kingdom of God has overtaken you."

Jesus seems to be involved in an exchange of arguments that is bound to be sterile. Each of the healers claims to cast out demons by God, and therefore to be more effective and more orthodox, whereas his rival works through the devil. We find ourselves in the middle of mimetic competition in which each casts out the other, like Oedipus and Tiresias, the rival prophets in Sophocles' *Oedipus Rex*. Violence is pervasive and everything can be reduced to a question of force, as the sequel to the passage implies. The presentation of the relationship between the two methods of casting out devils is almost a caricature: "Or again, how can anyone make his way into a strong man's house and burgle his property unless he has tied up the strong man first? Only then can he burgle his house" (Matt. 12:29).

The first strong man in this context is the devil, who is presented as the legitimate houseowner, or at least the original occupant of the house. The stronger man who overcomes the former is God. This is not Jesus' viewpoint. God is no common housebreaker. Jesus adopts the language of his interrogators, the language of rivals in the casting out of demons, in order to reveal the system of violence and the sacred. God is certainly stronger than Satan, but if so, in the sense implied in this passage, he would be just another Satan.

This is precisely how the Gerasenes interpret the explosive effect Jesus has on their community. They have a strong man among them, the demoniac Legion. This strong man leads them a tough life but he maintains some sort of order. Now comes Jesus, who must be even stronger since he makes their strong man powerless. The Gerasenes fear that Jesus will plunder all their possessions. That is why they are determined to ask him to go away. They have no wish to exchange one tyrannical master for a still more tyrannical one.

Jesus adopts the language of his universe—which is usually also the language of the Gospels. The evangelists are not too sure of what is happening. Their text is extraordinarily elliptic and possibly even mutilated. Matthew at least understands that everything should not be taken literally. There is an irony in the words we have just read that must be exposed, a wealth of meaning that escapes us on the immediate argumentative level, which is the only one apparent to the interrogators of Jesus, and to most modern readers; Matthew precedes the quotation with an important warning: "Knowing what was in their minds, he said to them. . ."

Mark's warning is different and even more revealing; he alerts us to the fact that it is a *parable* (Mark 3:23). This seems to me to be important in defining a parable which is an indirect discourse that can but need not include narrative elements since in this passage there are none. The essential factor in the Gospel use of parable is Jesus' willingness to be imprisoned within the representation of persecution from the persecutors' standpoint, and to do so for the sake of his listeners who cannot understand any other viewpoint, since they are prisoners of it themselves. Jesus uses the resources of the system in such a way as to warn people of what awaits them in the only language they understand. By doing this he reveals both the impending end of the system and the incoherence and internal contradiction of the discourse. He hopes to destroy the system in the minds of his listeners and at the same time to make them understand another meaning, truer to his words, but more difficult. This meaning, being a stranger to the violence of persecution, can reveal the effect of imprisonment on each one of us.

In the light of our analysis a second meaning can easily be perceived. The text actually says more than we have drawn from it here. It summarizes our conclusions and clearly formulates the principle I have uncovered, that violence casts itself out by violence, as the foundation of all human societies. As I have already observed the idea that a divided community is headed for destruction would appear to be true but is only a piece of common sense. To begin the debate, Jesus makes a suggestion to which everyone will agree. The second sentence then appears as a particular instance of the first. What is true of every kingdom, city, and house must be true of the kingdom of Satan.

But the kingdom of Satan is not one among others. The Gospels state explicitly that Satan is the principle of every kingdom. How is that possible? By being the principle of violent expulsion and the deceit it produces. The kingdom of Satan is none other than the violence that casts itself out in all the rites and exorcisms alluded to by the Pharisees, and even before that in the original, hidden deed that serves as a model for all these rites, the unanimous and spontaneous murder of a scapegoat. This is the complex and complete definition of the kingdom of Satan provided by the second sentence. It announces not only what will finally destroy Satan but also what originally brought him into existence and established his power, his founding principle. What is strange is that the founding principle and the principle of ultimate destruction are one and the same. This is disconcerting to the ignorant, but nothing in it need disconcert us. We know already that the principle of mimetic desire, its rivalries, and the internal divisions it creates are identical with the equally mimetic principle that unifies society: the scapegoat.

This is the process that is repeatedly unfolded for us. It is the reason for the quarrel between fraternal enemies that precedes the murder of John the Baptist, just as we have seen at the beginning of innumerable myths. The one finishes *normally* by killing the other in order to provide men with a *norm*. Far from being the simple application of a principle that was stated in the first sentence, the second sentence states the principle that is applied in the first sentence. The order of these sentences must be reversed. The text should be reread starting with the end. Then we understand why the first sentence remains in peoples' memories. There is something in it which goes beyond the everyday wisdom that was at first apparent. The Jerusalem Bible, from which I quoted, does not convey this very well because it does not repeat the initial adjective *every*, which appears twice in the original Greek. *Every kingdom divided against itself is heading for ruin, and every city or house, divided against itself.* The repetition of *every* emphasizes the impression of symmetry among all the forms of community mentioned here. The text enumerates all the human societies, from the greatest to the smallest, the kingdom, the city, the house. For reasons that at first elude us, care is taken not to omit any category, and the repetition of *every* underlines that intention even more, although its importance is not apparent, immediately. This is not fortuitous or an accident of style that has no relation to the meaning. There is a second meaning that cannot escape us.

The text is, in fact, insisting that all kingdoms, all cities, and all houses are divided against themselves. In other words all human communities without exception are based on the one principle, both constructive and destructive, that is found in the second sentence; these are all examples of the kingdom of Satan, and it is not this kingdom of Satan or kingdom of violence which serves as one example of society, in the empirical sense of sociologists. Thus the first two sentences are richer than they seem; an entire sociology or basic anthropology is summarized in them. That is not all. We can now begin to understand the third, and particularly the fourth sentence, which seems the most enigmatic: "And if it is through Beelzebul that I cast out devils, through whom do your own experts cast them out? Let them be your judges, then."

Why should the spiritual sons, the disciples and imitators, become judges of their masters and models? The word for judges is *kritai*; it evokes the idea of crisis and division. Under the effect of mimetic escalation, the internal division of every "satanic" community is exacerbated; the difference between legitimate and illegitimate violence diminishes, expulsions become reciprocal; sons repeat and reinforce the violence of their fathers with even more deplorable results for everybody; finally they understand the evil of the paternal example and curse their own fathers. They pass negative judgment, as implied by the word *kritai*, on everything that precedes them just as we do today.

The concept of the existence of an all-powerful divine violence seems to emerge from our text; it is even explicit as in the account of the miracle of Gerasa. But if the reader goes beyond a certain point, the interpretation is reversed by the observation that divine expulsion does not exist or, rather it only exists for the representation of persecution from the persecutor's standpoint, for the spirit of reciprocal accusation otherwise known as Satan himself. The force of expulsion always originates in Satan, and God has nothing to do with it; it is more than enough to put an end to the "kingdom of Satan." These men are divided by their mimeticism, "possessed" by Satan, each in turn casting the other out to the point of total extinction.

If self divided against self (mimetic rivalry) and the expulsion of expulsion (the scapegoat mechanism) are principles of both decomposition and composition for human societies, why does Jesus not mention the latter in all his final apocalyptic pronouncements? Perhaps I am right in identifying mimetic violence as the source of both order and disorder. Possibly the text is as grossly polemic, as unconsciously mimetic and grossly dualistic as the immediate reading suggests.

It seems that Satan has never ceased to expel Satan, and there is no reason to believe he will cease in the foreseeable future. Jesus speaks as if the satanic principle had used up its force for order and as if all social order would henceforth succumb to its own disorder. The principle of order is merely alluded to in the first two sentences, like a stylistic effect, something that has more or less come to its end, condemned to follow the path to destruction, which constitutes the only explicit message that is accessible to most readers.

The meaning of order is there, but it is precisely its presence that determines the vestigial character of the treatment of it. The reason lies in the fact that the violence of the cultural order is revealed in the Gospels, both in the account of the Passion and in all the other episodes we have read, including this one, and the cultural order cannot survive such a revelation. Once the basic mechanism is revealed, the scapegoat mechanism, that expulsion of violence by violence, is rendered useless by the revelation. It is no longer of interest. The interest of the Gospels lies in the future offered mankind by this revelation, the end of Satan's mechanism. The good news is that scapegoats can no longer save men, the persecutors' accounts of their persecutions are no longer valid, and truth shines into dark places. God is not violent, the true God has nothing to do with violence, and he speaks to us not through distant intermediaries but directly. The Son he sends us is one with him. The Kingdom of God is at hand.

If it is by the Spirit of God that I cast out demons, then the Kingdom of God has come upon you. The Kingdom of God has nothing in common with the kingdom of Satan and the kingdoms of this world based on the satanic principle of internal division and expulsion. It has nothing to do with expulsion. Jesus agrees to debate his own action in terms of expulsion and violence because those are the only terms his questioners understand. But he is telling them of an event that has nothing in common with this language. If it is by the Spirit of God that I cast out demons, then soon there will be no more demons or expulsions for the kingdom of violence and expulsion will rapidly be destroyed. The Kingdom of God is at hand *for you*. His listeners are addressed directly. The Kingdom arrives like a bolt of lightning. Like the bridegroom of the foolish and the wise virgins, it has delayed a long time but has suddenly arrived.

The Kingdom of God has arrived for you who are listening to me now, but not for those Gerasenes whom I have just left without saying anything to them because they have not yet reached the point you are at. Jesus intervenes when *the time has come* or, in other words, when violence can no longer cast out violence and internal division has reached its crisis. The victim-scapegoat is at the point of no return. Though for a while he may seem to bring back the old order, in reality it is destroyed forever. Instead of casting it out he is himself cast out, thereby revealing to men the mystery of expulsion, the secret on which rests the positive dimension of Satan's power, its organizing force of violence.

Ever attentive to the historical aspects of the revelation, Matthew, in his account of Gerasa, includes a statement by his two possessed that suggests a temporary separation between a universe that is based on the law and one that is not: "What do you want with us, Son of God? Have you come here to torture us before the time?" (Matt. 8:29). This complaint is significant in the context of our current analysis. I pointed out that the crowd of Gerasenes is less like a mob than the shepherdless flock to which Jesus usually preached. The Gerasene community is still more "structured." Paganism is responsible for this. This does not mean we should rate paganism more highly than Judaism. It suggests, rather, that paganism has not yet reached the same critical point in its evolution.

The final crisis that determines the final revelation both is and is not specific. In principle it is the same as the disintegration of all sacrificial systems that are based on the "satanic" expulsion of violence by violence. For better or for worse, the Gospel revelation makes the crisis inevitable. By exposing the secret of the persecutors' representation it prevents the mechanism of the victim from ever functioning and creating, at the height of mimetic disorder, a new order of ritual expulsion that replaces the old.

Sooner or later the ferment of the Gospels will cause the breakup of the social order it infiltrates and of all similar societies, even so-called Christian societies that claim to be based on it. This claim is partially true, but rests upon a partial misunderstanding, a necessarily sacrificial misunderstanding, which is rooted in the deceptive similarity between the Gospels and other religious mythological charters. "And if a house is divided against itself, that house will not be able to stand," Mark tells us, but that collapse is not just a stronger expulsion initiated by God or Jesus. It is the end of all expulsion. That is why the coming of the Kingdom of God means destruction for those who only understand destruction and reconciliation for those who always seek reconciliation.

The logic of the kingdom that cannot stand if it is always divided against itself has always been true in the absolute but was never true in reality because the hidden scapegoat mechanism always restored sacrificial differentiation and expelled violence by violence. Finally, that logic becomes a historical reality in the Crucifixion, first for the Jews and then for the pagans, the Gerasenes of the modern world who have always behaved a little like the people of Gerasa while claiming to be guided by Jesus. They are happy to think that nothing so drastic can happen to their communities, and are convinced that the catastrophes announced by the Gospels are imaginary.

An initial reading of the account of the demons of Gerasa gives the impression that everything is based on a logic of double expulsion. There were no decisive results from the first expulsion. It was a petty squabble between the demons and their Gerasenes who got along like thieves at a fair. Jesus was responsible for the second expulsion that made a clean sweep of the whole place and its inhabitants.

The same double expulsion, the one within the system it stabilizes, the other external to that same system that it destroys, is explicitly mentioned in the text we have just read: *"And if it is through Beelzebul that I cast out devils, through whom do your own experts cast them out?"* A more profound comprehension reveals that the divine power is not destructive; it does not expel anyone. The truth offered to mankind unleashes the forces of Satan, the destructive mimeticism, by taking away its power of self-regulation. The fundamental ambiguity of Satan makes divine action superficially ambiguous. Jesus brings war into the divided world of Satan because, fundamentally, he brings peace. People do not or pretend not to understand this. The text is admirably suited to be read by both those who understand and those who do not. The sentences dealing with communities divided against themselves and Satan casting out Satan indicate both the power of satanic mimesis to regulate itself and the loss of that power. The text does not explicitly identify the principle of order and disorder, but conveys it in sentences with double meaning. The endless fascination of these sentences lies in the chiaroscuro of the truth they contain that must not be highlighted if it is to function in the text exactly as it functions in reality. Those who do not see it remain in Satan's universe, on the level of the immediate reading, believing that there exists a divine violence, the rival of Satan's violence, and remaining prisoners of the persecution mentality. Those who see the truth understand that Satan's kingdom is headed for destruction because of the revelation of the truth about it, and they are liberated from the persecution mentality.

Thus we come to understand what is involved in the Kingdom of God and why it does not represent for men an unmitigated blessing. It has nothing to do with a flock of sheep grazing in an eternally green pasture. It brings men face to face with their hardest task in history. Compared to ourselves, the people of Gerasa are honest and sympathetic. They do not yet behave like imperious users of the consumer society. They admit that it is difficult for them to live without scapegoats and demons. In all the texts we have read the demonological perspective persists but is subverted. To get rid of it completely we only need to broaden a little the jurisdiction of the *skandalon* as defined by Jesus, whose prodigious power can be seen in operation everywhere. The texts I have interpreted are representative of all the synoptic Gospels. To put an end once and for all to the demon, we need only focus on the notion of scandal and all that goes with it to help us understand the problem of mimesis and its expulsions.

Mark and Matthew have good reason to warn us not to take too literally the greatest of all Jesus' demonological statements. We need only consult a dictionary to learn that the parabolic distortion of a text involves a certain concession to the mythological representation of violence that results from the collective murder of a scapegoat. *Paraballo* means to throw the crowd something edible in order to assuage its appetite for violence, preferably a victim, someone condemned to death.

Obviously, this is a way out of a very difficult situation. The speaker has recourse to a parable – that is, a metaphor – in order to prevent the crowd from turning on him. Ultimately, there is no discourse that is not a parable. All human language, and other cultural institutions, in fact, originated in collective murder. After some of Jesus' most hard-hitting parables the crowd often makes a movement of violence, but Jesus escapes because his hour has not come.

By warning the readers that Jesus speaks in parables, the Evangelists alert the readers to the distortion of persecution. Here we are clearly being warned about the language of expulsion. There is no other alternative. If we do not recognize the parabolic dimension of the expulsion we will be duped by violence. Our reading will have been of the type that Jesus warned must be avoided but was inevitable;

Then the disciples went up to him and asked, "Why do you talk to them in parables?" "Because," he replied, "the mysteries of the kingdom of heaven are revealed to you, but they are not revealed to them. For anyone who has will be given more, and he will have more than enough: but from anyone who has not, even what he has will be taken away. The reason I talk to them in parables is that they look without seeing and listen without hearing or understanding." (Matt. 13:10–14)

Mark at this point connects the parable even more clearly than Matthew to the persecution mentality. For those caught in it everything *appears* in parables. Instead of freeing us, the parable, when taken literally, reinforces the walls of our prison. This is the meaning of the following lines. It would not be accurate to conclude that the parable is not aimed at converting the listener. Even here, Jesus is talking to his disciples:

To you has been given the secret of the Kingdom of God, but for those outside everything is in parables; so that they may see and see again, but not perceive; may hear and hear again, but not understand; otherwise they might be converted and be forgiven." (Mark 4:10–12)

EVEN IN THE TEXTS generally described as "archaic," belief in demons may seem to flourish but in reality always tends toward suppression. This is true in the dialogue on expulsion we have just read and also in the miracle of Gerasa. We are not aware of the ultimate suppression because it is expressed in the contradictory language of the expulsion that is expelled and the demon that is cast out. The demon is sent back to the nothingness with which he is in a way "consubstantial," the nothingness of his own existence.

This is the meaning of Jesus' expression: "I watched Satan fall like lightning from heaven" (Luke 10:18). There is only one transcendence in the Gospels, the transcendence of divine love that triumphs over all manifestations of violence and the sacred by revealing their nothingness. A careful reading of the Gospels shows us that Jesus prefers the language of *skandalon* to that of the demonic while the opposition is true for the disciples and editors of the Gospels. We should therefore not be surprised to find a certain contrast between the fulgurating words attributed to Jesus, which are often not very coherent, and the narrative passages, particularly the accounts of the miracles, which are better organized from a literary perspective but lag somewhat behind the thought that emerges from the direct quotations. All of this would be understandable if the disciples were really as described in the Gospels themselves, very attentive and full of good will but not always capable of understanding fully what their master did and said. The description of Peter's denial already suggested that conclusion. The narrative passages are more likely to be directly dependent on the disciples than the transcription of Jesus' words.

Only Jesus can master the language of *skandalon*: the most important passages clearly reveal that the two languages are applied to the same objects, and they show us Jesus translating the demonic *logos* in terms of mimetic scandal. This is achieved in the famous admonition to Peter: "Get behind me, Satan! you are a scandal to me [an obstacle] because the way you think is not God's way but man's." Did Jesus in that moment see in Peter someone *possessed* by Satan in the sense that the witch-hunters used the expression? The next sentence which shows Peter's action as typically human proves that this is not so: "the way you think is not God's way but man's."

The language of *skandalon* substitutes for the salutary but blind fear of hell an analysis of the reason why men fall into the trap of mimetic circularity. By exposing Jesus to the contagious temptation of his own worldly desire, Peter transforms the divine mission into a worldly undertaking that must inevitably come up against rival ambitions which it arouses or by which it is aroused, Peter's own for example. In this context Peter plays the role of Satan's substitute, *suppositus*, the model-obstacle of mimetic desire.

A close correspondence exists between what the Gospels tell us of demons and the truth of mimetic relationships as defined by Jesus and as revealed in certain great literary works or in theoretical analysis. This is not true of most texts that reflect a belief in demons, but most contemporary commentators fail to recognize such a distinction and consider all such texts to be contaminated by the same superstition without ever really examining the content. The Gospels, in fact, are not only superior to all the texts placed in the category of magical thought but are also superior to all the modern interpretations of human relationships. Their superiority lies both in the mimetic concept and in the combination of mimesis with demonology found in a text such as Gerasa. The demonological vision powerfully incorporates the unity and diversity of certain individual and social attitudes in a unique way. This is why great writers such as Shakespeare and Dostoyevsky, or George Bernanos later, have resorted to the language of demonology in order to avoid the useless platitudes of the pseudo-scientific knowledge of their epoch and ours.

By acknowledging the existence of the demon we recognize the force of desire and hatred, envy and jealousy, at work among men. Its effects are far more insidious and twisted, its reversals and metamorphoses more paradoxical and unexpected, and its consequences more complex than anything man has since imagined in his eagerness to account for human behavior without supernatural intervention. Yet its principle is simple, almost simplistic, since the demon is both very intelligent and very stupid. The mimetic nature of the demon is explicit since, among other things, he is the monkey of God. In speaking of the uniformly "demonic" character of trance, ritual possession, hysterical crisis, and hypnosis, we are confirming the true unity of the phenomena, the common basis that must be identified if psychiatry is to make progress. That basis is the conflictual mimesis that Jean-Michel Oughourlian traces.

But the superiority of the demonic theme is shown in its unrivaled ability to assemble in one concept the divisive force (*diabolos*), the "perverse effects," the generative power of all disorder on all levels of human relationships on the one hand and the power of union that creates social order on the other. This theme accomplishes effortlessly what sociology, anthropology, psychoanalysis, and cultural theory have constantly attempted without success. The Gospels provide us with the principle that allows us to distinguish social transcendence and the immanence of individual relations and simultaneously unify them by controlling the relationship between what the French psychoanalysis call the *symbolic* and the *imaginary*.

The demonic allows, on the one hand, for every tendency toward conflict in human relations and for the centrifugal force at the heart of the community, and, on the other hand, for the centripetal force that brings men together, the mysterious glue of that same community. In order to transform this demonology into true knowledge we must follow the path indicated by the Gospels and complete the translation that they begin. It is obvious that the same force that divides people by mimetic rivalry also unites them by the mimetic unanimity of the scapegoat.

Clearly, this is what John is speaking of when he presents Satan as "liar and the father of lies" because he is "a murderer from the start" (John 8:44). This lie is discredited by the Passion which shows the victim's innocence. If Satan's defeat is so closely linked to the precise moment of the Passion this is because the truthful account of this event will provide men with what is needed to escape the eternal lie and recognize that the victim is slandered. Thanks to his well-known mimetic ability Satan succeeds in making the victim's guilt credible. Satan, in Hebrew, means the *accuser*. All the meanings and symbols are interwoven so carefully that they constitute a structure of flawless rationality. Could this be pure coincidence?

With the deepening of the mimetic crisis, desire and its conflicts become more immaterial because they have lost their object. As the situation becomes more "perverse" it even fosters belief in a purely spiritual mimesis; relationships inevitably become increasingly obsessive and autonomous. Demonology is not completely duped by this autonomy since it tells us of the absolute need that demons have to *possess* a living being in order to survive. The demon is not capable of existing apart from that possession. But its existence is strengthened as men's resistance to mimetic urges weakens. The principal examples of this are to be found in the great scene of Jesus' temptation in the desert. The most important of these is the last, which shows us Satan desirous of taking God's place as an object of adoration, as a model of a necessarily frustrated imitation. This imitation makes Satan the mimetic *skandalon* we see in Jesus' response which is almost identical with the response he gives Peter when he treats him as Satan. The same Greek verb, *upage*, begone, appears in both episodes, and the scandalous obstacle is implied. To adore Satan is to aspire to world domination. It involves reciprocal relationships of idolatry and hate which can only end in false gods of violence and the sacred as long as men maintain the illusion. When that illusion is no longer possible, total destruction will follow:

Next, taking him to a very high mountain, the devil showed him all the kingdoms of the world and their splendour. "I will give you all these," he said, "if you fall at my feet and worship me." Then Jesus replied, "Be off, Satan! For scripture says:

You must worship the Lord your God,
and serve him alone." (Matt. 4:8–10)

CHAPTER FIFTEEN

History and the Paraclete

ALL THE PASSAGES we have studied in the Gospels refer to phenomena of collective persecution that are either discredited or condemned in the sense that we discredit or condemn similar phenomena in our own history. The Gospels contain a range of texts that fit diverse situations — everything, in fact, that is needed for the critical analysis of representations of persecution from the persecutors' standpoint and resistance to the mimetic and violent mechanisms in which they are imprisoned.

The undermining of mythical beliefs begins with the acts of violence against those the Christians call *martyrs*. We see them as innocent people who are persecuted. This truth has been transmitted by history, and the perspective of the persecutors has not prevailed. The victim would have to be glorified as a result of the persecution in order to have sacredness in the mythological sense. The crimes imagined by the persecutors would have to be accepted as real.

In the case of the martyrs, there was no lack of accusations. Rumors were rife, and they have been believed by distinguished writers. These were classical crimes of myth, the typical reflection of mob violence. Christians were accused of infanticide and other crimes against their own families. Their intense communal life aroused suspicions of incest. These transgressions, associated with a refusal to worship the emperor, assumed a social dimension for the populace and for the authorities. If Rome burned, the Christians probably set fire to it.

There truly would be a mythological genesis if all these crimes were incorporated in the final apotheosis. The Christian saint would become a mythological hero. He would embody aspects of both supernatural benefactor and all-powerful troublemaker, capable of punishing each act of negligence or indifference toward him by sending a plague. What is essentially characteristic of the mythological quality of the sacred is its dual nature—it is both harmful and beneficial. It leaves the impression of a double transcendence, a paradoxical conjunction, because we understand it from a Christian perspective considered by us to be the norm, whereas in fact it is unique.

The innocence of the martyr is never in doubt. "They hated me [without a cause]." The Christian passion produces its first fruit. The spirit of vengeance leads vigorous rear-guard actions, but the martyrs nonetheless pray for their executioners: "Father, forgive them, they know not what they do."

Admittedly, innocent victims were rehabilitated before Christianity. Socrates, Antigone, and others are rightly mentioned in this context. There are aspects similar to the Christian understanding of the martyr, but they are isolated in nature and do not affect any society in its totality. The singularity of the martyr is due to the fact that his sacralization fails to take place even under conditions that are most favorable to the creation of the sacred—the crowd's emotion and their religious passion for persecution. The proof is that all the stereotypes of persecution are present. From the perspective of the majority, the Christians constitute a disturbing minority, richly equipped with the selective signs of a victim. They belong mainly to the lower classes, and many of them are women or slaves. But nothing is transfigured; the persecution is portrayed as it really is.

To canonize someone is not the same as to make him sacred. Admittedly, there are traces of the survival of the primitive quality of the sacred in the glorification of the martyrs, and later in the lives of medieval saints. I mentioned some of them in connection with Saint Sebastian. The mechanisms of violence and the sacred are a part of the fascination exerted by the martyrs. There might be said to be a virtue in the blood spilled in ancient times that became exhausted unless it was renewed from time to time by new blood. This is certainly true of the Christian martyrs, and we should be aware of its importance in the distillation of the phenomenon and the strength of its diffusion. Nevertheless, the essential element lies elsewhere.

Most observers these days, even Christians, dwell primarily on the sacrificial traces. They believe they have discovered the link between the theological aspects of Christianity, which are purely sacrificial, and its social efficacy, which is also sacrificial. This concept is real but secondary and should not conceal from them the specifically Christian process, which acts as a revelation, in a way that is contrary to sacrifice.

That two contrary actions can be combined only appears to be paradoxical. Or rather it re-creates the entire paradox of the Passion and the Gospels which lend themselves to secondary and superficial mythological crystallizations because they must reproduce the mythological process with extreme exactitude in order to reveal and completely subvert that process.

Even a purely sacrificial theology of the Gospels must ultimately be based on the Epistle to the Hebrews and certainly does not justify the exclusive importance given to the sacrificial fringe in the phenomenon of the martyrs. The Epistle does not succeed in defining the real singularity of the Passion, but it makes an attempt and accomplishes something important by portraying the death of Christ as the perfect and definitive sacrifice, which makes all other sacrifices outmoded and any further sacrificial undertaking unacceptable. This definition still does not uncover what I have tried to reveal—the absolute specificity of Christianity. But it does prevent a pure and simple return to the repetitive and primitive tradition of sacrifice, the kind of return we find in readings that limit martyrdom to mechanisms of violence and the sacred.

The failure of mythological genesis, in the case of the martyrs, makes it possible for historians to understand *in a rational light* for the first time and on a large scale the representations of persecution and their corresponding acts of violence. We come upon the crowds in the course of their *mythopoetic* activity, and it is not as pretty a sight as our theoreticians of myth and literature imagine. Fortunately for anti-Christian humanism, it is still possible to deny the presence of the process that gives birth to mythology in every other context.

Because of its revelation by the Passion, the scapegoat mechanism is no longer capable of producing true myth. Therefore there is no direct proof of the involvement of that generative mechanism. If, on the contrary, it had maintained its efficacy, there would have been no Christianity but merely another mythology. Everything would have come to us in the transfigured form of truly mythological themes and motifs. The end result would have been the same: the generative mechanism would still not have been recognized. Anyone who recognized it would have been accused of mistaking words for things and inventing the existence of a real persecution behind the noble mythological imagination.

I hope I have succeeded in showing the possibility and, indeed, certainty of proof, but it must take the indirect paths that we have followed. The Passion always acts as a model in the lives of the saints, and finds a way into the particular circumstances of such and such a persecution. But this is no mere rhetorical exercise or formal piety. Any critique of representations of persecution must begin here. Such a critique may yield rigid, clumsy and only partial results, yet the process was inconceivable until then and demands a long apprenticeship.

The rehabilitation of martyrs will draw accusations of partisanship that are rooted in the community of belief between victims and defenders. "Christianity" only defends its own victims. Once victorious, it becomes, in turn, a tyrannical oppressor and persecutor. As for Christianity's own acts of violence, it bears witness to the same blindness as its own persecutors.

All of which is true, just as true as the martyr's sacrificial connotation; but again, a secondary truth is only concealing the primary one. A formidable revolution is about to take place. Men, or at least certain men, will not allow themselves to be seduced by the persecutions that are claimed by their own beliefs and especially by "Christianity" itself. The resistance to persecution arises from the very heart of the universe of persecution. I am thinking of the process that I described at length earlier, the demystification of witch-hunts and a society's abandonment of the crude aspects of the magical concepts of persecution.

During the course of Western history representations of persecution from the persecutor's perspective gradually weaken and disappear. There are not necessarily fewer or less intense acts of violence; but it does mean that the persecutors could no longer permanently impose their own perspective on those around them. Centuries were needed to demystify medieval persecutions; a few years suffice to discredit contemporary persecutors. Even if some totalitarian system were to control the entire planet tomorrow, it would not succeed in making its own myth, or the magical aspect of its persecution, prevail. The process is the same as for the Christian martyrs, but it has been cleansed of the last traces of the sacred and radicalized since it demands no community of belief among the victims and those who demystify the system of their persecution. This is evident in the language that is always used in preference to any other.

In classical Latin *persequi* bears no connotation of injustice; the term simply signifies; to prosecute before a court. The Christian apologists, especially Lactantius and Tertullian, are responsible for the modern implications of *persecutio*, which stems from a very un-Roman sense of legal apparatus in the service not of justice but of injustice, systematically warped by the distortions of persecution. Similarly, in Greek, *martyr* signifies witness, and it is the Christian influence that developed its current sense of an innocent person persecuted, a heroic victim of an unjust act of violence.

When we exclaim: "The victim is a scapegoat," we resort to a biblical expression that no longer has the same significance as it had for the participants in the ritual of that name. It has the meaning of the innocent lamb in Isaiah or the Lamb of God in the Gospels. Every explicit reference to the Passion has disappeared, but the Passion is always juxtaposed with representations of persecution from the perspective of persecutors. The same model serves as a cipher for decoding, but it is so well assimilated that it is used mechanically without any explicit reference to its Judaic and Christian origins.

When the Gospels proclaim that Christ henceforth has taken the place of all victims, we only recognize grandiloquent sentimentality and piety, whereas in the Gospel reference it is literally true. We have learned to identify our innocent victims only by putting them in Christ's place, as Raymond Schwager well understood.[1] The Gospels, of course, are interested not in the intellectual operation they enable, but in the ethical change that they can possibly, but not necessarily, trigger:

"When the Son of Man comes in his glory, escorted by all the angels, then he will take his seat on his throne of glory. All the nations will be assembled before him and he will separate men one from another as the shepherd separates sheep from goats. He will place the sheep on his right hand and the goats on his left. Then the King will say to those on his right hand, 'Come, you whom my Father has blessed, take for your heritage the kingdom prepared for you since the foundation of the world. For I was hungry and you gave me food; I was thirsty

---

1. Schwager, *Brauchen wir einen Sündenbock?* This book sheds important light on the power of the Gospels in revealing mythology.

and you gave me drink; I was a stranger and you made me welcome; naked and you clothed me, sick and you visited me, in prison and you came to see me.' Then the virtuous will say to him in reply, 'Lord, when did we see you hungry and feed you; or thirsty and gave you drink? When did we see you a stranger and make you welcome; naked and clothe you; sick or in prison and go to see you?" And the King will answer, 'I tell you solemnly, in so far as you did this to one of the least of these brothers of mine, you did it to me.' Next he will say to those on his left hand, 'Go away from me, with your curse upon you to the eternal fire prepared for the devil and his angels. For I was hungry and you never gave me food; I was thirsty and you never gave me anything to drink; I was a stranger and you never made me welcome, naked and you never clothed me, sick and in prison and you never visited me.' Then it will be their turn to ask, 'Lord, when did we see you hungry or thirsty, a stranger or naked, sick or in prison, and did not come to your help?' Then he will answer, 'I tell you solemnly, in so far as you neglected to do this to one of the least of these, you neglected to do it to me.' And they will go away to eternal punishment, and the virtuous to eternal life." (Matt. 25:31–46)

The text has the quality of a parable. In order to speak to violent people who are unaware of their own violence, it resorts to the language of violence, but the real meaning is completely clear. Henceforth, it is not the explicit reference to Jesus that counts. Only our actual attitude when confronted with victims determines our relationship with the exigencies brought about by the revelation which can become effective without any mention of Christ himself.

When the Gospel text speaks of its universal diffusion, this does not imply utopian illusions about either the nature of the attachments to it or the practical results of the parallel process of penetration. It foresees both the superficial attachment of a still-pagan universe – the "Christian" Middle Ages – and the indifferent or ill-tempered rejection of the succeeding universe. The latter is secretly more affected by the revelation and often constrained for this reason to oppose the pagan Christianity of former times with anti-Christian parodies of the Gospel imperative. The death of Jesus is ultimately decided not by the cry of "Crucify him" but rather by "Free Barabbas" (Matt. 27:21; Mark 15:11; Luke 23:18).

The evidence of the texts would seem irrefutable, but every reference to it raises a veritable storm of protest, a chorus of henceforth almost universal exclamations, for the last titular Christians readily join in. Perhaps the texts are so strong that from now on just to quote them and indicate their relevance will seem polemical and indicative of a persecutor. Many, however, still cling to the modernist, traditional vision of Christianity as persecuting. This vision is based on two types of ideas that are too different in appearance for their agreement not to appear decisive.

Beginning with Constantine, Christianity triumphed at the level of the state and soon began to cloak with its authority persecutions similar to those in which the early Christians were victims. Like so many previous religions, ideological, and political enterprises, Christianity suffered persecution while it was weak and became the persecutor as soon as it gained strength. This vision of a Christianity that persecuted as much as or more than other religions is strengthened rather than diminished by the modern Western world's very aptitude for decoding representations of persecution. As long as this aptitude was limited to the immediate historical environment, i.e., the superficially Christianized universe, religious persecution – violence sanctioned or instigated by religion – appeared as a monopoly of that universe.

On the other hand, in the eighteenth and nineteenth centuries, Westerners made an idol of science and believed in an autonomous scientific spirit of which they were both the inventors and the product. They replaced the ancient myths with those of progress, which might be called the myth of perpetual modern superiority, the myth of a humanity that, through its own instrumentality, gradually became liberated and divine.

The scientific spirit cannot come first. It presupposes the renunciation of a former preference for the magical causality of persecution so well defined by the ethnologists. Instead of natural, distant, and inaccessible causes, humanity has always preferred causes that are *significant from a social perspective and permit of corrective intervention* – victims. In order to lead men to the patient exploration of natural causes, men must first be turned away from their victims. This can only be done by showing them that from now on persecutors "hate without cause" and without any appreciable result. In order to achieve this miracle, not only among certain exceptional individuals as in Greece, but for entire populations, there is need of the extraordinary combination of intellectual, moral, and religious factors found in the Gospel text.

The invention of science is not the reason that there are no longer witch-hunts, but the fact that there are no longer witch-hunts is the reason that science has been invented. The scientific spirit, like the spirit of enterprise in an economy, is a by-product of the profound action of the Gospel text. The modern Western world has forgotten the revelation in favor of its by-products, making them weapons and instruments of power; and now the process has turned against it. Believing itself a liberator, it discovers its role as persecutor. Children curse their fathers and become their judges. Contemporary scholars discover traces of magic in all the classical forms of rationalism and science. Instead of breaking through the circle of violence and the sacred as they imagined they were doing, our predecessors re-created weakened variations of myths and rituals.

In reality these myths have little importance. They are merely the outposts of a stubborn resistance. By decoding mythology, revealing the role of scapegoats in every culture, and resolving the enigmas of primitive religion, we inevitably prepare the way for the forceful return of the Gospel and biblical revelation. From the moment we truly understand myths, we can no longer accept the Gospel as yet another myth, since it is responsible for our understanding.

All our resistance is turned against the light that threatens us. It has revealed so many things for so long a time without revealing itself that we are convinced it comes from within us. We are wrong to appropriate it. We think we are the light because we witness it. But as it increases in brightness and scope it turns to itself for enlightenment. As the light of the Gospel extends to mythology it reveals its own specific nature.

The Gospel text is therefore in the process of justifying itself in the course of an intellectual history that seems foreign to it because that history has transformed our vision in a way that is foreign to all the religions of violence with which we foolishly confuse the Gospels. We have reached a new stage in the progress of this history which, though minor, bears heavy consequences for our intellectual and spiritual stability. It dissipates the confusion and reveals the meaning of the Gospel revelation as a critique of violent religion.

If that were not the meaning of the Gospels, then their own history would have escaped them; they would not be as we see them. But that is the meaning, under the rubric of the Holy Spirit. The great texts on the Paraclete enlighten the process that we are now experiencing. Their apparent obscurity is beginning to dissipate. The texts on the Holy Spirit are understood not because of the decoding of mythology, but because the light of the Gospels has penetrated myths and reduced them to nothing, elucidating words that seemed meaningless and full of violence and superstition, because they proclaim this process in the form of Christ's victory over Satan, or the victory of the Spirit of truth over the Spirit of falsehood. The passages in John's Gospel devoted to the Paraclete group together all the themes of this book.

All these thoughts are found in Jesus' farewells to his disciples, which constitute the high point of the fourth Gospel. Modern Christians are somewhat bothered by seeing Satan reappear at such a solemn moment. John tells us that Jesus' justification in history and his authentification are one with the annulment of Satan. This single and double event is presented to us as already consummated by the Passion and also not yet consummated, still to come since it is invisible to the eyes of the disciples.

> And when he comes,
> he will show the world how wrong it was,
> about sin,
> and about who was in the right,
> and about judgement:
> about sin:
> proved by their refusal to believe in me;
> about who was in the right:
> proved by my going to the Father
> and your seeing me no more;
> about judgement: (John 16:8–11)

There is between the Father and the world an abyss that comes from the world itself and from its violence. Jesus' return to the Father signifies victory over violence and the crossing of the abyss. But at first no one perceived this. For those who are in the world of violence Jesus is merely dead like others. There will be no astounding message from him or his Father after his return to his Father's side. Even if Jesus has become divine, the process will take place constantly in the style of the ancient gods, in the perpetual circle of violence and the sacred. Under these circumstances, the victory of the representation of persecution by the persecutors seems assured.

Yet, Jesus tells us, that is not how things come to pass. By maintaining the word of the Father against violence until the end and by dying for it, Jesus has crossed the abyss separating mankind from the Father. He himself becomes their Paraclete, their protector, and he sends them another Paraclete who will not cease to work in the world to bring forth the truth into the light.

Even if the language astonishes us, even if the author of the text sometimes seems dizzy before the breadth of vision, we cannot help but recognize what we have just been discussing. The Spirit is working in history to reveal what Jesus has already revealed, the mechanism of the scapegoat, the genesis of all mythology, the nonexistence of all gods of violence. In the language of the Gospel the Spirit achieves the defeat and condemnation of Satan. Based on the representation of persecution, the world inevitably does not believe in Jesus. It cannot conceive of the Passion's power of revelation. No system of thought is truly capable of creating the thought capable of destroying it. To confound the world, therefore, and show that it is reasonable and just to believe in Jesus as sent by the Father and returning to the Father after the Passion (in other words as a divinity that shares nothing in common with those of violence), the Spirit is necessary in history to work to disintegrate the world and gradually discredit all the gods of violence. It even appears to discredit Christ in that the Christian Trinity, through the fault of Christian and non-Christian alike, is compromised in the violence of the sacred. In reality, the world's lack of belief is perpetuated and reinforced only because the historical process is not yet complete, thus creating the illusion of a Jesus demystified by the progress of knowledge and eliminated with the other gods by history. History need only progress some more and the Gospel will be verified. "Satan" is discredited and Christ justified. Jesus' victory is thus, in principle, achieved immediately at the moment of the Passion, but for most men it only takes shape in the course of a long history secretly controlled by the revelation. It becomes evident at the moment when we are convinced that, thanks to the Gospels and not despite them, we can finally show the futility of all violent gods and explain and render void the whole of mythology.

Satan only reigns by virtue of the representations of persecution that held sway prior to the Gospels. Satan therefore is essentially the *accuser*, the one who deceives men by making them believe that innocent victims are guilty. But, who is the Paraclete?

Parakleitos, in Greek, is the exact equivalent of advocate or the Latin *ad-vocatus*. The Paraclete is called on behalf of the prisoner, the victim, to speak in his place and in his name, to act in his defense. The Paraclete is the universal advocate, the chief defender of all innocent victims, *the destroyer of every representation of persecution*. He is truly the spirit of truth that dissipates the fog of mythology.

We must ask why Jerome, that formidable translator who was rarely lacking in boldness, hesitated before the translation of the very ordinary, common name of *parakleitos*. He was literally taken by surprise. He did not see the term's relevance and opted for a pure and simple transliteration, *Paracletus*. His example is followed religiously in most modern languages. This mysterious word has continued to put in concrete form not the unintelligibility of a text that is actually perfectly intelligible, but the unintelligence of its interpreters, that of Jesus' accusation of his disciples, a lack of intelligence that history is slowly changing to comprehension.

There are, of course, innumerable studies on the Paraclete, but none provides a satisfactory solution, since they all define the problem in narrowly theological terms. The prodigious historical and cultural significance of the term remains inaccessible, and the general conclusion is that, if he is truly someone's advocate, the Paraclete must become the disciples' advocate with the Father. This solution invokes a passage in the first Epistle of John: "but if any one should sin, we have our advocate with the Father, Jesus Christ, who is just" (2:1). . .

In John's text Jesus makes himself a Paraclete. In the Gospel by the same author, Jesus effectively is shown as the first Paraclete sent to men:

I shall ask the Father,
and he will give you another Advocate
to be with you forever,
that Spirit of truth
whom the world can never receive
since it neither sees nor knows him; (John 14:16–17)

Christ is the Paraclete, par excellence, in the struggle against the representation of persecution. Every defense and rehabilitation of victims is based on the Passion's power of revelation. When Christ has gone, the Spirit of Truth, the second Paraclete, will make the light that is already in the world shine for all men, though man will do everything in his power not to see it.

The disciples certainly had no need of a second advocate with the Father, as long as they had Jesus himself. The other Paraclete is sent among men and into history; there is no need to get rid of him by sending him piously into the transcendental. The immanent nature of his action is confirmed by a text from the synoptic Gospels: "And when they lead you forth to deliver you, do not be preoccupied with what you will say, but say what is given to you at the moment for it is not you who will speak but the Holy Spirit."

This text is problematic in itself. It does not quite say what it intends to say. It would seem to say that martyrs need not be anxious about their defense because the Holy Spirit will be there to defend them. But there cannot be a question of an immediate triumph. The victims will not confound their accusers during their trial; they will be martyred; there are many texts to confirm this; the Gospels do not imply that they will put an end to persecutions.

It is a question neither of individual trials nor of some transcendental trial in which the Father plays the role of *Accuser*. This sort of thinking, even with the best of intentions — hell is paved with them — constantly makes the Father into a satanic figure. There can only be a question of an intermediary process between heaven and earth, the trial of "heavenly" or "worldly" powers, and of Satan himself, the trial of the representation of persecution in its entirety. Because the Gospel writers are not always able to define the place of trial they make it sometimes too transcendent or too immanent, and modern commentators have never escaped this double hesitation, not understanding that the destiny of all sacred violence is at stake in the battle between the Accuser, Satan, and the advocate for the defense, the Paraclete.

What the martyrs say has little importance because they are witnesses, not of a determined belief, as is imagined, but of man's terrible propensity, in a group, to spill innocent blood in order to restore the unity of their community. The persecutors force themselves to bury their dead in the tomb of their representation of persecution, but the more martyrs die the weaker the representation becomes and the more striking the testimony. This is why we use the term *martyr,* which means witness, for all the innocent victims, regardless of differences of belief or doctrine, as the Gospels proclaim. Just as in the word *scapegoat,* the popular usage of *martyr* goes further than scholarly interpretations and suggests for theology things that are as yet unknown.

While the world is still intact it cannot understand that which transcends the representation of persecution; it can neither see the Paraclete nor know him. The disciples themselves are still encumbered with illusions that only history can destroy by the deepening influence of the Passion. Thus the future will revive words to the disciples that were not able to claim their attention at the time because they seemed to be deprived of meaning: "I have said these things to you, while still with you; but the Advocate, the Holy Spirit, whom the Father will send in my name, will teach you everything and remind you of all I have said to you." (John 14:25–26)

> I still have many things to say to you
> but they would be too much for you now.
> But when the Spirit of truth comes
> he will lead you to the complete truth,
> since he will not be speaking as from himself
> but will say only what he has learned;
> and he will tell you of the things to come.
> He will glorify me,
> since all he tells you
> will be taken from what is mine. (John 16:12–15)

Of all the texts on the Paraclete, this, finally, is the most extraordinary. It appears to be made up of heterogeneous pieces and fragments, as if it were the incoherent fruit of a mystical schizophrenia. Actually, it is our own cultural schizophrenia that makes it appear that way. It cannot be understood so long as we use the principles and methods that inevitably belong to our world and can neither see nor know the Paraclete. John strikes us with so many extraordinary truths at such a pace that we neither can nor want to absorb them. There is a great risk of projecting on him the confusion and violence that are always to some extent present in us. The text may have been affected, in certain details, by the conflicts between the Church and the Synagogue, but its real subject has nothing to do with contemporary debates on the "anti-Semitism of John."

> Anyone who hates me hates my Father.
> If I had not performed such works among them
> as no one else has ever done,
> they would be blameless;
> but as it is, they have seen all this,
> and still they hate both me and my Father.
> But all this was only to fulfill the words written in their Law;
> *They hated me for no reason.*
> When the Advocate [Paraclete] comes,
> whom I shall send to you from the Father,
> the Spirit of truth who issues from the Father.
> he will be my witness [ekeinos *marturesei* peri emou]

And you too will be witnesses, [kai humeis de *martureite*]
because you have been with me from the outset.

"I have told you all this
so that your faith may not be shaken.
They will expel you from the synagogues,
and indeed the hour is coming
when anyone *who kills you will think he is doing a holy duty for God*.
They will do these things
because they have never known either the Father or myself.
But I have told you all this,
so that when the time for it comes
you may remember that I told you. (John 15:23–27; 16:1–4)

This text unquestionably evokes the struggles and persecutions at the time of its writing. It cannot directly evoke any others. But indirectly it evokes all the others since it is not dominated by vengeance but rather dominates it. To regard it as purely and simply a prefiguration of contemporary anti-semitism, under the pretext that it has never been understood, is to give in to scandal, to transform into scandal what we are told has been given to us to protect us from scandal and foresee the misunderstandings caused by the apparent failure of the revelation.

Apparently, the revelation is a failure; it ends in persecutions that seem likely to smother it but ultimately bring it to fulfillment. So long as the words of Jesus do not reach us, we have no sin. We remain at the level of the Gerasenes. The representation of persecution retains a certain legitimacy. The sin is the resistance to the revelation. Inevitably, it becomes externalized in the hateful persecution of the one who brings the revelation, in other words God himself, since he is the one who disturbs our more or less comfortable little arrangements with our familiar demons.

The persecutor's resistance – Paul's for example, before his conversion – makes the very thing that it tries to hide obvious. As a converted persecutor, Paul is the archetypal Christian:

He fell to the ground and then he heard a voice saying, "Saul, Saul, why are you persecuting me?" "Who are you, Lord?" he asked, and the voice answered, "I am Jesus, and you are persecuting me." (Acts 9:4–6)

I see in this the perfect theoretical recapitulation of the evangelic process that is described in all the texts discussed in the preceding pages. The same process also takes place in history and develops from now on as history; it is known to the whole world, and it is the same as the advent of the Paraclete. When the Paraclete comes, Jesus says, he will bear witness to me, he will reveal the meaning of my innocent death and of every innocent death, from the beginning to the end of the world. Those who come after Christ will therefore bear witness as he did, less by their words or beliefs than by becoming martyrs and dying as Jesus died.

Most assuredly, this concerns not only the early Christians persecuted by the Jews or by the Romans but also the Jews who were later persecuted by the Christians and all victims persecuted by executioners. To what does it really bear witness? In my thinking it always relates to the collective persecution that gives birth to religious illusions. It is to this that the following sentence alludes: "the hour is coming when whoever kills you will think he is offering service to God." Witch-hunters are encompassed by this revelation, as are totalitarian bureaucrats of persecution. In future, all violence will reveal what Christ's Passion revealed, the foolish genesis of bloodstained idols and the false gods of religion, politics, and ideologies. The murderers remain convinced of the worthiness of their sacrifices. They, too, know not what they do and we must forgive them. The time has come for us to forgive one another. If we wait any longer there will not be time enough.

Index